After the Texans...

Declan Milling

Clink
Street

London | New York

Published by Clink Street Publishing 2016

Copyright © Declan Milling 2016

First edition.

ISBN: 978-1-911110-81-1 - paperback
978-1-911110-82-8 - ebook

Table of Contents

Prologue 1

1 5
2 12
3 20
4 23
5 33
6 37
7 50
8 60
9 71
10 83
11 92
12 102
13 110
14 120
15 130
16 135
17 143
18 149

19 161
20 167
21 171
22 178
23 184
24 193
25 199
26 205
27 214
28 221
29 227
30 232
31 241
32 246
33 255
34 259

Appendix 263
Glossary 265
Author's Note 267

Prologue

They'd been in his hotel room, in Port Moresby.

"Oh, I'll be alright," she'd said. "I have my security detail. As usual."

As usual. That was ironic. Typical of her nonchalance to respond like that, considering how useless the security detail was in the past, but nothing was usual. It hadn't been for a long time. Not since Gordon Davies' murder. No, before that: not since Davies had been arrested – when that arsehole Bradlee Nelson had tried to stitch him up at the conference in Köln. Nothing had been 'usual' since then.

Then he'd left her in Moresby and headed up to Debepare. Just him and Dominik. How could anything ever be usual again after that? After killing Wiebe. And killing one of his 'boys' – that had been an accident – but the man was dead and he was responsible. Leaving Johanna in Moresby, on her own. Worse than just leaving her on her own, actually directing her into their hands.

"Here take this number, as well," he'd told her. "It's Gerry Johnstone's."

Talk about gullible.

"If there's an emergency, you can call him."

Emil, you naïve fool.

"Listen to me, Mr Pfeffer, listen very carefully and don't interrupt. If you value Dr Dorn's life, if you want to see her again, you

1

will do as I say. You will collect the data that you stole – the hard drives, CDs, DVDs – any and every copy that has been made from every location to which it's been copied. You will have it all in your personal possession within seven days. Once it has been recovered from you, you will forget about BKZ and anything or any person related to BKZ or the PNG projects. Dr Dorn will be kept as insurance that you comply."

The line had gone dead before he could say a word.

*****

"Emil, are you listening? Can you hear me? Emil, wake up!"

Betty G's rasping twang cut into his thoughts. He looked up. Betty and behind her his assistant, Sabrina, were standing there, their foreheads creased with concern.

"Finally, there's signs of life. Thank the Lord!"

"Oh, ah, Betty." Emil looked around, taking in his surroundings. He was sitting at his desk, in his office, in the Global Carbon Markets Organisation building in Bad Eschbach. The two women were looking down at him from the other side of the desk. Betty G fidgeting, hands in constant motion, as ever. Sabrina head and shoulders over her senior. "What's happening?"

"Apart from the fact that we've been trying to rouse you out of a catatonic state for the past ten minutes," said Betty G, "we're waiting for you to enlighten us on that score."

"What do you mean?"

"Well, about half an hour ago you resigned from this organisation and walked out the front door."

"Yes, I did, didn't I?"

"You took a call on your mobile, stood outside for a while, then came back in and sat down here at your desk. When Sabrina couldn't get a response out of you she came and got me. We've been trying to rouse you from your trance-like state ever since."

"I remember quitting and walking out. I remember the call, but not coming back."

"Well, you did. More to the point, does this mean now you're not quitting?"

Emil stared at the two women for a few moments. They could be mother and daughter, he thought, with their brown eyes and dark brown hair; except he knew for a fact that Betty G was a childless spinster.

"I guess it does."

"Good. I hoped you'd see sense," said Betty G. "I'll go tear up your resignation."

Both women left the office, leaving Emil still sitting at his desk. He lapsed back into his thoughts.

*****

Robert, from the Papua New Guinea Department of Justice, opening his eyes to the bullshit story Gerry had spun him about having a partner called Diana. The news of Johnstone's hurried departure:

"He left on a flight to Singapore," Robert had said.

The grey haired gent at the European Union diplomatic residence in Port Moresby:

"Well, I'm afraid you've missed Dr Dorn, Mr Pfeffer. She had to leave her work here and return to Brussels several days ago."

Then, back in Frankfurt, the call from Robert.

"I was able to get hold of the passenger manifest for the flight to Singapore the day you said. It shows she boarded that flight. But get this, mate, that was the same flight Gerry took."

In the hotel room, before they'd headed up to Debepare, Johanna had been crying. Angry and worried for them at the same time.

"Do you love me?" he'd asked her. Maybe she should've been asking him.

"*Bestimmt*," she'd mumbled between sobs: a German word *he* was always misusing. Her little joke.

"Then trust me to get back safely."

She'd only taken the first leg of the ticket, as far as Singapore. That had been Gerry Johnstone's destination, too.

1

He eased himself into the sofa and, tilting his head back, slurped the dregs of frothed milk out of the bottom of the cup. He looked into it expecting there should have been more, but not finding any, ran his finger around the inside rim for the coffee coloured remnants drying there, then licked it.

Cyril Barrington Griffith. Known as 'Bull'. Sometimes called 'CB', or 'Barry', but never Cyril. At least not to his face. The epitome of the self-made mining magnate – the poor boy made good story personified. His appearance bore out the characterisation in Australian sporting circles of Queenslanders as cane toads – that state's least popular export. Yellowy, olive-brown complexion, a lumpy face and slits for eyes under puffy lids, the product of years dealing with intense sunlight and coal dust. Greying, wavy brown hair combed back across his head, plastered to his scalp by hair cream. A flabby, bulbous neck that seemed to inflate and redden, like his face, when he was angry. Which was pretty often.

Satisfied he'd extracted all there was to be had from it, he put the cup down and picked up the morning's paper. The front page was devoted to the latest shift in climate change policy by the federal government.

"Geezuz, these bastards gimme the shits," he muttered for the benefit of the otherwise empty hotel suite.

He dropped the paper onto the coffee table and, heaving

his considerable bulk upright, went to the window and looked out on the waking city. The sun was almost up and in the distance he could see ferries and other craft plying up and down the harbour. He could make out the lights on a large cargo ship, gliding past the creamy sheen of Bennelong Point and the greenery of Mrs Macquarie's chair.

Not bad for these old eyes considerin' the hotel's all the way up in William Street, he thought, as they tracked the ship's departure. Garden Island navy base was lit up like a homing beacon for the annual Bogong moth migration. Must be some navy boys in. Way beyond it, silhouetted against a backdrop of glinting ocean swell, he could make out the shape of a cruise ship, just in through the Heads, processing up the outer harbour, probably to a berth at the Quay.

An unwelcome thought interjected, spoiling the serenity of the moment: maybe it was heading for Darling Harbour – full of Asian high-bloody-rollers, being ferried down to the casinos now coverin' the place like wallpaper. God, what're the bloody politicians doing to this place? It's one thing to sell coal and minerals to the Asians, but why'd they have to bring 'em here by the boatload?

Thirty years ago they were tryin' to stop boatloads of the bastards arriving here, turnin' them back for the Indonesians to sort out. Now they were practically paying 'em to come! And once they're here, you damned well can't get rid of 'em. They buy up all the real estate they can find and offload the extended family down here for schoolin'. The country has well and truly gone to the dogs, and those fuckwitted bastards sitting on their arses down in Canberra, along with their corrupt, state-based cronies, they were the culprits.

He sat down in an armchair adjacent to the window, exasperated by his own vitriol, and picked up the paper again. Why'd he bother with a rag like this, with its chardonnay socialist slant on everything? The Melbourne rag wasn't any better. Same publisher, same load a' bullshit. He was glad he'd finished his business here and was headin' home. He hated coming south. At least the paper in Brizzie didn't have as much of this leftie rubbish. One of these days he might even start his own paper, redress all the left-wing crap, put some balance back into the media. Might talk to his mates over in the US about that – they had some good stuff on their cable channels. Here, if it wasn't this climate change crap, it was gay-bloody-rights, or bloody refugees, or paedophile-bloody-priests, or some other rubbish in your face at every turn.

What about the people who actually worked for a livin', spent their days sloggin' their guts out to keep the country tickin' over? Where did they fit into all of this? No, they were only good for one thing: coughin' up more tax so the bastards in Canberra could keep their snouts in the trough. Well, he'd had enough of it, and unlike the lethargic, complacent bastards down here, *he* was gonna do something about it.

He loosened his tie and undid the top button of his shirt. Just thinkin' about it was making him hot.

*****

The trip had been an utter waste of time. But he'd had to try. His partners expected it. Those two bastards, Mendicane and Hounganis, didn't want to hear what he had to say. But he'd told them anyway. And he'd tell 'em again, if he had to. As for that smarmy little monkey, Mendicane, who had him to thank for being resident in the Lodge: well, just as he gave, so he could take away.

They'd met a couple of days earlier, in Canberra, the Prime Minister's suite at Parliament House. Mendicane's chief of staff had shown him in.

"Bull, good to see you, *mate*," Mendicane had said, looking at Bull over the top of his reading glasses, a mannerism he had picked up since becoming Prime Minister. His minders had coached him into it as a way of giving him more *gravitas*, something in which he was sorely lacking. With his hunched, rolling gait and big ears, the satirical cartoonists were showing no mercy.

Shaking the offered hand, Griffith wondered what had possessed him to throw his substantial wealth and political clout behind such a nincompoop. It had guaranteed Mendicane success in the party-room coup that Griffith himself had orchestrated, after one too many anti-mining policy decisions by the previous incumbent. But why, why, had he supported Michael Mendicane MP, the gaff-prone member from a snooty part of Melbourne? He shook his head in a private acknowledgement of his own stupidity.

"I invited Tony to pack down with us."

"Uh, the other half of the dynamic duo," grunted Griffith as Tony Hounganis, Mendicane's Deputy and Treasurer, waddled in through the door from his adjoining office suite.

Griffith looked around the office: behind him, a wall of redwood-panelled doors concealed cupboards and who knew what else, although he guessed they would be pretty much empty; in front, a cluster of armchairs and sofa that looked like giant, spongy, cup mushrooms, inverted; cream-coloured on the outside and brown in the middle. At the far end of the room a large, simple redwood desk on which some papers were scattered, and behind which more redwood shelves were sparingly arranged with family photos and a couple of mementos of official visits.

To Bull Griffith, there was little evidence of any serious activity.

"I see you've settled in."

Mendicane gestured for them to sit in the armchairs and Griffith deposited his ample frame in one.

"I'll get straight to the point. If you go ahead with this policy review you've been gabbing about in the press, that's the end of it. You'll have lost my support, just like your predecessor did. And don't forget, that's how you got to where you are now."

He fixed them both with his hard, squinting stare.

"Fair go, Bull," said Mendicane, "you wait until the High Court dumps us on the bottom of the ruck, then you start putting the boot in!"

"Don't gimme that High Court excuse bullshit, Mick. You

know as well as I do that the government could legislate to get around that."

"Bull, look, be reasonable," said Hounganis. "The High Court's just about threatening us. Their judgment was so critical of the government – it said if we keep funding Queensland's activities with the coal loader and port facilities, we'd be breaking the law. Not just our own laws, international law, too!"

"I told you – you can legislate your way 'round it."

"It's not that simple, Bull! We've got the bloody tourism industry virtually camped in our offices."

"Those poofters! 'Camped' is about right! Wait'll you get a few miners moving in here."

"And you might have noticed there were a couple of hundred thousand protesters out in the streets of the capital cities each of the last three weekends."

"Lefties with nothing better to do. What about the silent majority?"

"Jeez, anyone would think we were facing the West Indies speed attack from the nineties, we've had so many bouncers bowled at us lately," said Mendicane. "We've been ducking and weaving, rolling with the punches, as far as we can, but we've got to start hitting some runs soon, Bull. That's what the polls are telling us."

"You're only interested in saving your own skins, you weak bastards. These policy changes you've been talkin' about – they'll wreck this country's economy. They're pure populist fairy floss. Wind and solar – them so-called 'renewables' – they're never gonna replace coal in this country."

He poked a finger in Hounganis's direction, making him pull back instinctively in fright.

"And if you think you'll ever balance a budget without exportin' coal, just go ahead and try. You'll never do it."

"Now, Bull, you don't need to get like that," Hounganis responded. "We've got a very difficult political situation here, mate. Politically, the coal loader is dead in the water."

"Bull, mate, we've got to listen to what the people are yelling at us. Think of it like a Test match. Over the five days, you've got to adapt your tactics to suit changes in the pitch, and the weather, you change your fields, and your bowlers, to suit the batsmen, play to their weaknesses. We've got to adapt our strategy, otherwise the crowd's going to get restless and, and..." Mendicane searched for the right sporting analogy to finish the point he was making, "... and start a Mexican wave."

Griffith jumped to his feet – surprisingly quickly for such a big man. As far as he was concerned, the meeting was over. These two boofheads simply weren't listening, so there was nothing left to discuss.

"Well, they'll be wavin' good-bye to thousands of jobs, billions of investment, and to this country's future. That's just for starters. And they'll be waving bye-bye to you two and this government!"

"Bull, what the-bloody-hell else do you think we can do faced with a front-row of liberal, left-leaning High Court judges – they're not binding straight, but the ref's not watching, is he?" pleaded Mendicane.

"I don't know, Mick, that's what you and Tony are here to sort out. That's why *I* helped put you here!"

"We might be on the canvas, Bull, but we're not down for the count!" Mendicane tried.

"I don't care, Mick, that's it for me. The next lot of political funding I provide is goin' into my own party and my own candidates, not you and your lot. At least, then, I know I'll get what I pay for."

*****

The mobile phone lying on the table buzzed.

"Yeah?"

"We've got it, it's sorted. Deal's done," said the voice at the other end of the line.

"Watch what you're sayin' – phone's probably bugged. The bastards've been tappin' into everything since I became rich enough to be noticed."

Bull Griffith clicked the phone off, dropping it back on the table.

He sat a while, deep in thought, looking out at the brightening harbour, the already congested roads leading up from it, ant-sized people scurrying along the pavements and crossing the streets twenty floors beneath him. The view from his office was better. Cleaner, less congested. Story Bridge, the river and Kangaroo Point, then on all the way out to Moreton Bay. Even better, he had his little offshore hideaway where he could get away from it all. At least he'd managed to get that sorted out with the two-faced bastards in Sydney and Canberra, before they became born-again greenies.

Eventually, he got up and set about packing his suitcase. When he'd finished, he called down on the room phone to the concierge, for his car to the airport. Then he stood looking out the window again, still thoughtful, before collecting his things and heading downstairs, all the while thinking about the implications of the message; the possibilities that would now be opened up to him.

How he would exploit them.

How he was going to deal with those bastards.

2

"Do you remember telling me that size *does* matter?"

It was Luxembourg. They were in bed, a room at the Sofitel *Le Grand Ducal*. Resting after their early morning exertions.

"Yes," she'd smiled.

"And?"

"Also, technique is important."

"Are you trying to tell me something?" he said, pretending to be offended.

"Just that you have good technique," she'd said, smiling again. "With your tongue." Then she'd rolled onto him, plunging hers into his mouth.

The tongue.

The bundle of muscles, blood vessels and nerve endings sitting in the bottom of one's mouth. With all those nerve fibres it was sensitive. Sensual. Erogenous. He dwelt on the word. Erogenous. Yes, it was erogenous. Particularly so when it was in contact with another tongue. His mind needed little encouragement to head further down this side-track.

Abruptly, the background monologue stopped, bringing him out of his thoughts, back to the present. There was a loud *ka-choo* and, shortly after, the tingling of fine aerosol settling over him and those sitting alongside him in the front row. Profuse excuses were issued. The speaker at the lectern resumed his monologue.

Emil tried to refocus on his distraction, to put out of his mind the possibility that he might have just been the recipient of a virus bearing transmission from mucosae located around the very same tongue that had started him thinking about the subject in the first place. The thought of locking tongues with the speaker suddenly jumped, unbidden, into his mind. Ugh. He squirmed at the prospect. Oh, no thanks! Not with a guy. Especially not this overweight, sweaty one. He tried to steer his thoughts back to Johanna. But that fleeting visit was over, she was gone.

Tongues. He'd been thinking about tongues for a reason. He had in mind something for this speaker's tongue. He turned his attention back to it. Sago palm – called *saksak* locally. It had come up in conversation the second time he'd dropped into the Centre where she'd worked in Port Moresby. The starch extracted from the trunk was an important staple for the nationals. He'd tried it many years earlier during his time in Papua New Guinea.

"It's horrible," he'd told her. "Not my taste at all."

"You don't know what you're missing out on." He smiled to himself, remembering what he'd thought when she'd said that. "You can cook up its leaves and eat them, too," she'd said, but his mind had been on things other than cooking sago palm leaves with her. Then, for a reason he couldn't now recall, they'd got on to discussing its merits as a food staple.

That wasn't what interested him now. He wasn't planning a new low fat diet for the speaker. He was thinking about the sago palm thorns. The short, poisonous ones.

After the deaths of Davies and the others, he'd become interested in *sangguma* – traditional New Guinean witchcraft – Sepik River, to be precise, usually carried out on the orders of sorcerers. He'd researched it on the internet and been reading up. Somehow it made him feel closer to what had happened there, to the people who'd been murdered, and to Johanna. But there was another reason he was thinking about it now: that was its immediate application. The particular technique he had in mind involved the insertion of the short, poisonous thorns into the base of the victim's tongue. These would cause swelling and then loss of speech, which was precisely what he had in mind. More poisoned thorns could be inserted in the victim's vital organs causing infection and, eventually, death.

In his mind's eye he could see himself applying this technique to the speaker, with gusto. It was very uncharitable. And nasty. But most satisfying, all the same.

Emil stopped himself. Was he becoming more extreme? Was he a nastier person? Or had he always been like this and it was just coming out now? Maybe it was a coping mechanism. He considered it a moment or two. The image of a small, lifeless body on the edge of a jungle clearing, misty with rain, appeared in his mind's eye. The literally smoking gun, hot in his palm. No, he didn't want another death on his hands, he'd settle for the swollen tongue and unable to speak bits of it. That'd be enough ... *well*, maybe just a little bit of asphyxiation ...

But for the fact that Emil's face was much more recognisable at these events now, he would have walked out on such a boring speaker. Voted with his feet. But it was a little difficult for him to make that sort of statement, with his official role, and with his higher profile on the climate change speaking circuit since the events in Papua New Guinea had become widely known. And especially now, sitting in the front row within spitting distance of the speaker. Literally, in the case of this one, he noted with some distaste.

"... in this respect the government is ... remains totally committed ..."

Yeah, yeah. Blah-de, blah-de, blah. Heard it all before. I wonder if these characters ever listen to themselves delivering these rote speeches? Should be forced to. Strapped in a chair, like Alex in *A Clockwork Orange*. Forced to listen to himself. The way he was just reading – not delivering – the speech. The dull monotone, pauses in the wrong places, emphasis where it shouldn't be. It sounded like the minister had collected it from his speechwriter just as he stood up to read it.

The hotel conference room was on level thirty-four of the Shard in central London: for the moment, Europe's tallest building. But, as was most often the case, the conference room itself was internal and windowless. So he couldn't even distract himself by looking out at the view.

Emil's mind drifted again. He'd come this morning with the best of intentions. He really had planned to pay attention and participate. He had wanted to contribute positively to the debate. He had intended to be a worthy substitute for his over-committed leader, Betty Greenhaugh, who regrettably had been unable to attend due to the pressing nature of her busy schedule. His resolve had lasted about ten minutes into the opening plenary. Then this junior government minister had got onto the podium and inflated himself like a puffer fish.

"… we continue to be world leaders in addressing climate change …"

No, he would not embarrass himself by revealing to anyone that he was here only because of Betty G's edict that he attend in her stead.

"Emil, I can't take any more of your moods," she'd said. "I've run out of happy pills to give you and I can't bear walking around this office every morning feeling like I'm in the suicide wing of the manic depressive clinic. Take some time off, go to this London event for me and come back in a better frame of mind, so you can get on with things and move on. That's an order."

So here he was, sitting in the front row, shortly to join the puffer fish and other speakers on the podium for the ensuing discussion session. Unstructured babble to follow the structured babble. She could, though, have picked something more captivating than the *Climate Change Future Policy Summit* to give his frame of mind a boost. He imagined someone pricking the minister with a pin, so that he would shoot off, whooshing around the room, like a deflating balloon. No, that wasn't an appealing thought either. On the other hand, might be less tedious than his presentation. Right now, he'd even settle for some Bradlee Nelson questions to the honourable minister, just to liven things up a bit ... his thoughts wandered back to the *C-world* Conference a year earlier.

"Why then, Mr Pfeffer," Nelson had hectored him, "is one of your colleagues, in fact one of your very own *integrity* staff, a Mr Gordon Davies, the senior manager responsible for *integrity* in the Asia-Pacific Region markets, currently under arrest in Papua New Guinea, and can you explain to this audience here what the charges are?"

Emil rejected that idea, too. Just thinking of that arsehole, Nelson, reminded him of everything which being here was meant to take his mind off.

It hadn't been like this the whole time since he'd returned from PNG. Initially, there'd been much to do. Quietly initiating inquiries through Johanna's work and the Singapore police about her disappearance. Chasing up and tying off all the PNG loose ends. He'd been a witness in the re-opened inquests into the deaths of Davies, Sir Gideon and the two boys. And the Market Integrity Unit had led the re-examination of the Debepare projects and carbon trading proposals.

Carbon trading was pushing ahead globally, in spite of setbacks over the years. The debacle with the Papua New Guinea scheme had been smoothed over by Betty G and the Global Carbon Markets Organisation supporters at the United Nations. Blame had been laid at the feet of the deposed government. There'd been much praise for the organisation's officers who helped expose the former PNG leadership's machinations, in league with rogue individuals. The full extent of the conspiracy, though, and the fact that there were substantial, but as yet unidentified parties standing behind the government, had been buried in the paperwork, much to Emil's disgust.

However, he could hardly make a big deal of it. It would pose too great a risk to Johanna, of whom he'd heard nothing since her disappearance. So far as he knew, she was still being held as insurance against him initiating more investigations. But it would also muddy the waters, derogating from the huge media and public relations boost the organisation had derived – mostly as a result of Betty G's tireless efforts. Besides, he was the hero of the hour. It would complicate matters for the new PNG government, too, if he broke ranks. It just wanted to get on with things, getting a new trading scheme up and running.

Realpolitik. That's what had come to the fore: the greater good would be the global success of carbon trading.

"Emil, you keep your eyes on the big picture," Betty G had counselled him.

Sideshows like his intended hunt for Hudson and the real backers of the former PNG leadership, were he in a position to continue, would not to be allowed to derail the main game. The big players were working hard to keep it on track. His report of Hudson's revelations seemed to have been ignored, or disbelieved, or deliberately buried somewhere in New York. He couldn't tell which. After all, he wasn't privy to the higher-level discussions and Betty G hadn't seen fit to share the details with him. He got the message, all the same.

"You will collect the data that you stole – the hard drives, CDs, DVDs – any and every copy that has been made from every location to which it's been copied. You will have it all in your personal possession within seven days."

He'd managed to retrieve the original hard-drive from the General, along with some of the copies the General had made (although he hadn't asked him, he was sure the General would have kept at least one). He had it all in his possession, as directed, within the seven-day timeframe. Then nothing.

He was still living in the hotel near the office, not having the inclination or spirit to commit to another apartment – even if it would be only for a matter of months – until Johanna had been released and was safely back with him. He couldn't bring himself to do it. In his mind, it would be, in a sense, moving on without her. He just couldn't do it.

The collected items – hard drive, Dominik's laptop and

the General's copies – had remained in a bag in Emil's hotel room waiting to be collected for weeks, until one evening when he returned from the office, they were gone. At first, he hadn't noticed. When he realised they weren't where he'd left them, he'd rushed around to make sure they hadn't just been moved, then checked with hotel management, to make sure the maid hadn't thrown the bag out. But no-one knew anything about it.

The days had stretched into weeks, then months, the passing of each now marking off another ebb in his hopes that today would be the day she reappeared. That she rang. That he heard of her release. That somehow, he heard something, from somewhere. Her mobile number no longer worked. Christmas and New Year were long gone, the year was beginning to slip by, but still there was no sign of her.

A subdued round of applause broke into his reflections, signalling that the minister had finished. The next speaker was a representative of the anti-market protest movement. The event organisers, one of those global 'consulting' firms that had grown out of a global 'accounting' firm, had cleverly bought off the protesters by giving them a voice at the table. Otherwise they would have been disrupting proceedings in any way they could. In fact, they'd been given many voices in both plenary and workshop sessions, to accommodate their diverse – and worrying – Hydra-like formation. Very smart, he thought. Someone in that firm had done their homework.

His thoughts drifted again. The one small, positive thing recently was that he had managed to conjure out of Robert, and the new PNG Department of Justice head, a request for an Interpol Red Notice on Gregory Hudson. This followed a national court order for Hudson's arrest, arising out of the prosecution of the former Prime Minister, whose defence had been that Hudson was responsible for everything. But of course, like Gerry Johnstone, Hudson had vanished into thin air.

On the other hand, there seemed to be nothing else at all

positive. No information from the Swiss banking regulator on where the money from Gerry Johnstone's secret account had been transferred. Dominik had promised this was coming, but it hadn't eventuated. Not yet, at least. Suddenly, the Swiss banking authorities seemed to be dragging their heels along with Dominik's German government friends at the BMU. So that lead, as well, was going cold.

As for Dominik himself, he still wasn't at work, only due back the following week. He was just out of hospital. It seemed that Wiebe had done a lot worse mischief to him than the medicos had first thought. His convalescence had been much longer than anticipated.

The protest movement speaker was wrapping up her vision for stopping climate change without trusting in market forces. She was well-informed, and intelligent, and articulate. A petite, pretty, rather young-looking thing. They all looked so young to him these days. He was beginning to feel his age.

Since he was about to join her on the podium, to represent the case that *did* involve market forces, he hoped her looks weren't masking an inner firebrand, a tigress waiting to bare her teeth at him – or worse.

"…and Mr Emil Pfeffer, head of the Market Integrity at the United Nations' Global Carbon Markets Organisation…" the session moderator announced.

He collected his official thoughts, carefully putting aside the unofficial ones that had occupied his mind most of the morning and, willing himself into a positive, corporate frame of mind, joined the other panellists being introduced to the audience.

3

"Thank you for your contribution, Mr Pfeffer."

Her nametag simply read 'Lesley'. She was from the host firm.

"Well, thank you for your invitation. It was my pleasure to be here and have the opportunity to participate. Our Director-General's misfortune was my good luck," he smiled back at her.

It was easy to smile at such a beautiful woman. Large, brown, day-dreamy eyes, high cheekbones dotted with fine freckles. Generous, smiling mouth. She looked to be a similar age to him, would probably have been even more attractive when younger, he thought. She was wearing a fawn coloured, woollen dress that hugged her figure. The short sleeves showing off her lightly tanned arms.

But before either of them could say more, the firm's managing partner snaffled her off to attend to some issue with one of the invited VIPs. Probably the honourable puffer fish, mused Emil.

He opened the programme and scanned the names of invited guests to avoid the awkwardness of being left standing on his own. He'd looked at them so many times already he knew them all by heart. At the bottom and over the page, the names of the host firm's personnel were listed, should any of the attendees wish to contact the firm. His eyes ran down the next page until, beneath the exhaustive list of partners, they settled on the name of the Head, Knowledge Management: it was Lesley – Lesley Beckwith.

"Hmm, I wonder," he said to himself, half aloud.

The one line of enquiry he was continuing to pursue – through Dominik and his connections, though, to avoid attention – was attempting to locate Rodger Beckwith, whom he suspected was still somewhere in Switzerland. It was the only possible remaining connection into Bankgesellschaft Kohlenstoffermäßigungen Zürich – Beckwith's former employer and funder of the PNG projects – which Emil could think of, now that the BKZ data had been retrieved and all the other leads had dried up. In coming to London, he'd tentatively sniffed around where the Bishopsgate Consulting offices had been, but they had gone the same way as BKZ, vanishing from the face of the earth. The auditing firm had sacked the staff that had been involved in the Debepare projects, so no leads to follow there, either. Beckwith was his last roll of the dice. But Beckwith had never really appeared again after the PNG ceremony debacle, and Dominik's searches were yet to bear any fruit.

"My apologies for leaving you like that. Are you looking for something, or someone?"

He looked up from the booklet. The large, dreamy brown eyes were back, looking into his.

"Your name, to be honest."

He didn't mean to flirt with her, but he was. Her cheeks glowed, almost imperceptibly, for a second.

"And have you found it?" An eyebrow flickered briefly.

She smiled again, not the corporate one this time. The 'this-could-be-interesting' smile.

"Yes, I see you're responsible for organising this excellent event."

"Well, not quite. I'm the Head of Knowledge Management, which does events like this, but there are a lot of other people involved. I'll pass your compliment on to them."

"Whose idea was it to get the anti-market protesters on

board? Whoever it was, they're brilliant – there's not a placard in sight."

"Campaigners, please, Mr Pfeffer, not protesters! And I'm happy to hang onto the plaudits for that one. It wasn't easy though, they're a fragmented lot. Reaching all the right people took quite some time and effort. But really, they'd have had to hire a helicopter to protest outside here, anyway."

"Or abseil, which they're not averse to doing. But, well done. I think you might find other conference organisers copy your approach, from now on."

"Thanks. Was there a particular reason you were looking for my name?"

"Er, no, not especially, well, I just noticed…" he tried to tone down the flirting: time to come clean with her, he thought. "Um, you weren't living in Switzerland recently, were you, by any chance?"

Her manner changed instantly, like he'd tossed a wet blanket over the conversation.

"What makes you ask?"

"I met someone called Beckwith there last year, he was involved with carbon trading. I was just wondering if you might have been related."

She was staring at him, her eyes still with the same dreamy softness, but when she responded, her voice had a sharp edge to it.

"That was probably my husband, Rodger."

"Is he in London now?"

"No, he's still there."

"Oh, whereabouts?"

"I thought you might have been going to ask me out for a drink or something, but you seem to be more interested in him. He could be in hell, for all I care. I should have said, my soon to be ex-husband."

"Oh, I'm sorry."

"I'm not. Excuse me," she said, moving past him and quickly striking up a conversation with another group.

4

Emil stepped out of the lobby of the Shard and crossed the concourse to the escalators for the underground. He wasn't taking the tube, his hotel was a twenty-minute walk along the Thames riverside and across Tower Bridge: this was the quickest way to get down to Tooley Street and through Hays Galleria to reach the riverside.

There had been the usual drinks session at the end of conference proceedings, kicking off (thankfully early, he thought) before five. As he hit the fresh air, momentarily, he regretted staying so long. Unlike Frankfurt, from where he'd come, there was still a chilly edge to the early April evening and he shivered as he felt it on his face. He probably shouldn't have had that last glass of sauvignon blanc. But it did taste pretty good. Another tick for Lesley Beckwith and her colleagues for the catering. Five or six glasses was more than his capacity for alcohol these days, but he'd performed all his official functions in attending, so why not have a few drinks? He might even treat himself to a few more over dinner then have a nice, long sleep in tomorrow. Besides, the walk back to the hotel would help sober him up a bit, before deciding where to eat.

He could have dined with the people he'd been talking to at the drinks. The group, an entertaining bunch of South Americans and Asians, were heading in the direction of Borough Market. They'd heard there were good restaurants there. Nice enough people, he thought, but he'd had enough of policy wonks for the day and decided to dine alone. Once he'd freshened up back at the hotel, he was going to see what was on offer along the river opposite his hotel, around Butler's Wharf.

As he headed down the escalator, ruminating on possible cuisine he might find, his eye was caught by the slim figure of a woman, not far ahead of him. It was a figure that had caught his eye a few times already throughout the course of the day. She was wearing a jacket now, but he still recognised the figure-hugging woollen dress: the figure in it belonged to Lesley Beckwith. What luck. A chance to redeem his earlier gaffe. The missed opportunity. She had a good head start on him, so he quickened his pace to catch her.

At the entrance to the underground he saw her turn left through the arches, in the direction of the Jubilee Line. Running to catch up, he whipped out his Oyster card and followed through the ticket barrier and down the long escalator. How should he approach her? Maybe he should try to explain himself first, justify questioning her about her husband and apologise. Maybe he could even still persuade her to tell him where her husband was. Then again, maybe he shouldn't mention Beckwith at all. Uncertainty now. Maybe he shouldn't have had that last glass of wine. Self-doubt. Maybe he was just going to make a fool of himself. But he kept going.

In the thicket of commuters, it was hard to make up the distance between them. At the bottom she headed for the eastbound platform and straight onto a waiting train. Trailing in her wake, Emil pushed and bumped his way through. It was well past peak hour, but still he had to force his way into the packed carriage, two doors along, just as they snapped shut. She stayed on for two stops, alighting into another crowd. Again, he couldn't bridge the distance through the intervening bodies, finding himself trailing fifty metres in her wake.

How would he approach her now?

It had gone well beyond a casual crossing of their paths. It crossed his mind that she might think of it as something sinister. A case of stalking. If he suddenly appeared from behind, following her, this far from the venue … But fuelled by the alcohol coursing around his veins, he let that thought slip out of his mind again. He kept going.

Before he knew it, he found himself behind her on a canal pathway, still about fifty metres back. The sound of his footsteps on the brick paving was echoing around the bland brick building facades that lined either side. It was darker and the crowd of commuters seemed to evaporate straight after the tube exit. There wasn't another soul in sight. More misgivings. The pathway itself was well lit, so if she was the nervous type and looked around, she'd see him there, following her, as clear as day. The only sounds, other than his reverberating footsteps, the occasional irritated squawking of ducks attempting to roost.

Better to hold back: if he hurried to catch up now, it would spook her even more in a place like this. He kept an even pace, neither gaining nor slipping, running over and over in his mind what he'd say, when he did catch up to her. If he did.

The path passed under a roadway then diverted left and for a while he lost sight of her. Reaching the corner, he saw that she was striding away into the distance around the side of a larger body of water from which the canal flowed. The water was covered in roosting ducks, water fowl, gulls, swans and other birds, all trying to settle down for the night. It surprised him, given the canal water was a hideous dark turquoise. It reminded him of a new variety of washing up liquid. He passed a sign, identifying the area as a former dock. To his left, above him he could just make out, in the darkness, the frame of a disused gasometer, looming over the path like a skeletal sentinel, observing the two of them.

She strode on, oblivious to his presence – at least, that's what he was hoping – crossing a road and turning over a small bridge above heavy wooden lock gates. The bridge steelwork was painted pink, with a mechanism on one side that would have been used for raising the roadway. The mechanism made it look lopsided; in the streetlight it appeared to him like a huge, pink, snail shell.

Across the bridge, she turned towards a brick building with a timbered second story. The Old Salt Quay pub. For a second, he thought she was going in, but she glided past, continuing onto a pathway along the river, in front of the pub. He picked up his pace, so as not to lose sight of her. She might turn into one of the buildings along the riverfront. It was a mistake. The pathway took a long diversion around another former dock inlet, meaning she would be virtually looking straight at him, as he followed up one side, while she was coming back down the other. The lighting wasn't quite as good along the riverfront as it had been along the canal, but she couldn't miss seeing him.

Then, abruptly, she turned up a short flight of steps and was inserting a key in the lock of the gate at the top. He started running, but she was already inside and opening the door to the apartment building by the time he reached the gate.

"Hello, hello! Excuse me, Lesley! Hello."

She stopped, letting the building door swing back closed.

"Who is it? Do I know you?" she called back, trying to see who was calling her name from the shadows the other side of the gate.

"Hello, yes, I'm sorry, it's Emil Pfeffer," he stepped back into the light where she could see him better. "We spoke at the conference earlier today."

She approached the gate, warily. "Have you been following me?"

"Yes, look, I've been trying to catch up. I wanted to apologise for upsetting you this morning with my questions."

"You haven't been trying very hard, if you've followed me all the way from Canada Water."

"You've got a very brisk stride," he smiled, apologetically.

She moved to where she could see him better, regarding him for a few moments, as if trying to gauge whether he was worth trusting, worth the effort.

"What do you want?"

"I thought we might go for that drink you mentioned, this morning."

Again, she took her time before responding, looking him up and down.

"I should tell you to get lost." She paused, still looking at him closely. "But since you're here, you might as well come in."

The apartment was up a single flight of stairs, the fall of the land towards the river putting it on the second floor. It was compact, neat and a little sterile. There were no ornaments, or any personal items, in the sitting–dining room. No pictures or photos graced the walls. The furniture comprised a heavy wooden dining table with four chairs at one end of the room and an L-shaped sofa in the middle, facing a television screen at the other. Behind the screen, the wall was covered entirely by cheap shelving, on which were piles of papers, some folders, a stack of newspapers and magazines, and items of clothing. Two windows faced onto the river, where Emil stood looking out. The Thames slithering quickly past, its surface rippling like the muscular body of a huge, coffee-coloured snake.

"This is a good location, nice view, handy to transport."

"I'm afraid it's already taken, if you're looking for somewhere."

"Er, funny you should say that: I'm living in a hotel at the moment, so I guess eventually I will be looking for somewhere. But that's in Frankfurt, not London."

"Well, it's not cheap here, but as you say, it's convenient. I needed somewhere like this, when I came back. I had to find work and I was lucky that there was an opening at my old firm. They were happy to have me back."

She had returned from the small internal kitchen with a bottle and two glasses, the same wine they'd been serving at the conference.

"No point in going out, when we can have a drink here," she said, seeing him look at the bottle.

She had been with the consulting firm for many years, until

the opportunity to move to Switzerland had come up. The offer to her husband had been too good to refuse, even if it meant sacrificing her career.

"Yes, I was living in London some years ago too, had a place in Islington. Of course, it wasn't as hip then, as it is now. Actually, back then, it was pretty moth-eaten. But it was comfortable and familiar."

"Why did you leave it?"

"An opportunity came up with this organisation, also too good to pass up."

He was trying to avoid touching on anything too private, too sensitive, like the split from her husband. But the alcohol in the blood running through his brain was conjuring perverse thoughts; being in this situation with her, it was scrambling his ability to think straight.

Now that he was here, talking to her, he was struggling to think of what to say, without leading back to her husband, just asking her straight out where he was. He was starting to notice how drunk he was. Not a good sign. Got to be careful here, he thought, as she poured them each another generous glass of sauvignon blanc.

"Do you have children?"

She stared at him from the opposite end of the sofa, her lovely eyes both engaging him and confronting him at the same time, assessing where he was going with the question.

"Why?"

"Oh, er, I was just thinking the flat might be a bit cramped, with kids running around."

"Do you see any running around?" she said aggressively, then looked away and sighed, before turning back to him. "I'm sorry. That was rude, as my husband would undoubtedly have pointed out, if he were here. Yes, we have two, a boy and a girl. They're in boarding schools. At least he pays for that."

This was becoming awkward, turning out to be a mistake. Emil sipped his wine and looked out across the snake sliding past the window. The sawtooth-stepped brickwork of the building directly opposite, with lights dotted through it, could have been the outline of a huge alien spacecraft that had landed in Wapping. In front of it, a tug glided noiselessly past, three barges loaded with waste containers, in tow.

"If you're here because you want to talk about my husband's work, I'm afraid I can't help you."

Emil looked back at her. She seemed older than when he had first spoken to her, that morning. Maybe she was just tired. It would have been a stressful day. She'd finished her glass and was pouring herself another.

"He told me nothing. I was in Luzern, with the kids. He was in Zürich. Gave up my career, with a supportive employer and the job I loved doing, to give him a second chance with his. I would have been a global executive with them, by now, if I hadn't left. Could've been based any-where in the world."

"But you're in an important position, here in London, aren't you?"

"Head of Knowledge Management, for the London office? You've *gottobe* joking. We're not even the main European office anymore, Brussels is. And Frankfurt's second. The real power's in the east: Shanghai, Hong Kong, Singapore."

"Oh, I didn't realise."

"I could have been a global executive," she repeated, "heading up a global team on something really important, in one of those places. But I gave it up. And how did that rat thank me?"

As emotion rose in her voice, she was starting to run words together. I hope I don't sound that pissed, he thought. She must have had even more to drink than me.

She threw down the rest of her glass and poured herself another.

"By dumping me in Luzern, with the kids. On my own. Amongst all those bloody Swiss."

She took a gulp of wine.

"And basing himself in Zürich, hardly ever coming home."

She was looking Emil directly in the eye. Her own big, dreamy, brown eyes now slightly glassy.

"It was only by chance, I found out why he was away so much. He was screwing her. His assistant. Another bloody Swiss. Now I don't even have the kids with me."

Having followed Lesley Beckwith with the intent of getting her to talk about her husband, Emil found all he wanted to do now was get her off the topic.

"My girlfriend has disappeared, so I'm alone as well." That didn't come out the right way, he thought, having said it. "What I mean is, she took a flight from Papua New Guinea to Frankfurt, but without any explanation, got off at Singapore. Nobody's heard from her since."

"Maybe it was for someone else."

"Yes, that's a possibility, I suppose." He paused, thinking. "But there's nothing to suggest that ..." his voice trailed off as he remembered, with a sudden uneasiness, what Robert had told him. She'd been on the same flight as Gerry Johnstone. And he'd been booked only as far as Singapore.

"People often do things you don't expect they would. It's the little signs, changes that you don't notice, don't pick up on. I didn't notice, until it was way too late. Even then, it was only because he slipped up."

"I think she might have been kidnapped ... by the people who were financing your husband's bank ..."

He looked at her and, in his increasingly wine-befuddled mind, got the feeling that she was looking at him somehow differently.

"Why do you think my husband would leave me for another woman? Don't you think I'm attractive, Emil?"

"I think you're, er, quite beautiful, actually."

Wrong answer! He knew, as soon as he'd said it.

"Do you think I'm sexy?"

"Well, er, yes, but..."

"Don't you think men would want to *fuck* me?"

The word hit him like a punch, a king hit, knocking him

off whatever remaining balance he had. She'd moved closer to him on the sofa. With a surprise, he felt her hand was on his knee.

"I think half the men in the firm would. But they'd just do it so they could boast to their friends. The rest of them are gay."

"I, I …"

"Do you want to fuck me, Emil? Is that, really, why you followed me?"

"Yes, no. No! Er, I mean…"

Suddenly, she was kneeling on the floor in front of him, between his legs. How did she get there so quickly? One hand trying to get his belt undone, the other working up and down his groin. He wasn't resisting as hard as he might have been.

"Lesley, stop, please. No, I don't think it's a good idea."

"That's not what this is saying," she said, continuing to rub the front of his trousers.

Resolve. Moral fortitude. Inner strength. A rash of inane expressions raced through his mind. With an effort, he tried to recover the situation.

"No, please, Lesley."

He grabbed her hand, but she started rubbing him with the other.

"No, Lesley, stop! Please! Lesley."

He sensed he was about to lose control.

"Mrs Beckwith! Stop!"

She stopped abruptly, looking up at him. Fiercely. Then her hand, still on the bulge in his trousers, closed quickly and tightly around it, squeezing it as hard as she could.

"Don't call me that! Don't *ever* call me that!" she said, squeezing even harder, staring wildly into his startled face. Then releasing him, she slumped forward, her sudden anger run out of steam in that one violent burst, forehead on her arm on the edge of the sofa next to him.

Emil exhaled the breath he'd been holding. The stinging!

Ahhhhh. All he could do was gasp in pain. And gasp some more. At the intensely sharp, burning sensation in his penis.

"Oww! Jesus Christ!! Yeowww!"

It was pulsing. Each time he would think it had stopped, it would be engulfed by another ferocious spasm.

Excruciating stinging!

He pushed down on it with both his hands, trying to reduce the intensity of each recurrence, unable to move from where he sat, beads of perspiration suddenly breaking out and running down his face.

Trying to breathe deeply.

Trying to relax.

Waiting for each burning throb to abate.

Finally, after minutes of pushing down on his still offended groin, when he felt recovered enough, unsteadily, he got to his feet. She was still where she had slumped, motionless, like a shapeless sack of potatoes.

"I'd better go."

He gathered his coat and hesitantly, fearful that any sudden movement would start the stinging again, padded slowly and awkwardly down the short hallway to the door of the apartment.

"If you want to know where my arsehole of a husband is, he's still shacked up with that Swiss slut half his age. They're in a chalet above the lakes near Luzern," she said, pushing herself up from the floor. "Here, I'll write out directions how to get there."

5

A burst of vibration from the bedside table announced an incoming call.

Emil was sitting at the small desk in his hotel room. Past the screen of his open laptop, outside the window, he could see the Thames was high, its movement indecisive, the ebb tide about to begin. He'd been sitting there for quite a part of the morning, wrestling with the online booking process for one of the many budget airlines now filling the airspace over Europe.

His own indecisiveness was, in part, due to the incipient hangover bubbling along under the surface. He knew it was there somewhere, just that it hadn't turned nasty yet. He'd been doing his best to make sure it wouldn't: drinking lots of water, several double espressos and an orange juice for breakfast, washing down a large vitamin B-complex tablet.

He'd just returned from the toilet, but could almost feel the need to go again – an unfortunate side effect spawned by the hangover amelioration measures. And the pain he was experiencing with each of these visits, was reminding him of the previous evening.

"Oh, fuck, not again already. Emil, you idiot!" He slumped forward in the chair, elbows on knees, the butts of his palms massaging bloodshot eyes. His morning had been bouts of guilt and self-recrimination, interspersed with satisfaction at finally having got a lead on Beckwith and BKZ.

After staggering back to his hotel, he hadn't bothered about dinner but just collapsed into bed. His own, thankfully, rather than hers, as it might have been. But he hadn't left her behind completely. He dreamt he was on a paddle steamer heading out of Luzern, onto the Vierwaldstättersee, with someone – the impression the dream left when he woke was that it was her. They were steaming down the lake, ahead to the left, the Rigi Kulm; in the distance, Rütli, where they would disembark for the remote location of Rodger Beckwith's love nest, to catch him at it, with his assistant.

He didn't find out what happened, when they got there. A ringing sound had broken into this thought stream. He could hear a telephone ringing very persistently. But where would there be a telephone on a paddle steamer in Lake Luzern? Somebody should answer the damned ... then, with disappointment, he'd woken up and realised it wasn't a telephone on a paddle steamer. It was the alarm on his mobile phone. He was not on a paddle steamer on Lake Luzern. He was not with Lesley Beckwith. He was in a hotel room, alone, in London.

After breakfast in the hotel bar, he'd returned to the room to book on the next available flight to Luzern. He wasn't going to wait and let Beckwith slip away like the rest of them, now that he had a lead. That was when the wrestling match with the budget airline's website began. You'd think they'd make it easy, he fumed. All he wanted to do was to buy a ticket, to give them his money. But no, first he had to provide vast amounts of personal information and each webpage was not letting him get past, until it had extracted every, last detail.

What was it these days? Everywhere you turned, there was someone wanting your personal information. Usually, just to sell it to someone else. Ignore the fact that it's *your* personal information; ignore the fact that they expect to get it for *free*. Worse than that, these sites would actually blackmail it out of you, so that you couldn't get what you wanted or needed from them – even though you were paying – until they'd got the information they wanted.

Emil reached over and picked up his vibrating mobile phone.

"That took a while: don't tell me you're actually relaxing, Emil?" Betty G twanged in his ear. "Having a lie-in?"

"I am a bit slow moving this morning, Betty, as a matter of fact. They served a nice drop of white after the event last night. I might have had a glass or two more than I should have."

"Good for you, Emil! How was the event?"

"You did well not to waste your time …"

"Well, one of us needed to be there, so you were helping me a lot, by being 'it'."

"Glad to be of assistance. By the way, I've decided to take your advice and have some time off, I was just looking up flights."

"I'm afraid you're gonna have to put that on hold, Emil. Maybe you can tack it onto the end of this job. We've just been contacted by the Australian Government. Came in through the Liaison Unit, but it's a market integrity matter. They want to have some discreet, off-the-record discussions, as soon as possible."

"You want me to go out there, or are they coming to Frankfurt?"

"Hong Kong. There's a team of lawyers there who can provide the background briefing, but basically it's to do with some legal case they're fighting. Has potential to affect their policy on carbon trading. They're worried especially about possible effects it will have on the market."

"Couldn't they just put all this in writing?"

"Politically, too sensitive. Too confidential, commercially. It's big. And it's important. At this stage, they're only willing to provide a face-to-face briefing. To you."

"OK, Betty. I guess I'll see you back in the office tomorrow, then."

"Too urgent. You're booked direct from London. Flight details and hotel booking are being emailed to you, as we speak. Your flight's at eighteen thirty-five, so you better get movin'."

After the Texans...

"*Tonight?*"
"You got it, Emil!"

6

There wasn't much he could do about it.

It was unfortunate, but the visit to Rodger Beckwith's mountain love nest would have to be postponed. And with it, the possibility of getting a lead on BKZ and, ultimately, on Johanna's whereabouts. He thought about asking Dominik to pay Beckwith a visit, but that might be expecting a bit too much, given he was only starting back at work in the next week and was still recuperating from the operation on his injuries.

Heathrow was congested and chaotic as he'd come to expect, even in the new terminal, which he discovered, too late, was a very long walk from the Crossrail station. Given his state after the previous evening's events, he wasn't really in the mood for overexerting himself, so he offered up a prayer of thanks for the diplomatic passport. At least that eased his passage through the security queues.

He didn't quite know why, but he loved Hong Kong and had visited many times. He'd even thought about the possibilities of working there when he first looked to get out of London. Then the Global Carbon Markets Organisation job had come up in Frankfurt. Maybe it had been for the better. Living here might have killed off the love affair, he mused, walking up the air-bridge into the terminal.

Once he had his luggage, he was quickly out of the airport and on the express train into Central. From there he took the free hotel bus, rather than a taxi. The early afternoon traffic was just as bad as ever, but the air was mild and a fresh breeze was making it seem clean, at least. The hotel was above Pacific Place, up the hill from Queensway, just before it reached Wan Chai and became Hennessey Road. He'd stayed here before, but not on the 'executive levels', where his room was this time (the thought crossed his mind that the Australian Government must be paying for it), so he took his time settling in, enjoying the view across the top of the Convention and Exhibition Centre and over the harbour, past the end of Kowloon towards the old Kai Tak airport.

The meeting with the Australian lawyers was in the Exchange Centre, adjacent to the main station. He remembered there was an automatic teller machine in the Pacific Place shopping mall, so he went via there to get some cash, before heading underground to take the MTR from Admiralty. When he emerged at Central, to his surprise, the weather had changed dramatically. Torrential rain was pelting down, the streets already turning into brimming currents. Dark storm clouds were sitting low over the buildings up towards the Peak. It had probably been building all day, he just hadn't noticed it when he arrived.

This is crazy, he thought, almost like the entire weather cycle had been moved forward three months. It was the thunderous, drenching sort of rain usually associated with the typhoon season, late in the summer, but here it was now, coming down in buckets. He made his way up to the elevated pedestrian walkway that provided a conduit between various shopping malls and office buildings. It was covered, affording an escape from the congested traffic around Central and at least partial respite from the weather. A godsend at any time, but in these sorts of conditions it came into its own.

He obviously wasn't the only one caught unawares – there seemed to be clusters of dripping, wet bodies everywhere. Some people were just milling about, seeking refuge from the rain; others actually trying, like Emil, to get somewhere. It was especially slow going around the entrances to shops and malls, and with the rain blowing in, only those needing to cross Connaught Road were venturing out onto the bridge towards the Exchange Centre and station entrance. He stood, momentarily shielded from the rain swirling on the wind, surveying his options: no signs of easing – there was nothing for it, but to make a dash.

Puddles were everywhere in the undulations of the concrete slab walkways. He tried to pick his way between the worst of them, but his shoes were quickly so wet he gave up. People were dashing around in all directions. He was getting soaked, they were soaked, collisions made it worse. Trying not to run into them, he kept moving, looking for the closest entrance on the other side to head towards. Whipped by wind gusts, the rain was scything across the walkway: it seemed to be getting more intense. He spotted the entrance to the railway station and headed for it. From there, he could enter the building complex from the inside, but getting to it, meant a further thirty metres or so along the walkway past the end of the bridge in the rain. His suit already felt like a used bath sponge – it would look like seersucker by the time he got to the meeting. Got to find a bathroom with a blower hand dryer, he thought, before I meet these guys.

As he got closer, it seemed all the pedestrian traffic was aiming for the same entrance. With people trying to exit through the doorways at the same time, it was backing up. Emil found himself hemmed in by the crowd. It was shielding him from the weather, but he was only inching towards the doors. He could feel his shirt and trousers sticking to him. It was bloody uncomfortable. Just barely creeping forward.

Then, he saw him.

The one person in the world Emil least wanted to see, but most needed to find.

And never expected to see. Not here. Not now.

It was as if someone had suddenly slapped him, or given him a fright. At first, all he could do was blink his eyes in disbelief, testing whether his vision was playing tricks on him. The rain, his discomfort – instantly forgotten.

But there was no mistaking who it was. His appearance. The attention to detail. Even in these conditions, he exuded elegance, composure.

He'd come out of the entrance to the railway station and turned, striding along the walkway, away from the crowd gathered around the doorway. Emil stood where he was, surrounded by wet, steaming, shuffling bodies for a few moments, too surprised to do anything but watch, as Gregory Hudson turned onto the next bridge along, back over Connaught Road, towards the Hang Seng Bank building. Assurance in every stride, moving swiftly but calmly, untroubled by the weather, turning the collar of his off-white Burberry raincoat up against the wind and rain.

He was about to disappear past the corner of the building on the other side of the bridge, when Emil reacted. Suddenly he was moving, pushing his way through the crowd, not worrying about the rain or water underfoot, not worrying about the people he was offending by forcing his way past them; then running, urgently, desperate not to lose sight of Hudson.

Back through the squalls, across Connaught Road, the walkway disappeared behind the Hang Seng Bank building, towards the Central Market Building. Reaching it, he almost slipped over as the concrete changed to the wet, tiled flooring of the passageway. It was wall-to-wall with shoppers, commuters and people trying to keep out of the weather. He pushed on through the crowd, wary of his footing, eyes quickly searching, skimming over every shopping stall and booth, left and right. The off-white Burberry was nowhere to be seen. Hudson could have disappeared into any of the multitude of shops and booths, or the labyrinth of passageways between them in the Market building. But Hudson didn't look like he was here for shopping and, if he were, would prefer somewhere a little more up-market. Figuring he must be somewhere up ahead, still in the crowd, Emil kept going.

A footbridge crossed Queens Road, leading onto the first of the moving footways and escalators that headed up the mid-levels. To one side, an escalator and, to the other, steps, led down to Queens Road, now traversed by the torrent gushing down Cochrane Street immediately beneath the walkway. Emil covered half the steps down and checked up Cochrane and along Queens Road: there was no sign of the off-white Burberry. He raced back up to the moving footway, now solid with people – why couldn't the idiots stand to one side to let others through? Instead, he leapfrogged his way up, around the people coming down the parallel set of steps. At the foot-bridge over Wellington Street, he searched up and down the teeming footpaths below. No sign of Hudson.

The next section of footway was clearer. He worked his way up it quickly, careful to avoid slipping on the wet metal surface. At Shelley Street, again he scoured the street for any sign of Hudson. As he strained his gaze into the murky streetscape, glimpses of white clothing here and there in the rushing crowds deceived him, half-tempting him to race down. Dismissing them, he was running again, to the first of the escalators up into Soho.

There were even fewer people ahead of him now. At the top end of the section of escalator, he could just make out trouser legs extending below the bottom of what could have been an off-white raincoat. The angle of the roof blocked most of his view so he squatted, trying to see the rest of the body above to the legs. It was an off-white raincoat, but he couldn't make out that much. Vaulting up the escalator two steps at a time, he caught sight, in the distance, of the Burberry disappearing into Staunton Street.

Reaching the top, he leapt out into the crowds of bar and restaurant goers milling about. The storm was moving on, the rain easing. But the off-white Burberry was nowhere to be seen in the profusion of alleyways, shops and street food stalls, run-off still gushing from their canopies in mini-waterfalls. He searched up and down the street, looking into the nearest establishments and alleyways for any sign of Hudson. But he was gone. And with him, the tiny, fleeting hope that had been engendered.

Or had it?

The Interpol Red Notice was in place. Of course! That was as good as an international arrest warrant. There was still a chance.

Emil made his way back to Central and down onto the MTR. The Hong Kong police force headquarters, he remembered, was in Arsenal Street, Wan Chai. Explaining that he needed to speak with someone about an Interpol Red Notice, he was directed to 'B' Department, Crime & Security, and the Commercial Crime Bureau, in another building along Arsenal Street. After more explanations, eventually he was ushered into a meeting room where he was joined by a serious looking officer, epaulettes bearing two pips over a bar.

"I'm Senior Inspector Tang," said the policeman, looking up from the business card, which Emil had presented to one of policemen to whom he had already told his story. "You are with the UN Global Carbon Markets Organisation in Frankfurt. Very good. Er, how do you pronounce your name?"

"'Feffer'. It's German for pepper."

"Ah, but you sound English, or Australian."

"Yes, well-spotted. But my name is of German origin."

"I am not aware of any carbon trading in Hong Kong, but I am sure it is here somewhere. So, Mr Pfeffer, how can I help you?"

"As I explained to your colleagues, in my work, I was involved recently in a matter in Papua New Guinea. Criminal activities were exposed on a significant scale, impacting both that country and my organisation's work. Four people were killed, including one of my staff. Following investigations, an arrest warrant was issued and the government requested Interpol to issue a Red Notice for the main perpetrator, a Canadian, called Gregory Hudson. I have just seen Hudson in Central."

"I see," said Tang, carefully regarding Emil, whose soaked shirt was sticking to him like an outer skin. "Are you here on official business?"

"I was on my way to a meeting in the Exchange Centre. As you can see," Emil gestured to his sopping shirt and suit coat, "I wasn't quite prepared for a pursuit up through the midlevels in a storm."

"So you chased after this man – he was aware that you were after him?"

"I don't think so. He was too far ahead of me, that's why I lost him. I think he got off the escalator at Staunton Street. At least, that's where I lost him."

"You're certain it was this man, this Hudson, and that there is currently a Red Notice in force in respect of him?"

"No doubt. I recognised him immediately. He was quite close initially, but I found it hard to catch him in the crowds – and in the storm," said Emil, holding his arms out to indicate again the impact it had had on his clothes.

"Yes, so I see, Mr Pfeffer." Tang considered this, tapping the edge of Emil's card on the table top while he thought. "If you can provide some details, including where you are staying and for how long, I will make enquiries with the Interpol Division of our Liaison Bureau. They work closely with the Department of Justice's Mutual Legal Assistance Unit, who coordinates all these types of requests."

Then he offered: "Will you be late for your meeting? I can arrange transport to the Exchange Centre."

Having provided a written statement and details of his hotel, with siren blaring and blue lights flashing, Emil was returned by police car to the Exchange Centre, like some very important person. However, getting out of the car with his drowned rat appearance, he wondered whether he didn't look more like a suspect being released after having been helping the police with their inquiries. Before he left the police head-quarters, he'd made sure Senior Inspector Tang would attach every priority to finding Hudson.

"This man, Hudson, is very dangerous, Senior Inspector. I can't emphasise enough, how important it is that you find him, as quickly as possible."

*****

"Good of you to show up."

Emil had finally located the Australian legal team.

"You should've checked the weather forecast first though, by the look of things."

It was the leader of the legal team, SJ Loftus, Senior Counsel, who greeted him, receiving his apologies with a shrug.

"Suppose we can't complain too much, seeing as you've come halfway 'round the world, at very short notice."

They were in a meeting room, looking out as the tail-end of the storm was disappearing over Kowloon in the early evening twilight. Loftus, tall and slightly stooped from his years spent standing at the bar tables of various courts, full head of greying hair, two-toning with his charcoal suit, made the introductions.

"Now that the hearing is drawing to a close, the rest of the team's departed. We've trimmed down to a lean machine of three. This is Marianne Carrone," he said, gesturing towards a mousey woman with tightly curled, auburn hair, dressed in a dark blue tailored suit, under which a cream shirt with lace collar was buttoned resolutely to the neck. "Marianne is our remaining support solicitor. And this," he said, turning to the other person in the room, who had a ruddy face and stout body, also in a suit, just more of it, "is Rita McCarty. Rita is my junior."

And she is undoubtedly a red wine drinker, thought Emil. Silk shirt open at the neck, garrulous and friendly although her short cropped hair made her seem a little butch. 'Junior' was not how Emil would have addressed her. He shook their hands, noting, as he did, the firmness of Rita's grip. Their business cards indicated they worked for a legal agency of the Australian Government.

"Some floors below us in this building, Mr Pfeffer, are the premises of the Hong Kong International Arbitration Centre. That's the reason we're here."

The meeting room was their temporary office, had been for the best part of the preceding year. The main table and side tables were littered with laptops, bulging lever-arch folders, and legal texts. Documents, extensively tagged with post-it notes, were strewn in arcs in front of where Marianne and Rita were sitting. It being close to when they normally broke for an evening meal, by the time he arrived, they'd sent out for refreshments. Each of them now had a drink in hand, Emil noting that Rita had claimed a large glass of shiraz.

"Please, it's Emil."

"I understand you're a lawyer, Mr Pfeffer." Either Loftus didn't hear Emil's entreaty to less formality, or wasn't going to alter his habit in spite of it. "Are you familiar with the concept of 'investor-state dispute settlement', by any chance?"

"I'll have to plead ignorance, I'm afraid. I might be in the business of public international law given my employer, but it isn't my *forte*."

"Ah, well, the Australian Government, in all its wisdom, over the last couple of years decided it would be a good idea to sign up to a number of agreements which include these so-called investor-state dispute settlement provisions. That, it now transpires, was a very bad move."

"I don't think it's quite correct, SJ," Marianne cut in, "to say they thought it was a good idea. The reality was, at the time the relevant agreements were negotiated, the government was under a huge amount of pressure from the industry. The lobbyists were really out in force."

"Yes, thank you for that, Ms Carrone. I'm being facetious; please grant me that one small indulgence, will you? As you can see," said Loftus addressing Emil, "we have our team pedant." Then raising his glass to Marianne, "And invaluable, she is too!"

"I assume, when you say 'industry', you're referring to the carbon market?" asked Emil. "The reason why I'm here?"

"Not just a pretty face!" Rita shot in quickly, reaching for the nibbles.

"Whether it was the weight of lobbying, political pressure to get the agreements signed, weakness on the part of the negotiators – or stupidity on the part of the decision-makers – is really neither here nor there. Fact is, we're stuck with these provisions and they're being used against us," said Loftus.

"I'm not up to speed on any of this, I'm sorry, you'll need to explain," said Emil.

"Okay, over to you Marianne, you've got all the background."

"Thanks, SJ." Marianne sat up straighter. With the high lace collar, she gave a good impression of being a Victorian schoolmistress. "Briefly, these types of provisions are generally seen as a legacy from World Trade Organisation free trade agreement negotiations going back thirty or forty years.

"Since free trade agreements provide for investment in each country by investors from the other, they needed a means of resolving any disputes which might arise, for example, between an investor from one country and the government of the other. Rather than resorting to the laws and courts of one or other of the parties, which might have given rise to perceptions of bias, these provisions became the norm."

"Problem is," Rita chipped in, "the mechanism they provide is arbitration, usually on a confidential basis, so there's little room for external scrutiny. Means less legal processes followed. No system of precedents, so there's a lack of consistency in the decisions. No appeals to the courts. Arbitrators may not even be lawyers."

"That *would* be a disaster!" Emil smiled.

"Indubitably!" Rita shot back. "The main focus of these tribunals is whether the investor has suffered any damage, not whether the government's laws or policies are legitimate. The processes are driven solely by the commercial outcomes."

"Well, that's a criticism that's levelled at this approach, Rita, but it needn't always be the case," said Marianne.

"Okay, point taken. But when the outcome affects government policy, and it's decided in secret, by people who aren't judges, then *that's* a problem!" returned Rita, again reaching for the nibbles, then replenishing her glass of shiraz.

"In Australia's case, we've been stung before," Marianne continued. "The 1993 Australia–Hong Kong bilateral investment agreement – the Agreement for the Promotion and Protection of Investments…"

"You're not delivering a university lecture, Marianne," Loftus interjected, "cut to the chase."

"On that occasion, a big tobacco company restructured its operations through Hong Kong companies, so that they could allege that the Australian Government's cigarette plain packaging legislation infringed their intellectual property rights in the packaging. Then they sought to have the dispute resolved by arbitration, under the investor-state dispute settlement provision in that agreement.

"Despite this experience, the government has signed up to a number of bilateral carbon trading agreements which include these provisions. It seems the investor lobby groups latched onto these as a way of protecting their members from swings in policy by governments. You'd have to agree, the Australian Government doesn't have a great record of consistency on climate change policy …"

"Yes, I'd definitely have to agree with that," observed Emil.

"Okay, thanks Marianne," said Loftus. "So, Mr Pfeffer, that's the context. What we have is a case of history repeating itself, except this time it's an even more extreme manipulation of the circumstances by the players involved."

"'Players' is a bit ambivalent isn't it, boss?" Rita again. "Shouldn't that be 'filthy rich, greedy foreign swine, intent on destroying our natural heritage'?"

"Alright, Rita. It might help Mr Pfeffer more if we outline the facts, before we attach our value judgments, don't you think?"

47

The glass heading for Rita's mouth was momentarily diverted upwards, a sign of acquiescence, before its contents were drained, then refilled again. Just the usual senior–junior banter, Emil guessed.

"As Marianne mentioned," continued Loftus, "Australian policy on climate change, and environmental matters generally, has wobbled about a bit. Recently, there's been an intense public debate about development of a massive new coal-loading terminal on the Queensland coast. Biggest in the world, it will be, when built. You might have read about it – scientific consensus is that it would hasten the final death throes of the Great Barrier Reef."

"Yes, I've seen reports on that. But I understood the government has said it's 'off the agenda'?"

"Exactly. But a lot of investment has been made, in anticipation of the expected continuation of federal government support for the project. Unfortunately, or perhaps fortunately, depending on one's perspective on the matter, after a number of political and judicial developments, the government has done a policy back-flip. As, I might add, it's perfectly entitled to do."

"Showed a bit of ticker, for once," added Rita.

"It's just that the investors who have been pouring money in, based on what they now claim was clear encouragement from the government, are not happy at all," Loftus concluded. "They want redress."

"Why don't they sue the government in the courts?"

"Unlikely to win. And in what must rank as one of the most cynical legal actions ever mounted," said Rita, again picking up the flow, "they've homed in on the investor-state dispute settlement provisions included in the bilateral carbon trading agreements to protect investors in carbon reduction projects.

"You see, the draftsmen never envisaged such a cynical ploy and weren't cautious enough with their phrasing of the provisions. The definition for 'carbon-related investments' doesn't make it clear that these should be only for emission reductions. It can be read equally to include investments that cause increased emissions. That's what they are arguing.

"So now, coal mining projects, and projects related to coal mining, that will cause vastly increased carbon emissions, are claiming for recovery of their anticipated losses. Losses, they claim, will run into the billions ..."

"All of this is, of course, a major problem for our government, but shouldn't unduly concern your organisation," Loftus explained, comfortingly. "Except," he paused, looking at Emil, beer glass held carefully balanced in his hand, "except, Mr Pfeffer, if we were to lose."

With that, SJ Loftus, Senior Counsel to the Australian Government, raised the beer glass to his lips and drank its contents.

7

It was two days before Tang got back to him.

On the first night, the meeting with the Australian legal team had gone late. There had been a lot of background for him to assimilate; there'd been a lot of glasses of wine consumed. He woke the next morning tired and flat. Not with a hangover, as the legal team had been doing most of the drinking. Emil had wanted to stay alert, in case Tang came straight back to him.

But Tang hadn't come back to him that night and he woke next morning with the same flat listlessness that, on such mornings in Frankfurt, was driving Betty G crazy: the reason she'd wanted him out of the office in the first place. It was a purposeless, directionless feeling like one woke with after drinking gin – not that he ever did much of that. But he knew what it felt like just the same.

"What am I doing here?" he asked no one in particular, sitting on the side of his bed, staring at the floor in front of his feet. "What the *fuck* am I doing here?" He'd been like that since waking half an hour earlier. Mornings he woke feeling this way, like a rudderless ship, generally followed nights when he'd dreamt of being with Johanna again, doing things, having conversations, sharing experiences with her, a jumble of memories and yearnings.

How many times had she told him that she loved him? How

many times had *he* told her? Not enough. He had an intense longing for her; a selfish need to fill the void she'd filled, but now left vacant. It made him feel empty. Then the self-recrimination would begin.

His thoughts drifted back to the hotel room in Moresby.

"I really didn't want you involved in all of this," he'd said to her, "but you're here now, so I guess that can't be avoided."

You're wrong Emil, it could have been avoided, if you'd just given a little more thought to her, instead of to stopping Hudson.

"You can do something to help us," he'd said, giving her the laptop – probably the reason they'd taken her. "If anything happens to me or if you haven't heard from me before you're scheduled to leave, contact this person in Frankfurt and give it to him. A journalist, he'll know what to do with it."

For all he knew, that'd probably made the journo a marked man, as well. Then he recalled how, earlier, it was he who'd been upset with Dominik for using Johanna as a go-between to contact him.

"He talks about these mysterious 'other people'," he'd complained to her about Dominik, "the ones that he thinks have a 'mole' in the organisation, and who broke into his apartment. The ones who are dangerous and are the reason he's more or less in hiding; but then he goes ahead and uses you as his agent, without even thinking that by doing so, he might be putting you at risk …"

Emil cringed at the recollection. In Bad Eschbach, he tried to not let these guilt trips take hold by launching himself into action, keeping busy, doing things aimed at finding her, at bringing her back. But this was becoming harder to do, with the drudgery of staff management and the daily routine imposing itself on him, offering fewer opportunities for diversion, for feeling that he was doing something positive; that he was making progress towards finding her. As time passed, the moods were coming over him more often.

This second morning in Hong Kong was worse than usual.

Since being in London, every now and then uncertainties would spill over and start seeping into his consciousness. When he'd been dreaming of intimacies they'd shared, the sudden recollection of Gerry Johnstone being on the same flight as Johanna, of them both leaving the flight in Singapore, would barge in and destroy the moment.

"People often do things you don't expect they would," Lesley Beckwith had said. "It's the little signs, changes that you don't notice, don't pick up on."

The awful doubt that the drunken conversation with Lesley Beckwith had left planted in his mind. The not knowing. He hated himself when he had these thoughts, but there was little he could do to stop them. They were there, in his head. Maybe his more intense sense of longing for her was a psychological counter-balancing of these thoughts. The answer was to find her. And the first step to doing that, was to find Hudson.

When it did come, Tang's call came early in the morning, as Emil was preparing to head down to the Exchange Centre.

In the two days since arriving in Hong Kong, he had barely stepped out of the meeting room that was the Australian legal team's base. Not being a member of either side's legal team, Emil wasn't admitted into the hearing room, six floors below. Under the rules of the arbitration body, hearings were private, unless the parties agreed otherwise. The other side had made it clear that things were to stay private – and that Emil was to stay out. The arbitration had been mounted by Hong Kong investors who claimed to have ploughed significant resources into developing real estate and infrastructure in and around that part of the Queensland coast adjacent to the site of the proposed coal loader development. Investment that would be worthless if the project didn't go ahead. Estimates of their claim ranged from two billion to five billion Australian dollars.

Despite Loftus's assessment that the outcome would be a finding in favour of the Australian Government's sovereign right to determine its own domestic policies, at this stage, really, they had no inkling of how the panel of three arbitrators would decide. If the ruling went in favour of the investors, the fallout for the Global Carbon Markets Organisation would be two-fold: firstly, the impact it would have on the Australian Government's support for carbon trading where, to date, it had been very active, helping to give the market much needed liquidity and depth. Secondly, they had no idea how many other bilateral agreements may contain similar provisions capable of manipulation by fossil fuel developing investors, posing risks to the countries involved. If the numbers were significantly large, it would certainly affect market confidence and even had the potential to bring the entire market crashing to an ignominious collapse. Given its fraught history to date, another global price collapse would probably signal the end of trading as a credible mechanism, once and for all.

"If the investors win, governments in countries involved in carbon trading will scramble to see if their bilateral trading agreements have these provisions. Then they'll be assessing whether they're capable of being construed in the way the investors are arguing here," Emil explained to Betty G and the rest of the Executive Board.

They'd convened a conference call, the preceding afternoon.

"Rather than alert governments now, provoking concerns that might turn out to be unfounded, we should find out what we can from our own research, first."

"But, Emil, many, if not most of these bilateral agreements contain confidentiality provisions, which means we really need to consult the parties in the first instance, anyway," cautioned Betty G.

"True, Betty, but I'd still like to get Dominik and the team to make a preliminary assessment, to see if we can get a better handle on the potential size of the problem."

"Alright, but I don't want to be caught short if this panel suddenly whacks the Australians, then other countries go into a flap. The first question they'll ask is why we didn't warn them – why *I* didn't warn them!"

"Based on the timetable for the arbitration and the fact

that both sides have just about finished presenting all their evidence, I'm guessing that the hearing will go at least a few more days."

"What about a ruling, Emil, how long before the arbitrators might deliver?"

"No idea, we'll just have to wait and see."

"Okay, Emil. Your unit's got forty-eight hours to find out what it can and brief me," Betty G had decided.

In the mood he was in this morning, Tang's news was not what he needed. "The Interpol Division and Justice are aware of this Red Notice, Mr Pfeffer," Tang reported, "but there is no record of a person by the name of Gregory Hudson having entered Hong Kong. Not for the last month."

Emil wondered whether the mood he'd woken in had been a premonition of what Tang would tell him. "Can you please check again, Senior Inspector, the earlier period? He could have entered Hong Kong any time since he was deported from PNG last year."

When Tang called back, Emil was in the meeting room. The situation hadn't changed. "We've searched back to the time you indicated this man Hudson was removed from Papua New Guinea. There is no record of a person by that name entering Hong Kong since that time. I'm sorry we cannot be of more assistance, Mr Pfeffer. Are you certain that the man you saw, the one that you followed, was this Hudson?"

"Absolutely. I'll get the Papua New Guinea authorities to send you through a photo."

"No need. There's a photo on the Interpol Red Notice listing. But that doesn't help, when our records show he hasn't entered Hong Kong. You have my contact details – the Liaison Bureau has asked me to act as contact point with you; so, if you see him again – don't take any risks, you said he is dangerous – please get in touch with me."

At least Tang was taking him seriously. He'd told him Hudson was dangerous, but was he, really? Only when he had his henchmen there to carry out the dirty work, Emil thought, remembering Wiebe. But then, *he* was the one who'd killed Wiebe – even if it was in self-defence. Maybe Hudson is the one who should be worried.

He didn't have time to dwell on it: he needed to be mobilising his people in Bad Eschbach, after the briefing with the executive. Later that day, he was engrossed on a call with Dominik and at first didn't notice the knock at the door. He was telling Dominik about his Hudson sighting, so their discussion had moved rapidly from the number of bilateral agreements the Market Integrity Unit had been able to access, to how Emil might go about finding Hudson in Hong Kong, if he was operating under a different name – the conclusion they'd both reached. The door of the room opened a little, and the profile of a young Chinese woman appeared through it, hesitantly.

Emil held the phone away. "Hello, can I help you?"

She turned, surprised. Her hand went up to cover her mouth and she made a little bow. "Excuse me."

He noticed was that she was very pretty; wearing a red suit, over a silk shirt, open at the neck to show a double string of small pearls. A businesswoman or professional, he guessed, judging from her appearance.

"Are you looking for someone? Can I help you?" then into the handset, "I'll call you back, Dom," he said, ending the call. It was almost the end of the afternoon session of the hearing, from which the others were yet to return.

"No. Thank you. I will call back. Thank you," she said, backing out of the room again.

"Can I take a message? Who was it you wished to see?" he tried, but she pulled the door shut behind her and was gone.

When the legal team returned, none of them had any idea of who it might have been or for which of them she might have been looking.

"An opportunistic thief?" suggested Marianne.

"Maybe she was just lost. There are plenty of rooms here, this place seems well patronised," offered Rita.

At the lunch recess on the following day, Emil joined the legal team outside the hearing room, heading out to a restaurant. He felt someone's eyes on him and saw the pretty Chinese woman again, watching him from inside the hearing room. She was part of the investors' legal team. She looked away as soon as he looked at her. He confided to Loftus after lunch.

"That's Ms Cheng, from Kok, Wei & Partners, instructing solicitors for the other side," advised Loftus. "She's the partner's 'gofer', whoops, I mean assistant solicitor." He ducked as Rita hurled a screwed up ball of waste paper at him.

"So do you think Kok, Wei sent her up here to see what she could find out while you weren't around?"

"I doubt it. We've made our case, so they know everything there is to know. They would have known it all six months ago, anyway, when we lodged written submissions to the panel. And, they're a reputable firm. Besides, if you hadn't been there, the door would have been locked. Maybe you should try asking her? She's very attractive, why don't you ask her out for a drink?"

"'fraid I'm spoken for."

Rather it was Loftus who approached her, at the end of the day's proceedings.

"Our colleague, Mr Pfeffer, said you called by our office yesterday," he said as they were leaving the hearing room. "Were you looking for one of us?"

"I think your colleague is mistaken. It must have been someone else. Perhaps we all look alike, to him."

Relations between the two sides over the course of the hearing had been standoffish, but cordial. Her response seemed just a little bit over the edge towards rudeness, which surprised Loftus. It seemed out of character for the other legal team, but also for the Cantonese who, as a rule, he found to be very polite. He took it no further, Cheng leaving him in her wake as she sped up to join her own, waiting colleagues. When he told Emil, they agreed it was a bit rude.

"Well, if that's what she's like, I certainly won't be asking her out for a drink!"

*****

The week ended and the arbitration panel drew the hearings to a close.

"Well, all we can do now is wait," announced Rita on the team's return to the meeting room that afternoon.

"Not so, my esteemed junior," responded Loftus. "Whatever the decision, we need to get this lot," he waved his arms around the room, "sorted and packed. So. Lots to do, more than just wait!"

Emil spent the following week marshalling his MIU team around the task of finding out what they could of the carbon trading agreements various countries had entered. He scheduled a call with Dominik first thing each morning, meaning early afternoon in Hong Kong, to check on their progress, but in reality ended up spending most of each day on the telephone to him.

The initial forty-eight-hour deadline from Betty G had been extended, but now that the hearings were finished and a decision was expected within the next week or so, the pressure was on to devise a strategy for all those countries whose trading agreements may contain similar provisions. After several more teleconferences with Betty G and the executive board, it was agreed that a general bulletin be sent to all countries engaged in carbon trading.

"What we'll be asking is that they advise us of any bilateral trading agreements they have containing investor-state dispute resolution provisions," he advised the executive. "We'll ask them to send copies, so Dominik's team can compare them with the provisions being considered in Hong Kong. That way, the Market Integrity Unit will be in the driving seat."

"And the hot seat, Emil, if things go badly for the Aussies!" said Betty G. "But that's good, we're on the front foot!"

The question was, whether it would stay there once the decision was handed down.

Emil was putting in long days by spending each evening hanging about the midlevels escalator until the pedestrian traffic thinned out, searching, waiting for another appearance by Hudson. On several nights, he was still there until after midnight. Before he retired to bed each evening, he'd speak to Dominik again, just to make sure everything was on track, so he wouldn't wake in the morning to learn of a derailment.

Towards the end of the week, returning to his hotel after an evening prowling around the midlevels escalator, he was surprised to see Ms Cheng, in the lobby of his hotel. She seemed to be looking, or waiting, for someone; or maybe she was just checking the place out. He stopped and watched her for a few moments, making sure that it was in fact her. As soon as she saw him looking at her from across the opposite side of the lobby, she left. At least that verified that he was right. It was Cheng who'd called in at the meeting room.

The next day, he told Loftus.

"Hmm. Maybe she's spying on you," mused Loftus. "Should I have a word to the partner she works for?"

"No, I hardly think that would be the case! It's not a big issue. Forget I mentioned it."

Some nights he found himself a vantage point at the window of one of the English-pub style establishments that lined the escalator route, and would linger for several hours over a single drink, or plate of food, a book or papers in hand, but his attention resolutely fixed on the passers-by. These exercises were fruitless: off-white Burberry raincoat lookalikes caught his attention a couple of times, but there were no further sightings of Hudson.

On the Saturday evening, he was at what was becoming his regular window position in the Yorkshire Pudding pub. Being the weekend, there'd been a lot more people out and about, and his eyes were getting tired from the constant flitting from one face to the next. Once or twice, he'd been tricked by the manner of movement of a man whose face he couldn't see; but each time, the person had turned around to disclose just another false alarm.

It was almost midnight and he was just about to leave, when his phone buzzed. It was Loftus.

"I know it's late, but I thought you'd want to know immediately: just got a text to say the panel is reconvening on Monday morning to deliver its decision orally."

"Pity I can't get in to hear it. So do they give it writing, as well?"

"Yes, the written version will follow later."

8

SJ Loftus was not a man to be overconfident. Thirty years at the bar had taught him that. Solid, reliable, invariably spot on when evaluating clients' prospects. Sound judgment. An entertaining performer, but unlike some of his peers, never a showman. Unemotional, incisive, to the point. That's the way judges liked it. That's the way he liked it.

He'd been running this arbitration case for the government from the start. Now they were into the home straight and he had a positive feeling as to the outcome. Not that he'd had any doubt in the correctness of his client's, his government's, position from day one. But all the resources had to be marshalled, all the grounds had to be covered, and all the research done; all the questions had to be answered, all the documents had to be drafted, all the timelines and deadlines had to be met, and all the costs covered; then all the strategy decisions had to be made, all the evidence had to be adduced, and all the arguments had to be put and drawn together as a coherent whole, before one could even begin to start thinking in terms of an outcome.

All those things had been done. It was coming to an end. He felt they'd scored points on their opponents in every aspect. Every matter raised by the investors in their statement of claim had been surgically dissected and dealt with – forensically, clinically. Every witness, every item of documentary evidence produced by the claimants had been rebutted thoroughly, powerfully, effectively. Every question raised by the arbitrators had been considered carefully, and answered directly, comprehensively.

The investors had tried some familiar lines of argument. The government had deprived them of their investments, they said, by imposing policies that effectively expropriated those investments. The government had breached its obligations to treat them fairly and equitably, based on the legitimate expectations they had formed from the course of their prior dealings. The government had impaired their investments by imposing policies that were unreasonable and discriminatory, policies that impaired the management, maintenance, use, enjoyment and disposal of those investments.

The 'legitimate expectations' argument had been tricky to deal with – given the government's flip-flopping on climate change policy – but, in the end, they'd managed to destroy the investors' arguments on that one as well, just as they had with all the other grounds of the investors' claim. And once the panel had decided in the government's favour, then Loftus would be putting to the panel the government's claim for its legal costs, which would be substantial, and which the investors would have the pleasure of paying.

It hadn't been a long haul. Not as long as some of these matters could be. In fact, in Loftus's experience it had been positively speedy, compared to some other international dispute settlements. But it had been hard: twelve months of intensive work, sixteen hour days, seven day weeks. Long absences from his family. Long absences from his chambers! Lord knows what crumbs the clerks would throw his way when he returned. But that wouldn't be until he'd had a long break with his wife and kids, a couple of weeks, to recharge the batteries; find out what they'd been up to, while he'd been tied up on this matter since he couldn't remember when.

But it was almost over, they were almost there. All they needed was the decision.

*****

Emil sat outside the closed doors of the hearing room.

He'd arrived after commencement of the session, so he hadn't managed to see the others before they'd gone in. He wasn't too bothered about missing them: the only person he had a mind to see and speak to that morning was on the opposition legal team, not the Australian Government team. Ms Cheng.

The previous evening, being Sunday, had been quiet and he'd returned to the hotel from his vigil at the midlevels' escalators relatively early. As he had entered the lobby, he'd been surprised again to see her there: this time, she'd been at the main reception desk and was just leaving. He tried to catch up to her in the lift lobby, but she'd already taken a lift down towards the exit to the shopping mall. He followed in another lift, but by the time he reached the exit to the mall, she had gone, melding into the crowds of diners looking for tables in the many restaurants dotted around the concourses.

Not long after returning to his room, there was a knock at the door. It was the concierge, delivering a small brown-paper-wrapped parcel to him. When he'd opened it, he'd found only a mini DVD computer disk. No name of sender, no addressee, no message. The concierge could only tell him a young Chinese woman had delivered it by hand, simply asking that it be delivered to him. No names, no message, other than that it was important it be delivered to Mr Pfeffer, personally, as soon as possible.

Intrigued, but against his better judgment, he'd put it in his laptop and checked the files on the disk. There were just two, both video files. He played the first: it was very short and showed what looked like a Caucasian couple walking up to a building with a child, a young boy. It wasn't very good quality, a little out of focus, but he could make out that the boy was Chinese and, from the background, it had been filmed in Hong Kong, possibly up in the midlevels, he guessed.

But what did this have to do with him? It was puzzling.

Curiosity induced him to run the second video file. The quality was better, the camera had been focused, but he wished it wasn't. As he sat there, waiting outside the hearing room, he was still sickened by the images it contained. Sickened and angered. So angered, he wanted to burst into the room and grab the man sitting in the middle of the table at the end of the room, and hurl him through the plate glass window behind where he sat. He wanted to see that disgusting specimen splattered over the pavement thirty-eight floors below.

The second video file had obviously been taken with a concealed camera, concealed inside a room of an apartment: a bedroom. This time, there was only the man and the boy. The images depicted were things Emil had never anticipated he would see, or ever have cause to look at. They were things he had never wanted to think about. Of course, like anybody, he knew this sort of thing happened. But like most people would, he'd avoided it, mentally filing it with other difficult images, such as depictions of extreme cruelty to animals, wanting not to be confronted by it. It was one of those things you heard about remotely, in the news, when people were being sent to gaol for a very long time. But this time he had to deal with it head-on.

His disgust and revulsion at the images churned his stomach. For a while he thought he might throw up, but didn't. He'd stopped the video as soon as he realised what was happening, but not before the camera had caught the man's jowly face, pink tip of a tongue darting in and out of his mouth like a big lizard. That face was a face Emil had recognised. It was the face of an eminent person. A person known far and wide for his expertise in the practice of alternative dispute resolution. It was the face of the man who now sat the other side of the closed hearing room doors, as chairman of the arbitration panel.

But now wasn't the time for dealing with him. Right now, it was the curious messenger, Ms Cheng, to whom Emil wanted to speak.

When he'd stopped the video on his laptop, he'd sat for a long time. Hardly breathing, hardly moving. Just thinking. For reasons he couldn't explain, the images had set him thinking about Papua New Guinea. Thinking about his time there as a younger man; about the whispering campaign against the now long dead Piers Birch; thinking about the taunts that he had endured at the hands of his peers, because of Birch.

He remembered, with painful irony, the name they'd used to tease him – 'BC' – short for 'Birch's catamite'. It still made him flush with anger. He'd remembered Johanna's reaction when he'd told her about it, how fiercely protective of him she'd been; the intensity of her anger. And her tenderness, too – the first time they'd had sex, which was shortly after.

It had been like a light turning on in his head. Almost as if Johanna had been sitting there with him, stirring his subconscious, spurring his memory. There was something in the film – the first video file. He replayed it. Then replayed it again and again. It was brief and not good quality, which might have been deliberate; maybe this, too, had been filmed with a concealed camera.

Eventually he'd realised what it was: it was the woman. It was blurry, so he couldn't be sure. There was something familiar about the woman, the way she tossed her hair, the way she walked, the way she carried herself – her deportment (if she'd been to a *proper* school, that is). He couldn't be certain, the footage was brief, but the way she moved, her bearing, gave him the overwhelming feeling that he'd met this blonde woman before. That he knew who she was.

That morning, he'd woken with a head full of questions, uncertain as to what was the best way to proceed. He had sat pondering it over his breakfast coffee, lost to the outside world, for a long time, until it gave him a headache and made him arrive late at the hearing room, after the doors had been closed for the start of proceedings.

He was puzzled as to the meaning of these videos, why had the disk been given to him? Was he being set up? The disk was essentially child pornography; he'd be in serious trouble if it was found in his possession. And why now, at this crucial time in the arbitration? Why did Cheng leave it for him? Why not give it to Loftus, or one of his team? Surely Rita or Marianne would have been a more appropriate person for Cheng to make the disclosure to. Maybe there was a reason why she hadn't. And why had the film been made in the first place? Was someone blackmailing the panel chairman? Perhaps it was Cheng's own clients, trying to ensure a victory in the proceedings.

But then, on the other hand, with Cheng being on the investors' legal team, maybe this was their insurance. If they lost, somehow the disk could be found in his possession – or if he were to disclose it. Then the decision itself, and the Australian team tactics in achieving it, could be discredited as involving blackmail. That was the trap – the reason why he had been selected to receive it: they were assuming that he would jump at the chance to claim the limelight by revealing it.

Sitting there outside the hearing room, still pondering all these imponderables, Emil was surprised when, suddenly, the doors of the hearing room opened wide and the investors' legal team strode out purposefully, passing him without so much as a glance. He stood, expectantly looking for Ms Cheng, but she wasn't with them.

Turning, to see if she was still in the room, he was stopped dead in his tracks.

Loftus's face showed no emotion, as usual. But the look of numbed shock on Marianne's face and the crimson mask of Rita's, told him the outcome. He knew which side the decision had favoured, without needing to ask.

They were all heading towards the door. Behind them, the room was empty. There was no sign of Cheng.

*****

"I still can't fathom it. I just, cannot, fathom it."

Loftus stood at the table in the meeting room, leaning

forward, supporting himself on the knuckles of his bunched fists.

It was late morning, the next day, and it seemed the legal team's post mortem had been on going, without a break, since the moment of decision the day before. Emil had only just arrived in the team's meeting room. He'd spent half the night on telephone calls to Betty G and Dominik, putting into immediate effect the strategy they had devised, in the event of the outcome that had now come to pass.

This morning he had been to the offices of Kok, Wei & Partners. They were the last word in legal office opulence, perched precariously high above the harbour on one of the upper floors of Two International Finance Centre. From up there, he had been able look down onto the very top of the building where he now was.

"Good morning. I'd like to speak with one of your solicitors, Ms Cheng."

"Ms Cheng has not arrived yet," said the receptionist. "Do you have an appointment?"

He explained it was private and was told he could wait there. So he'd sat in the lobby at Kok, Wei for two hours, waiting for her to show, looking out across the harbour at the amazing buildings going up in the Tsim Sha Tsui district, beyond Harbour City. There was one that looked like it must be at least a hundred floors and, next to it, one that looked like an upside down U. He shuddered at the thought of being on the lowest of the cross-floors, knowing that there was nothing beneath you for about thirty stories. The panorama was captivating, with all the activity on the harbour below, ferries constantly coming and going from the Star Ferry terminal, large and small vessels churning their way through the choppy swell of the shipping channels.

He was wondering if it was from Tsim Sha Tsui that she came in to work each day; or maybe from further out, in the New Territories, when the partner who had been at the hearing came out to see him.

"Cheng is not here, Mr Pfeffer. Is there something I can help you with?"

"No, no thanks. I'd like to speak with her personally, if that's alright. Will she be in today?"

"We assume so. It's not like her to be late without a reason. Normally, she would call if there is a problem, but as far as I am aware, she hasn't. Would you like to leave a message?"

That was one thing Emil certainly didn't want to do. So he gave the partner his business card, then left.

"I can't understand where, how, we went wrong," continued Loftus, rocking back and forward, still supporting himself on his knuckles on the table top. It must have been hurting, but he didn't seem to notice.

"Don't go getting too Jesuit with yourself, boss. Keep the self-flagellation to a minimum, please!" Rita tried. "We won't get a proper handle on the reasons until they provide the written version."

"Sorry to interrupt, but did any of you see Ms Cheng, yesterday morning?" asked Emil.

"No, we were all a little too preoccupied going down the tubes for a couple of billion dollars," said Rita abruptly, almost angrily. "You seem to be more interested in her, than anything else going on here!"

"Yes, I thought you said you were spoken for?" said Loftus, momentarily drawn out of his reverie.

"Look, it's not what you think. I'm just trying to find out why she keeps showing up in my hotel lobby," Emil deflected them, at once regretting having raised it in the first place.

They went back to what they'd been doing. Rita and Marianne sorting out the case materials still strewn over every available surface, except the one they'd cleared for Emil to work at. Loftus back into his reverie.

Emil got on with the emails he needed to send, to follow up his overnight calls. In a strict legal sense, the panel decision was of no precedent value. However, there was no doubting that other countries, whose bilateral trading agreements contained such provisions, would need to be alert. As news of the decision filtered out through the media, there was the possibility that investors in those countries, disgruntled by policies that impacted their activities, would be looking long and hard at how they might pursue a similar course.

"It might be a financial body blow for the Australian Government, Emil," Betty G had said on their call at about two o'clock that morning, "but if it reacts by cancelling its bilateral agreements and pulling back from carbon trading, that's gonna be a massive hit for the global market. I shouldn't need to spell out for you what that means for this organisation!"

"No, you don't need to spell it out, Betty."

"You need to get down to Canberra, Emil. I want you personally to find out how the policy there is gonna change, then brief me. As soon as you're finished in Hong Kong, okay?"

That directive meant the end of any prospects of him ever getting to Luzern, to find Rodger Beckwith. And the few straws of hope he still had to cling onto were here in Hong Kong, not in Australia.

His laptop buzzed with another incoming email. It was Betty G, asking for any details he could obtain on the actual decision itself. He looked over at Loftus.

"My Director-General is asking what, if any, details of the decision you are able to disclose at this time?"

"The decision is in favour of the Claimants. The amount of the award we're not supposed to disclose yet, but I can tell you, off the record, that the figure is approaching three billion Australian dollars. When you add in the costs we've incurred running the matter, and the other side's costs that we will need to pay, I'd put it at three billion."

Emil shook his head. It was a huge disaster for all of them, but particularly for Loftus. Not many lawyers, not even top counsel, ever lost that much on a single decision.

"Decision itself – if it was politics, I suppose you could say they divided along party lines," continued Loftus. "The panel member appointed by the government was in our favour; the panel member appointed by the investors was in their favour. And the chairman, well, he came down in favour of the investors, obviously."

Emil looked at Loftus and the others.

"Yes," he said, knowingly. "Obviously."

*****

Not far from the Exchange Centre, at Police Headquarters in Arsenal Road, Wan Chai, Senior Inspector Tang was sitting at his desk, reviewing reports of recent arrests and incidents that his officers had investigated. His unit was generally ahead of the curve when it came to case clear-up statistics, which was just as well if he was going to stay on the promotion fast-track. However, recently it had been slipping a bit, a fact noted to him that morning by the Assistant Deputy Commissioner: a none-too-subtle reminder of the expectations that were being placed on him. Trouble was, the ADC had told him, he was *too* accommodating, too willing to accept the jobs his peers would say they had no time for. But, as Tang had told the ADC, if someone wasn't willing to do these tasks – like chasing up Red Notice reports from visiting round-eyes – they would slip through the cracks and eventually come back to bite someone, perhaps even someone more senior than Tang himself.

As he sat there, skimming through the pile from his in-tray, reflecting on the conversation, he wondered whether the ADC would think he was being a bit too cheeky by saying that, or would he accept that Tang was just genuinely concerned. His phone rang. It was a colleague in Operations.

"We have just received a report, a missing person report. I am sending it over to you."

"Why are you doing that? What has it got to do with me?" he snapped. "The ADC told me only this morning to stop accepting these matters from other units."

"You are shown acting as the liaison for a round-eye who reported sighting an Interpol Red Notice offender?"

"Has he gone missing?"

"No. His name appears in this missing person report. You will need to be involved."

9

It was like having a radioactive isotope in his pocket. The DVD disk. It felt warm against his leg, a constant reminder that it was there. But he wasn't taking any risks: rather than leaving it in his room, he was going to keep it with him, wherever he went. In the back of his mind, he was still wrestling with what he should do with it, what to do about it. But, for the moment, those questions were secondary to his need to manage the organisation's response to the arbitration decision. Still, he could feel it there, in his trouser pocket.

He picked up his mobile and dialled Dominik for the umpteenth time that day.

Dominik provided his latest update on the interactions with national bodies in various carbon trading countries. So far, the responses had all been positive and reassuring. The early intervention by the GCMO was helping to dampen what, otherwise, could have been an inflammatory situation. Betty G was relaxed. For the moment. He knew he had to keep the news positive, so she would stay that way.

"Betty has been around here a few times today, asking about your plans for meetings with the Australian Government," reported Dominik.

"Damn, that's one thing I haven't even had time to think about yet. Thanks Dom, you'd better get Sabrina to make some bookings, so it'll look like I'm moving in that direction.

Can you also make some inquiries with the department in Canberra – see if they can recommend which ministers I should try to see."

The trip down under was something he had to do, but the longer he could postpone it, the more hope it gave him of getting a lead on Hudson. And sorting out what he was going to do about the DVD. He had to find a way to get in touch with Cheng. He ended the call, leaving Dominik to do the legwork. His mobile rang again almost immediately. It was Betty G.

"Emil, what are your arrangements with the Australians?"

"Oh, hi Betty. I'm just setting up the meetings. As soon as they're all locked in I'll send you the details."

"I can help there. I've had Jorge speak with their Prime Minister's office." Jorge, an Argentinean, was Betty G's new deputy. "They recommend that you speak first with the relevant minister, then set up a joint meeting with the minister and the Treasurer. So let's get this moving."

"Okay Betty, I'm onto it. It's the Minister for Energy whose portfolio covers climate change policy."

"Not for this one. It's all being consolidated under the Attorney-General. Sounds ominous to me, like they're already setting in motion the steps to unwind their trading arrangements. The sooner you get there and we get an understanding of their thinking, the better."

The call ended.

"Shit!" he muttered. He had to get some breathing space, time to sort things out in Hong Kong. But with Betty G on his case, that possibility was rapidly evaporating. Just like his not-happening visit to Beckwith, in Luzern.

"Shit, shit, shit!"

He looked up. Loftus, Marianne and Rita had all stopped whatever they'd been doing and were watching him.

"Oops. Sorry, excuse me."

"Bad news?" asked Rita.

"Something we can help with?" added Loftus.

"Not unless you can make me be in two places at once. But

thanks, I appreciate the offer." He considered it for a couple of moments. "Actually, I might have a chat with you about your minister, I could use your advice, before I go and speak with him."

"Well, Rita and Marianne normally have a lot more exposure to the Attorney than I do, but I'm sure we can all chip in our two cents' worth."

The two women nodded their agreement.

"Thanks. What about we do it in more convivial surroundings? Say, Kerry's Bar in Wan Chai, later in the week, maybe Thursday evening?"

Having got that important piece of business sorted out, Emil went back to managing his team in Bad Eschbach; Rita and Marianne pressed on with their tasks; Loftus remained inert, lapsing back into his reverie of case analysis and self-analysis, staring out the window at the harbour.

One practical measure Emil had put in place while Dominik was recuperating in hospital, was to purchase two unregistered, pay-as-you-go mobile phones that they could use for communications concerning their on-going, off-the-record inquiries into BKZ. Late that afternoon, as the others were making noises about leaving, Emil's mobile buzzed with a message from Dominik, saying that he would call him. A short time later, Emil's mobile rang.

"Are you free to speak?"

"Yes, the others have all just left for the evening. I'll probably head off soon, too."

"Are you still looking for Hudson?"

"Yeah, I'll probably take up my usual spot in the Yorkshire Pudding pub tonight."

"I checked it on 'street view'. Looks like a good place to watch the escalator."

"Yes, it's a good spot, but it's a waste of time sitting there if he doesn't come past. Anyway, what have you got for me?"

"What's that saying you use sometimes 'No news is good news'? Remember I told you a week ago that the police had tracked down the waiters from the PNG ceremony?"

"Have they admitted it was them?"

"Nothing so easy. But two of them have disappeared!"

"You mean they've done a runner? That's as good as admitting it was them, isn't it?"

"I'm a bit worried that's not what happened. You see, the third one the police interviewed, I've just learnt, is dead. He was the victim of a hit-and-run, after he'd left the police station. No witnesses. The police don't have any leads."

"Isn't it possible it could've been an accident?"

"Sure. But together with the other two disappearing, makes me a little suspicious."

"Well, you'd better take some precautions, Dom. Stay with your friends again, don't go out alone, especially while you're still recovering from the surgery. It may still just be an accident, but I'm sure you're aware of what you need to do. More so than I would be, at any rate."

"You should be careful too, Emil. Out there on your own, you're much more exposed than I am here."

"Thanks! What are you trying to do, make me nervous or something?"

"One other matter. There was a call for you, a woman. She was reluctant to say much. Just that her name was Lesley, from London, and you would know where to reach her."

He detected something disapproving in Dominik's tone of voice.

"That's Beckwith's wife. She was running the event in London that I attended in place of Betty – it was an amazing coincidence. Things have been moving so fast I had completely forgotten about it. She gave me a lead on where we could find Beckwith, near Luzern, but I didn't have time to do anything about it before Betty hijacked me to here."

After Dominik, he made three calls before leaving the meeting room and heading up to the midlevels. First, to Lesley Beckwith.

"Did you go to Luzern?"

"Not yet. Unfortunately, the day after the conference I had

to travel to Hong Kong, urgently. That's where I am now. I really don't know when I'll get to Luzern, the way things are going."

"You don't need to bother, you've missed your chance. There's been an avalanche."

"Great! So what's the situation?"

"That arsehole husband of mine and his Swiss slut are listed as missing, presumed dead. It wiped out the chalet where they'd shacked up. So now my children might not have a father. I don't even know what provision that rat has made for us in his will. God only knows how I'm going to pay their school fees, if he hasn't left us anything."

She sounded like she'd started to weep. It didn't seem to Emil like the tears were for Beckwith, so much as for herself. He tried to console her, but whatever he said sounded a bit thin, coming from the opposite side of the world on the telephone, and given he only knew her from their one, brief, drunken encounter. He wondered if she realised that if they didn't find Beckwith's body, his estate may remain in limbo until he was declared dead. Or whether she'd considered that by directing Emil how to get there, she might have been sending him to his own death. Maybe that's why she'd rung – to check. He thanked her for the news and ended the call, promising to call again.

The other two calls were to the European Commission. The first to Johanna's boss, Mathias, who was almost like a brother to Emil now, a fellow traveller in Emil's quest to find Johanna. From their various conversations, Emil felt he'd learnt more about her professionally than he had from Johanna herself.

"She's well on her way to becoming quite an authority on tropical birds," Mathias had advised him on an earlier call. "*The* authority, perhaps, one day. But I can't see her staying with us very long if she wishes to pursue it – I'm afraid tropical birds are not a priority here at the Commission."

But for the moment, she was an integral part of his team and he wanted her back. Both of them were intent on finding out where she was, what had happened to her, on securing her safe return. But Mathias had little news to buoy him.

"The investigation is continuing, the police and the airport authorities in Singapore have the matter in hand, but that's all they will say."

It had been the same response for months.

The second call was to Luisa, the trainee who'd worked with Johanna in Port Moresby, but he didn't manage to reach her. So he packed up and headed for the Yorkshire Pudding.

Taking up his usual seat, a stool right on the corner of the bench that ran the length of the bar facing Staunton Street, then turned at right angles and ran up the side along Shelley Street. The wall along Staunton Street was glass panels that slid away opening it to the street, all the outside noise and bustle part of the bar room ambience, competing with the two large screens, one at each end of the bar, continuously show-ing sporting events. American football, US league baseball, cricket from India, football from Europe, darts champion-ships, snooker competitions, motor racing, athletics champi-onships, there seemed to be no end to it. If there was sport being played somewhere in the world, it would be on those screens, twenty-four-seven.

Emil ordered a pint of lager, which the waitress delivered along with a bowl of peanuts. Many evenings over the pre-ceding couple of weeks, that had been his only sustenance; and frequently the pints of lager were left in the glass to go flat. Sitting on the stool, leaning on the bench, sipping from his pint, he could feel the DVD in the pocket of his trou-sers, against his leg. A reminder of the matter he must resolve. Finding Cheng. And finding Hudson – his last remaining lead to Johanna – now his lead through Beckwith was gone for good. But there was precious little time left for him to do either. With Betty G breathing down his neck, what time remained was rapidly running out.

"Don't you think you're overreacting a little, Dom?" he'd asked, when they'd spoken.

"Emil, you heard Hudson just as I did – his associates are very vindictive. If you ask me, they'll be tying off the loose ends here in Frankfurt: that means we both need to be careful."

"At least they're active, showing themselves. This might be just what we need – might provide us with a chance to find out who they are."

He mulled over their conversation. When it all boiled down, so far as BKZ was concerned, really all he had left was to find Hudson. But already the seeds of doubt, sown by Tang, were beginning to niggle at his recollection of the sighting: doubt over whether it really had been Hudson that he'd chased up here, after all. Had it all been just his imagination? Maybe Tang was right. Was he wasting his time sitting here every evening?

What would Hudson be doing here, anyway, if it is him? He ran through the possibilities: was he hiding from the authorities? Was there an extradition treaty between Hong Kong and the US? With Canada? Emil didn't know; that would be something he could check tomorrow. Surely there were better places for Hudson to hide? No, if it was him, then he must be here for a purpose, Emil reasoned. He must be up to something, which to Emil's mind could only be bad, whatever it was. All the more reason to find him, to smoke him out.

Then there was the disk. What the hell was he going to do about it? The panel chairman. His companion, the blonde woman. Emil worked his way through the possibilities again. Whatever it meant, he knew he couldn't sit on it, keep walking around with the disk in his pocket, indefinitely. Sooner, rather than later, he needed to act. He'd need to hand it over to the Australian legal team, before they left town. Or, the other possibility was that he hand it over to Tang and get him to arrest the chairman. But then, these options raised further questions: he would need to be able to explain how the disk came into his possession: but would they believe him, any of them? Cheng was the answer. He definitely needed to talk to her.

Emil looked at his watch: it was after eleven. Where had the evening gone? There were few people in the street now, the bar behind him almost empty. He realised that he'd been sitting there all evening without looking at any passers-by. He'd been so consumed by his thoughts that Hudson could have danced a jig in the street in front of him and he wouldn't have noticed. The pint glass stood in front of him on the bench, three-quarters full of flat lager. Emil got up from his stool, nodded goodnight to the bored bar staff leaning on the counter and headed back to his hotel.

He was still puzzling over all the questions and issues as he wandered through the lobby of the hotel, towards the lifts – so preoccupied that he didn't see Senior Inspector Tang, standing in front of him, until he walked straight into him.

"Good evening, Mr Pfeffer."

"Oh, Senior Inspector, you gave me quite a start then!"

"I'm sorry, I thought you had seen me, that's why you were walking directly over to me."

"No need to apologise, Senior Inspector, it was my fault. I was deep in thought and not watching where I was going. Are you here to see me? I hope you're going to tell me you've found Gregory Hudson."

"No. Unfortunately nothing so exciting as an arrest on a Red Notice. But I am here about someone we are looking for."

"Oh. Does that involve me?"

"Is there somewhere quieter, more private, where we can talk, discreetly?"

Emil looked around the lobby. "That corner of the bar looks pretty quiet – will that do?"

They settled themselves into oversized, leather lounge chairs, adjacent to the massive glass panes overlooking the jumble of buildings down the hill. Emil ordered them each a glass of mineral water.

"So, Senior Inspector, how can I help you?"

"Mr Pfeffer," said Tang, watching Emil very closely, "do you know a lawyer, a young, Chinese, woman lawyer called Cheng?"

As Tang said the name, every pore in Emil's body seemed to gush sweat. He felt relaxed, but not in control of his body's physiological reaction to the mention of Cheng's name.

"Only that she is on one of the legal teams, in the matter which brought me to Hong Kong."

In his trouser pocket, it felt like the DVD disk had just exploded into flames and was burning a hole in his leg.

"Ah. I see. Which side is she on?"

"She is with the lawyers acting for the other side. I'm afraid most of the details are confidential, but I can tell you that the Australian Government is one of the parties. They are the ones who asked me to come to Hong Kong. Is she the person you are looking for? Can I ask what she has done?"

Tang ignored the questions. "Have you been speaking with her very much, during the hearing of this dispute matter, Mr Pfeffer?"

"Not at all. Since I am not a member of one of the legal teams, I haven't been allowed into the hearing room." He checked himself. "Oh, sorry, no, I tell a lie. I spoke to her once, when she appeared at the door of the room the Australian legal team is using. But when I asked her what she wanted, she just ran away."

Tang looked at Emil quizzically. "She was scared of you?"

"No, no. When I say 'she ran away', what I mean is, she said she didn't want to speak to me and went out the door again, very quickly, as if she had made a mistake, or was embarrassed. I was on the telephone, so I didn't get up to see where she went. At that time, I didn't even know she was from the other legal team."

"I see."

Tang sat back and seemed to relax into his thoughts. Emil took a sip from his mineral water, noticing, as he did, how wet the palms of his hands had become.

Tang sat forward again, eyeing Emil intently. "And have you seen her again, after that?"

"Yes, of course. The hearing is now finished, they've just

given the decision, but while it was on-going I saw her on several occasions outside the hearing room. That's when I found out she was on the other side. But I haven't spoken to her."

Tang sat staring at Emil for a few moments before continuing.

"Mr Pfeffer." Tang's stare was beginning to unnerve him. "Did Cheng come here to see you, in this hotel?"

Tang must have already spoken to the concierge. Emil could feel his sweat glands going into overdrive again. He wondered was it obvious yet to Tang? Damp patches showing through under his arms. Tell-tale trails of perspiration running down his temple.

"Yes, Senior Inspector, she did come to this hotel, but not 'to see me', as you put it. She left an envelope for me with the desk. That was all. We never spoke."

"And what was in this envelope?"

"Look, Senior Inspector." He was getting a bit fed up. It seemed to be a cross-examination. "What has that got to do with you? What has she done that brings you here to grill me?"

"Just answer my question please, Mr Pfeffer, or we may have to continue down in Arsenal Street. That is where the grilling takes place." Tang's even, almost friendly tone of voice hadn't changed. But the threat was clear.

"It was some material I had left, accidentally, outside the hearing room."

His mind flashed back to Johanna, his hotel room in Bad Eschbach – she'd been lying face down on the bed, he had been massaging her shoulders and neck.

"I've decided to go to India, to see what Dominik has found," he'd announced.

"I thought you would. As soon as I saw you read it, I knew."

"I'm not that transparent, am I?"

"Yes, it's what I like about you, Emil."

He hoped his ability to lie had improved since then. Tang continued watching him.

"Why couldn't someone from the Australian legal side

deliver this to you? Why could Cheng not just give it to you the next day?"

Tang continued to stare, taking in every movement, every flinch, every twitch, every flicker of Emil's eyes, looking for signs of hesitation, uncertainty; looking for signs of weakness, signs of dishonesty, in his responses.

Emil kept his composure. "The answer to that, I'm afraid Senior Inspector, I don't know. You'll have to ask Ms Cheng, herself."

"Well, I will ask *you* this, Mr Pfeffer: why did you go looking for Cheng at her place of work?"

"To thank her, for returning the material," he lied.

"You waited two hours to do that?" Tang's look had changed. He was openly sceptical. His expression challenging the veracity of Emil's answers, without calling him a liar. Not yet.

Fuck, Tang's already carried out a full-blown investigation, he thought. "Is that a problem, Senior Inspector?"

"Not if it's the truth. Where have you been this evening?"

"After I left the Exchange Centre, I had a meal in Soho." Mostly true, at least, he thought. "Look, Senior Inspector, I'm still at a loss as to why you have come here to my hotel, late at night, asking me all these questions, as if I'm a suspect in the commission of some crime."

"Ms Cheng's parents have reported her missing. She has not returned to her home for a number of days. Everyone I have spoken to says this is completely out of character for her. From the information I have been able to gather, I understand that the last time she was seen, anywhere, by anyone, was here in this hotel, leaving an envelope, or parcel, to be delivered to you. If there has been a crime committed, Mr Pfeffer, I think that makes you a person of interest, would you agree?"

Emil remained silent, watching Tang. He could feel the wetness of his shirt, clinging to his body, beneath his suit jacket.

"However, at the moment, all we have is her unexplained disappearance. If she contacts you, or if you see her again, please get in touch with me immediately."

Tang stood and left. His glass of mineral water remained where the waiter had put it on the coffee table, untouched, sitting in the pool of condensation that had formed around it.

10

By Thursday, Emil was ready for a drink. Tang's unexpected visit put a dampener on a week that had already begun badly. Betty G's increasingly frequent and agitated calls for him to 'get down under', were making it worse.

Late on Thursday afternoon the Australian legal team had just about finished sorting and packing their materials. The meeting room was tidy for a change and, once the couriers had come and taken the boxes of materials, it looked quite empty. They would be returning to Australia that weekend, which meant Emil's justification to Betty G for remaining in Hong Kong would be gone. He wouldn't have the meeting room any longer, or any reason to remain.

Earlier in the week the team had returned for one last session, to have the bad news about costs confirmed by the panel. The investors' legal costs were outrageously inflated, in keeping with the opulence of Kok, Wei & Partners offices, but in the context of the overall award of damages, a mere drop in the ocean. Or, at least, that's how Rita put it, when they returned to the meeting room. It was a sombre group that clinked their glasses in a silent toast, sitting at a table in Kerry's Bar, by the time they reconvened on Thursday evening.

"So, what do you think about this business with Cheng?" asked Emil, when they'd all sampled the wine.

"We thought you might be the one to enlighten us, given the interest you'd been showing in her whereabouts."

"Very funny, Rita. I don't take kindly to the police waiting in my hotel, putting me through the third degree, at midnight."

"We all had a visit, Emil," said Marianne. "I don't think they were singling you out."

After what Tang had said, Emil wasn't sure he agreed. He wondered whether any of them had mentioned to Tang his repeated sightings of Cheng in the hotel lobby.

"Don't worry, Emil, your secret's safe with us." Rita must have been reading his mind.

He pulled a face at her. It wasn't that funny, but they all laughed anyway. Release of tension. Exhaustion. Deflation, after the result. Even Loftus was less remote tonight than he had been at any time since the decision.

"I'll probably be seeing you again soon, once my appointments with the Attorney and the Treasurer have been locked in."

Emil had been using whatever time was available during the week to find out as much as he could from Marianne and Rita about their minister, the Attorney-General. He'd been feeding this into emails back to Betty G, to give the impression that he was doing some useful background digging with the legal team in Hong Kong. It had worked for a day or two, but there was a limit. And Betty G reached hers pretty quickly.

"Emil, this research you're doing is all well and good, but just sort out your meeting arrangements and get down to Canberra," she ordered. "You need to talk to Canberra before they fix on a policy position that's bad for us and that we can't influence. Anything more you can find out in Hong Kong won't help us if the decision's been made in Canberra before you get there!"

Rita poured out the remains of the first bottle into their glasses, and then topped them up from the second, which had been uncorked, ready to go. Tonight they were all drinking red.

"What's the Canberra scene like these days? What do I need to know, before I get there?"

"We've been away for the best part of twelve months, so we're not up to speed on the latest gossip ourselves," said Marianne.

"We've already told you what a 'yes man' the A-G is for the PM, which, I've got to say, puts him pretty low down the pecking order since the PM is just a 'yes man' for Bull Griffith," added Rita.

"Bull Griffith? That coal mining ratbag? Is he still around?"

"The very same. Australia's richest man, according to the annual list that's published in the papers."

"Word is, he's the one pulling the strings for this government," said Loftus. "When the coal lobby says 'Jump!' the government says 'How high?'"

"Bloody hell. But hang on, if that's the case, how did the government end up in this arbitration mess? Surely Griffith wouldn't have agreed to them pulling the rug out from under this port development by Queensland?"

"He didn't," said Loftus. "That's why there was a Cabinet putsch. PM was rolled by his own people. The gossip is that Griffith orchestrated it and arranged for the current nong to be installed. Now he's double-crossed Griffith on the coal loader as well."

"You mean Michael Mendicane? I thought he was meant to be the man of the people, the uniter of factions?"

"Man of the people, where'd you get that hogwash – from his PR unit?" said Rita. "More like 'return to the planet of the apes'!"

"Yes, the cartoonists are giving him a real working over," said Loftus, allowing himself a chuckle.

"From what you're saying, maybe it's Griffith I need to meet."

"Now that *would* be a complete waste of your time," said Loftus, Rita and Marianne murmuring their concurrence. "Not to say that you'll get any further with the A-G, or the

Treasurer. Hounganis announced a couple of weeks ago that there's a fifty-billion-dollar black hole in the budget. This debacle we've just presided over here has added another three to that. I don't think they'll be too receptive to anything which isn't adding dollars to the country's bottom line."

A third, then a fourth, bottle of red came and went. Emil hadn't been keeping track of how many glasses he'd had. He was relying on Rita's greater capacity for red wine consumption to make sure he didn't over indulge, especially as their 'dinner' amounted to a couple of bowls of nibbles (which Rita *did* get the lion's share of) followed by two cheese plates with crackers. Hardly nutritious, but hopefully it was soaking up the alcohol.

A fifth bottle of red appeared at the table, minus its cork.

"This has got to be my last, folks. Much and all as I'm enjoying your company and insights into the Australian political scene – tomorrow is another day. For me, possibly not a very happy one, if my boss isn't satisfied I'm on my way to Canberra."

"Are you sure you don't want to join us at that Szechuan place in Lockhart Road?" asked Marianne. "Need to stave off the munchies."

But Emil finished his glass and, refusing a refill from Rita, bade them all a good evening. Looking at his watch as he stepped out of the bar, he realised there was little of the evening left. He'd been trying to drink a glass of water between each glass of wine, as a way of reducing the impact. But stepping outside, the consequence of this strategy was immediately apparent: a full bladder. He decided to get back to his hotel as quickly as possible, rather than use the bar's toilet and risk being trapped, *en route*, into another 'last drink'. His sudden urge to urinate wasn't helped by the fact that, even though it couldn't be called cold, it was noticeably cooler than it had been inside the bar. It had rained heavily again, earlier in the evening, and there was still a light drizzle.

From Wan Chai to the hotel wasn't far, less than a kilometre.

Emil took the raised footways along and over Harcourt Road and Queensway, thinking back over the evening's conversation. At the start of the evening he'd been mulling over whether to tell them about the DVD. To test the water, he'd asked whether they thought the chairman of the panel was kosher, the real McCoy, a truly independent third member of the panel. All three agreed that he had conducted himself with absolute impartiality. Couldn't have been fairer, was Rita's observation. He'd tried another tack: what could they do if they found out he was bent – that he'd found against the government for improper reasons? Emil had even tempted fate by suggesting, what if he'd been bribed, or even … blackmailed?

"I can answer that," Loftus responded. "It's quite straightforward: under the Hong Kong Arbitration Ordinance, it's open to a party to apply to the High Court, in the first instance, on the grounds of a serious irregularity affecting the tribunal, the proceedings or the award. It's quite a broad remit given to the Court. What amounts to a 'serious irregularity' is defined. It includes the award being obtained by fraud, or the way in which it was procured being contrary to public policy. I think that would cover the situations you're talking about, don't you? Why do you ask?"

"No, no special reason. Just wondering. By the sounds of things, you've analysed it pretty closely, though, yourself. Were you worried about something like that happening?"

"No more than necessary. You forget I have overall carriage of the matter. The Arbitration Ordinance is the legislation that ultimately governs proceedings, so, of course, I need to be familiar with it."

Emil let the subject drop. He still wasn't sure that disclosing the disk and its contents to them was the right way to go – it was still troubling him why Cheng hadn't given it to one of them, in the first place. The other reason was the blonde. He was becoming more and more convinced that he recognised her, that he knew her. And if that was the case, he wanted to find her, too, and get answers to some questions, like how she came to be here in Hong Kong, involved in such a filthy activity. If Cheng had decided to go to ground, he was going to have trouble finding out anything from her. That made the blonde even more significant.

Striding along above Harcourt Road, trying to keep his mind off his increasingly desperate urge to pee, Emil hadn't been paying much attention to his surroundings. Directly below, an occasional vehicle would swoosh past through the storm water still lying there, the sound eventually breaking into his train of thought. It made the roadway seem like a river gorge between the flanking walls of skyscrapers, he mused. For some reason, he found himself listening to his own footsteps. Apart from him, the walkway was deserted. His footsteps were echoing along the hard surface of the long concrete box. Then, with a start, he realised why he was listening to his own footsteps: the echo wasn't quite right. It seemed not quite in synch, a fraction of a second out of time; as if there was a second set of footsteps, trying to mimic the sound of his.

He kept walking, reminding himself he'd been drinking, ever more conscious of the need to get to a toilet. But with each step, he was becoming surer it wasn't his imagination. He started walking slightly more briskly, then abruptly stopped. No mistake. The second set of steps was as clear as a bell.

He spun around, eyes searching the darkness at the end of the long, neon-lit slab. No one there. He was alone in the concrete box. Or was he? There were slots on either side, for stairs, back before the walkway turned over Harcourt Road. It would be easy, he thought, for someone following to slip into the shadows if they thought they'd been heard. He decided to make a dash for it. He was desperate to get to the toilet anyway.

Immediately, he could hear running footsteps. More than one set. Running after him. He reached the end of the walkway, leaping down the steps, two at a time. Another twenty metres, then he was through the doors into the mall beneath the hotel. Seconds behind him, he heard the doors crash open again. He was sprinting up the escalators, two flights, heart pounding at the sudden, unwelcome exertion. Past the hotel doorman, into a waiting lift. Hotel room security key already out of his pocket, in his hand. He ran it across the reader in the lift. As the doors slid closed, he caught the briefest glimpse of two thickset, sweating, Chinese faces in the gap; then the doors came together, and the lift was moving; quickly, straight up to his floor. Thank God for hotel security keys. Especially the ones that only let guests access their own floors, he thought, passing it by the reader at the door to his room and going straight into the bathroom.

Having relieved himself, he noticed that his toiletries were scattered in and around the hand basin. That's odd. He thought for a moment: the room had been cleaned when he'd called in to drop his briefcase, before going down to meet the others. He was sure of that. He couldn't remember whether he'd looked in the bathroom, at that time. Maybe the maid had missed it.

But then, he thought, he didn't leave the bathroom like that in the first place. He never would. Someone must have come in here and scattered them around like that.

Puzzled, he went into the bedroom and turned on the lights. His clothes and personal effects were all over the floor, papers were scattered everywhere, briefcase lying open and empty on the floor. His suitcase had been upended and the bedding had been pulled off the bed, the room completely ransacked.

He picked up the house phone: there was a dial tone. At least that was working. The front desk assured him a manager would be straight up. Ever since the episodes at his former flat in Bad Eschbach, he'd become more careful about collecting evidence when incidents like this occurred. He took out his mobile phone and photographed everything.

As he finished photographing, there was a knock at the door. The manager was mortified. Nothing like this had ever happened in the hotel before, he said, bowing. He rang for staff to come and help Emil move to another room, then rang security. The police would need to be informed. He asked Emil to make a list of missing items and went to check the hotel's closed-circuit television.

Emil began gathering up his clothes and papers. So far as he could tell, nothing seemed to be missing. There was another knock at the door.

"That was quick!" said Emil, greeting a stony-faced Senior Inspector Tang.

"What do you mean?"

Emil stood back, gesturing for the policeman to enter.

Tang surveyed the upended bedding and suitcases. He turned back to Emil: "What happened?"

"That's what you're here to investigate, isn't it Senior Inspector?"

"I am not here for this," said Tang, his expression cold, unchanging.

"Then what are you here for, Senior Inspector?"

"I am here because Cheng has been found. Dead."

"Oh, no!" Emil felt an immense tiredness wash over him. It was as if all his muscles were exhausted, his body wanting to slump. "Where? What happened?"

"She lived with her parents at Chai Wan, at the eastern end of the island, a public housing estate – one of the smaller home ownership scheme developments, Hang Tsui Court. Her body was found in the park next to it. That park had been searched, so it is clear the body was put there afterwards, possibly tonight. Where were you tonight?"

"You're not serious, are you?"

"Where were you tonight?" Tang repeated, more firmly.

"At a bar in Wan Chai, with the Australian legal team."

"You will need to make a statement and account for your time for all of this evening."

"That won't be a problem, Senior Inspector." A sudden impulse to tell Tang about the DVD came and went.

Tang sensed Emil's thoughts. "Do you want to tell me something, Mr Pfeffer?"

"Er, no. I, ah, I was just going to ask how Ms Cheng died."

"She was strangled. From the bruising on her neck, by someone with very strong hands. They gripped her neck so hard it snapped. From marks on her wrists, her hands had been tied very tightly."

Tang continued staring at him. Outwardly calm, but anger simmering like a pot about to boil over into flames. His voice, when he spoke, was laced with contempt.

"I don't know yet how you are involved, Mr Pfeffer. But I have no doubt that you *are* involved, somehow, in Cheng's disappearance and death. I will find out. I will find out what you were doing with her."

"You're totally mistaken, Senior Inspector."

"Why, then, does the closed-circuit television show her in the lobby here on three separate occasions? Your Australian colleagues even said, you mentioned these visits to them."

Before he could answer, there was a knock at the door. The manager returned with the news that security had advised there was no closed-circuit television on the individual floors, apparently for reasons of guests' privacy.

"That's fantastic, isn't it? It works in the lobby and you use that to raise implications against me, but it doesn't work up here, to show who broke into my room. What are you going to do about my room being ransacked, Senior Inspector?"

"That will have to wait. The murder investigation has priority."

"Well, if it has to wait until after this Sunday, it's too late, because that's when I'm flying to Australia."

"That will not be possible, Mr Pfeffer. You are a material witness in this investigation. It is now a murder investigation. I must ask you to remain in Hong Kong, until you are excluded from inquiries. You will only be able to leave with my permission. But for now, you must stay. Please, give me your passport."

11

"What are you employed for, Emil?" What *the hell* are you employed for?" Betty G shouted down the telephone at him, before abruptly hanging up.

He'd rung her to explain he wouldn't be able to leave Hong Kong as soon as she wanted. She rang back, once she'd cooled down, and apologised. He explained the situation to her without mentioning the DVD, which remained in his trouser pocket. He assumed Tang and his colleagues would be listening to his telephone calls, so he gave her the same story he'd given Tang, about Cheng leaving the parcel for him at reception, and his subsequent visit to her workplace to thank her.

It didn't help the situation, but at least he was still on speaking terms with Betty. He would be there a little longer, but what good would it do him? Cheng's death removed his main reason for wanting to stay. After the usual morning round of calls, he chewed over his options and decided what he needed to do. Sitting in the pub in Soho was a waste of time. He had no reason to think that Hudson would go past again. It was just clutching at straws. He had to take a more positive approach and that meant going after the arbitration panel chairman, confirming his suspicions about the blonde and, if possible, finding her.

It seemed to Emil the people who'd filmed the video must be responsible for Cheng's death, so he'd make sure her death was on the chairman's conscience. Something for the sick pervert to think about while he sits in his prison cell, in the paedophile wing – if such things exist in the Hong Kong prison system.

He'd learnt from the Australian legal team where the chairman lived. That was one useful titbit of information he'd garnered over the drinks in Wan Chai. He finished work while there was still daylight and took the number six bus from Admiralty over to Stanley, grabbing a seat upstairs at the front window.

The route over Stubbs Road to Stanley was single lane each way, steep slopes falling away below it in many places, from which pencil thin blocks of apartments would stretch forty or fifty floors into the sky. He'd travelled over many times before, to shop in Stanley Market or meet friends there for meals, being amazed (and horrified) at the way the drivers threw the double-decker buses around the sharp corners above the precipitous drops. It still gave him the creeps.

The road ran past the chairman's residence. He'd been told it was a freestanding house, above the beach at Repulse Bay. The building, painted lemon, with a grey tiled roof, was easy enough to spot – it was the only freestanding house there, all the other buildings being apartment blocks. The scumbag must be loaded, he thought, as the bus trundled down the hill past it.

The early evening light was fading and, through the foliage along the roadside fence, he could see there were lights on in all the small windows along the first floor. Below, he could see there was an archway entrance to what must have been a garage, and through the open gate he could see a silver Aston Martin and a large BMW saloon gracing the paved apron in front of the building.

Emil stayed on the bus until it reached Stanley, then took a taxi back up to the house. The gate to the driveway was still open, so he walked in, security lights flooding the area in bright, white light as he did. It enabled him to see where the front entrance was situated. The BMW was where he'd seen it, but the Aston Martin had gone.

A Filipino housemaid answered the door. No, her boss wasn't available. It was his night to go to his club.

"It is important that I speak with him tonight. Where is his club?"

"Aberdeen. The yachting club, sir."

Emil had asked the cab driver to wait. They set off for Aberdeen – looked like it was going to be a long evening, lucrative for the cabbie. He hoped it would be money well spent. It took a while, but the driver eventually found the entrance to the Aberdeen Boat Club – insisting there was no club called the Yacht Club.

At the reception, Emil drew a blank.

"Mr Law. Mr Howard Law."

"Sorry, sir, there is no member shown with that name."

"H-O-W-A-R-D. L-A-W?"

"That's right, sir. No name with that spelling."

Emil returned to the cab. He was directing the cabbie to take him back to Central, when there was a tap on his window.

"Ah, sir, are you sure it was the Boat Club, and not Aberdeen Marina Club?"

"No, I'm not. Where's the Marina Club?"

"Just along this road, you can't miss it." The man gave instructions to the cabbie in Chinese.

At the Marina Club reception, he was advised that the club could not give information about members, nor would he be allowed in to look around. Guests could only enter accompanied by a member. But if he'd like to wait, they'd see if they could help him.

Emil stood at the glass wall, looking out the front entrance to where his cab waited with its meter ticking over. Behind it, a backdrop of yacht masts swaying gently from side to side, like a profusion of arrhythmic metronomes. Behind them, clusters of matchstick apartment blocks rose up the green sides of the surrounding hills, slowly becoming more indistinct in the darkening haze of the evening. He stood there, gazing into the middle distance, trying to formulate words around his thoughts. Trying to construct what it was he wanted to say, if he did get to speak to the chairman.

"You want to speak to me?"

The voice surprised him. He turned and looked into the same jowly face he's seen in the video. It repulsed him; he restrained his urge to hit it. He needed to be coherent and objective if he was going to get the information he wanted.

"Yes, you may or may not remember me, I was with the Australian legal team in …"

"Yes, yes, what do you want?"

The chairman was clearly unimpressed at being disturbed.

"Is there somewhere private, where we can talk?"

"Here's just fine." Impatiently, full of self-importance. "What do you want?"

"Okay, if that's the way you want it. I have a DVD – given to me by someone who is now dead. Murdered. That DVD contains video footage. Video footage of you. Do you want me to go on?"

"I want you to get out of my sight." The jowly face had reddened alarmingly. "Get out of here," he shouted, "right now!"

He turned and called to the reception desk. "This man is leaving now! Get him out!"

Emil, ignoring him, went on. "The footage is of you and a young boy. I'd guess he's about nine, or maybe ten years old."

The chairman was walking quickly back past the reception, into the club. He wasn't looking back, but as he passed the desk, turned to the receptionist.

"Get him out NOW!"

Emil tried following him.

"You're sexually molesting him, Mr Law. You're raping him!"

But the chairman was out of sight and Emil was only shouting at the security guards who had appeared in front of him, blocking him from following the chairman any further. They grabbed his arms and, turning him around, frogmarched him towards the entrance. Emil didn't resist, but kept shouting.

"That's a crime! Raping a child! A serious crime."

The security guards took him out through the entrance before releasing their grip on his arms.

"Leave these premises now, please."

The two guards stood watching as Emil climbed into the cab. Damn it, he hadn't got anywhere. All he'd done was put the scumbag on notice. Hadn't asked about the blonde.

The driver sat impassively, waiting for instructions on the next destination, as if this was all just part of the normal daily routine. Emil leaned forward:

"Can you go back over to..." In front of them, the silver Aston Martin was easing its way out of the club car park onto the roadway. Then it accelerated away from them.

"Follow that car!" he shouted, pointing after it. "Quickly, follow that car!"

*****

Emil adjusted his weight onto the other leg. He was standing across the road from the entrance to an apartment block in the midlevels; leaning against a wall, trying to look inconspicuous. An impossibility, given that it was late evening, there was no-one else around and he'd been loitering up and down past this spot for the preceding two hours. But it wasn't too hot, and it wasn't raining. That was something.

They'd followed the Aston Martin back over towards Central, then up into the midlevels. At first, it had been difficult to keep in sight. But as the cab driver warmed to his task, Emil needed to get him to back off, especially as they wound their way up through the narrow streets leading to Conduit Road where, at times, the taxi was virtually tailgating it.

The Aston Martin had disappeared into the underground parking of an apartment building, not far from the top of the midlevels escalator. Emil thought about keeping the cab waiting again, but in the end, decided to let it go. None of the names on the tenants' directory for the building meant anything to him, so he had no idea into which of the apartments the chairman could have gone. But what he did know, was that he recognised the outside of the building: it was the same apartment building that appeared in the first short video clip on the DVD, which was still warming his pocket.

Earlier he'd noticed, a little further along the road, that there was a look out for viewing the city below. It had a seat and since he was tired of standing, went and sat there. Once upon a time, it might have provided a nice view of the harbour as well, but that was well and truly hidden by the forest of apartment blocks and office buildings now standing in front of it. The pavement here was wider and by sitting sideways along the seat, he could still observe the entrance to the apartment building. Abundant foliage along the edge of the footpath partially hid the seat from that part of the road, which meant he wasn't obvious to anyone approaching the building on foot.

He sat a while longer, but nothing was happening. It was getting towards midnight; another wasted evening. Since he'd been sitting there, a Chinese couple had walked up – probably off the midlevels escalator – and entered the building. Otherwise, there'd been no-one entering or leaving the building. Or even walking in the street. It was very quiet, for such a large block, he thought. Except for the garbage collection truck he could hear working its way along the street towards where he was, the whole area seemed unnaturally quiet.

The truck went past and pulled up in front of the apartment block. He waited until the workers finished loading the waste from the bins beside the building entrance, then stood up and stretched: it was time to call it a night. That scumbag either wasn't coming out again, or had sneaked out and he'd missed him. Either way, Emil was leaving. He'd have to try again in the morning. Maybe he would take the DVD and what information he had to Tang. Let him sort it out. The garbage truck disappeared around a curve in the road. He felt tired and began walking slowly after it, towards the top of the midlevels escalator.

Suddenly, everything was dark. Something was over his head. A hood, or cloth sack, of some sort.

He raised his arms to get it off, but they were pulled back down, quickly, pinned to his sides.

Strong hands pinioning him. Where'd they come from? Hadn't been a sound. Not a footstep. Nothing.

He struggled, twisting, trying to free himself. But the hands had him in a vice-like grip, on both sides. He heard a tearing sound. What was it? He recognised it: gaffer tape; being unwound from a roll, very quickly. Being wound around him, just as quickly. Trapping his arms by his side, more around his ankles. Something hard hit him on the back of the head. Then nothing.

*****

Everything was black.

He was conscious again, but everything was black. Was he blind? It was the hood: he realised there was a hood over his head. He was lying on his side, being tossed about. From the movement, the sounds, he guessed he was in the back of a truck or van. His head was aching where he'd been hit; he was tightly bound, arms to his sides – he remembered the gaffer tape. The tightness of it around his chest and the cloth of the hood were making it hard to breathe.

Relax. He told himself. Relax. Breathe slowly and deeply.

He imagined pictures he'd seen of terror suspects subjected to 'special rendition' by the CIA and its cohorts. Why would they do this to him? No, that was crazy. It wasn't the CIA.

He thought of calling out, but his throat was dry and all he did was cough. His head throbbed. He closed his eyes again. No one would hear him over the noise of the vehicle anyway. Concentrate on breathing, he told himself.

The vehicle had been bouncing along – quickly on an

uneven road surface, he guessed, but now it slowed. It was turning, making Emil roll over, until a boot stopped him and rolled him back. He hadn't realised there was someone with him in the van or whatever it was.

"Hello? Hello?" he tried. "Why are you doing this to me?"

Nothing.

"Where are we going? Where are you taking me?"

No response.

The vehicle seemed to be turning continuously, causing him to roll. The boot pushed him back over, then rested hard on the side of his neck, preventing him from moving, the unspoken order: shut up. It seemed to be turning in a tight circle, no, not a circle he realised, a spiral: it was descending. From the change in sounds, it must have left the road, must be descending a sort of spiral driveway.

There were other noises now. Machinery. Trucks. The loud, warning blah-blah sounds of reversing trucks. And the smell. Even from where he was, on the floor in the back of the vehicle, with a hood over his head, it was unmistakable. It was the smell of all the restaurant back alleyways of Hong Kong Central, concentrated in one place: the powerful, pungently sweet stench of rotting organic waste, unmistakably Chinese food waste.

He realised he knew this place: he'd been here once before – done a tour, years ago. There couldn't be another waste facility in Hong Kong with the same spiral entrance as the Island West Transfer Station. The vehicle levelled out and came to a halt. Doors opening, he could feel someone pulling at his legs. Someone lifted his shoulders, presumably the owner of the boot who'd been sitting over him in the back. He was standing upright outside the van. Through the black material of the hood he could sense very bright lights all around him.

Someone was holding him upright, there was a voice close to his ear:

"*Zàijiàn!*"

Then, a little push.

He was tumbling, he could feel himself tumbling through space, hooded, bound up like an Egyptian mummy, falling end over end, terrifyingly, through a black void. His feet hit something soft, it seemed like he was sinking into it. Not water. Firmer. The smell. The waste! Putrescible waste. Food waste. God, the smell!

He landed almost upright, but buried up to his waist. Gasping for air. Suddenly, it seemed like there was no air. The waste – aerobic decay. He dragged at the air, sucking the cloth of the hood onto his mouth, now wet, onto his tongue: an astringent, disgusting taste. He couldn't wipe it off. He puffed his cheeks and blew to get the cloth off his mouth, trying to work saliva around his tongue to obscure the fucking awful taste.

Other sounds: harbour sounds – he was in a waste container. Jesus! He started wriggling, but the gaffer tape was tightly around him. With the movement he was sinking deeper into the muck.

"Help! Help me!" It came out as a coarse moan. No one would hear it.

He thought: from here, containers are loaded on barges to the West New Territories Landfill. Fuck! Got to get out before they close it.

More waste was dumped on top. Suddenly, no light. Completely buried.

Writhing, struggling, it was hard to breathe. Hood soaking wet, barely keeping the muck out of his mouth. Wet slurry permeating the cloth. In his eyes, ears, nose. Fuck! Can taste it.

The weight of waste was pushing down on him, making it even harder to move.

He could feel the wetness through the gaffer tape, in his clothes. Soaked.

The smell – he recognised hydrogen sulphide momentarily, then couldn't even distinguish that.

Waste won't be compacted until it gets to the landfill, he

thought. Still some air here. Conserve energy. Breathe slower, shorter.

He tried to imagine being back in the pool, swimming, relax; just little breathes; feeling drowsy, wet, close eyes to keep muck out, hard to keep open …

12

"Ladies and gentlemen, the Prime Minister!"

Michael Mendicane strode into the garden outside his office and up to the lectern in front of the assembled members of the parliamentary press corps. His minders had orchestrated this new, US-presidential style arrangement for press briefings, another attempt to endow him with *gravitas* – something he was badly in need of. With his rolling gait, like he'd just stepped out of the saddle he'd been sitting in for years, long arms lolling by his side as he made his way in, it was easy to see how the political cartoonists derived their inspiration. The minders would have been tearing their hair out.

The Prime Minister got straight down to business.

"I've called this briefing, this afternoon, my fellow Australians, to inform you of a serious financial setback the nation has suffered on our road to national economic recovery. This setback is on a scale many of you may find hard to grasp. I have trouble coming to terms with it myself. It is on a scale that has serious implications for the policies of this government, going forward.

"I like to think we're all on the one team here: Team Australia, which is why I called this briefing. As your captain, I have a duty to make sure team members understand the team tactics. It's no good keeping bad news from the rest of the team, if this means the other players don't understand

102

the team strategy. We've all got to be singing from the same whiteboard, er, hymn sheet.

"So, it's my duty to inform you, that the government has had a significant international arbitration decision against it. Unfortunately, there is no scope for appeal to the video umpire; there is no television match official or Hawk-eye. The cost of this loss runs into the billions of dollars.

"Coming on top of the budget deficit, this is a double king hit. The government will need to revisit and again review public spending.

"Treasury is considering the implications. The Cabinet will be reviewing government policies concerning, in particular, the carbon trading and climate change, from which this disaster has arisen. I will be making a statement on the impacts, to the Parliament, in the coming weeks, once a full and thorough assessment has been made of the damage.

"However, I want to reassure all of you, my fellow teammates, that this government will not be sacrificing any of you for the sake of a few carbon emissions. Nobody who is performing gets dropped from my team! Food on the table, in the homes of families battling to survive these tough economic times – that's what this government is about. Jobs, for people who want to work. That's what your team captain is about!

"And if that means we have to be a little less 'touchy-feely' in some areas … like, for instance, the environment, well, I make no apologies if that's how it's got to be. We cannot afford to keep our hands off the sacred cows forever. Even … that holiest of sacred cows … the Great Barrier Reef … in these tough economic times.

"Now, I'll take couple of questions …"

Predictably, the questions all focused on where the cuts would come from, who was going to pay. Mendicane waited until there were a few along the same themes, then produced his own knockout lines.

"Just to answer those questions about cuts. Let me be quite clear. In spite of the situation this latest setback leaves us in; in spite of the double king hits, this government will do everything within its power to generate growth, to score more points, rather than make cuts on top of cuts.

"We're not trying to defend a non-existent lead, we want to put more runs on the board. We are about growing the economy, scoring tries, touchdowns and goals, fostering and developing team skills, not reducing them. Encouraging new development, not stifling it. Growth is our best response, when it comes to the economy! And so that's what we'll be looking to do."

In his office suite along from the Prime Minister's, Tony Hounganis sat watching a live feed of the press conference on a television screen, together with his chief of staff and press officer.

"Vintage stuff, Mick. Pure vintage performance," he chuckled.

"Don't get too cocky, Tony. Mick might be able to fool some of the punters with his common man touch, but the polls still show we've got a real battle on our hands – you've seen them, it's neck-and-neck," said the chief-of-staff.

"Yeah, sadly, this bloody arbitration business is a double-edged sword. I just need to be able to make Mick understand that. He's all fired up to use it as an excuse to reverse the policy on the bloody coal loader, but I don't think he's taken enough time to think how angry people are. He's already forgotten the protests. Hundreds of thousands of *his* 'little Aussie battlers' – the voters he's thinking he's got in the bag. If we're not careful, they'll be out of the bag and on the streets again. Not what we want, in the run up to an election."

"Well you better make sure he does understand. Otherwise we'll be out on the streets too – without jobs!" said the press officer.

"Don't worry mate, we'll still throw a few crumbs your way if we end up in opposition," said Hounganis, laughing.

On the television, the press conference had finished.

"You've got a meeting with him later this afternoon, Tony,

so you can start working on him straight away," said the chief-of-staff, clicking off the screen.

*****

Thunderstorms were brewing in the hills around Canberra. The light was dull in the garden outside the Prime Minister's office. Parliament House staff were busy clearing away the last of the chairs and technical equipment that had been set up there for the earlier press conference.

Inside, Mendicane and Hounganis had been discussing 'the way forward' for the last hour, without making much progress. Hounganis was having trouble getting his message through to his erstwhile political soul brother.

"Mick, all I'm saying is that we need to be careful. Attorney Generals are saying this bloody arbitration is going to cost upwards of three billion, mate. That's on top of the existing situation. Where are we going to find that sort of money?"

"You're the Treasurer, Tony."

"Yes, Mick. And you're the bloody captain who's going to take the ship down with him, if he's not careful."

"What do you mean?"

"What I mean is that we're just about to start the run in to the next election, as you bloody-well know. We can't afford to have people back on the streets, protesting about the Barrier Reef. Street protests are bad news in an election campaign."

"I know, mate. It's the curse of these damn three year terms. We've got to start moving towards longer terms – like the yanks, or five-year jobs, like the pommies have. We should get this moving in the next parliament."

"If we're still here!"

"Time for a drink, I think."

From a bar fridge behind one of the redwood panels lining the wall, Mendicane produced a bottle of beer for Hounganis and a tomato juice for himself. Hounganis tried to set it all out for Mendicane, again.

"So, on the one-hand, we have the risk of street protests if we even look like we're going back to supporting the coal loader – not to mention the fact that we'll look like we're just caving in to these Hong Kong crooks." He took a swig of beer from the bottle. "And, on the other hand, we've got to find a way to claw the budget back out of this black hole, which is now compounded by the bloody arbitration disaster, without hitting our 'little Aussie battler' constituency in the hip pocket."

"Better get those boffins of yours at the Treasury onto this Tony. It's time that lot earned their keep."

Before Hounganis could respond, the door opened and Mendicane's chief-of-staff poked his head around it.

"Sorry to interrupt, Mick, but is Bull Griffith meant to be joining you?"

"What? No, no bloody way! Tony and I are discussing strategy."

"Well, he's here to …"

The door swung open wider and Bull Griffith pushed his way past the chief-of-staff, with the Minister for Mining and Energy, Barry Phelong, following closely on his heels. Griffith turned and, elbowing Phelong out of the way, closed the door in the chief-of-staff's face. Phelong was the member for a West Australian electorate and had been included by Mendicane in his ministry, under sufferance, to placate the factions and keep Griffith on side. He was a career party hack-cum-politician and the way he crept around behind people made Mendicane think of him as a hyena. He certainly didn't trust him. Nor did Hounganis.

"If you're talkin' strategy, Mick, you need to be talkin' to me," said Griffith. He pointed at the beer in Hounganis's hand. "I wouldn't mind one of those myself. Which door is it?"

Mendicane, mouth open in surprise, gestured to the panel that concealed the bar fridge. He and Hounganis sat there speechless, while Griffith selected a bottle, opened it then flopped into one of the upturned, spongy cup mushroom armchairs, facing them, without bothering to offer a drink to Phelong. He took a long pull at the beer, then put the bottle on the table beside his armchair. Phelong took up a subordinate position, standing behind the armchair.

"I liked your press conference performance this afternoon, Mick," he said, eyeing the two of them like a slave trader might evaluate a couple of prospective acquisitions. "It's just what you needed. Start the ball rolling. Steal a march on the Opposition. They think you're in complete disarray. In fact, from the feedback I'm getting, most of the country thinks the entire government is in disarray, has lost its way. Now's the time for you to act and you'll catch your opponents on the hop."

Mendicane was nodding his head. Slowly. He wasn't quite sure where Griffith was going with this, but after their last fractious meeting, he felt he'd better humour him.

"I'm with you Bull, I'm with you. Rope-a-dope – that's what you're talking about, isn't it? The old 'sucker punch' routine. Am I right?"

"Somethin' like that, Mick. Yes, somethin' along those lines."

Griffith took another swig of beer.

"I've been giving a lot of thought to your predicament – *your* budget predicament," he said, looking at the Treasurer in a way that gave Hounganis an unhappy feeling deep down in his bowels, causing him to squirm a little in his seat.

Hounganis loosened his tie and undid the top button of his shirt.

"What, with this arbitration business, on top of an already unacceptable deficit situation. More borrowing's not an option. And you don't want to put up the tax rates, do you? I think you need your friends," he continued, now giving them both the most genial look he could muster.

"And a friend in need, is a friend indeed!" spouted Mendicane, coming to life.

"That's right, Mick. That's so right." Griffith took a sip

from his beer bottle. "I have some friends. Business associates. Colleagues. Friends. I'd like you to meet them. These gentlemen are good friends of mine. Of ours", he said, waving a hand behind his head at Phelong, who was nodding his agreement, "from the US, which you know has always been a great friend of Australia. They've told me they're very interested to invest in our beautiful country. Interested in helping your government through these tough times. Investing in helping us develop our resources. Investing big-time!"

"Bull, that's music to my – our – ears. Isn't it, Tony? Isn't it Barry," said Mendicane, giving Houganis a look of encouragement and Phelong a more guarded one.

"Sounds good, Bull. So far." Houganis smelt a rat. "What's the story?"

"I'll tell you what the story is, Tony," Griffith snapped back at him, "these associates of mine are willing to pour billions of dollars of investment into this country, in spite of the great fuckin' mess you two and the rest of the idiots in your Cabinet have made of government policy."

Behind him, Phelong's expression changed to one of hurt indignation.

"Why are they willing to do this? Because they can see what a great land of opportunity Australia still is, for hard workers, willing to put in the hours, and investors, willing to put in the money. And because I've told them that *your* government is the one to back, the one that investors can rely on, to get the policy right. To support investors. In spite of your mismanagement. In spite of this cock-up in Hong Kong."

He finished his beer and stood up. Mendicane and Houganis stood up, too. Deferentially.

"They believe me. They trust me. And they're the sorta people who put their money where their mouth is. They can get you through this crisis. They can make the arbitration loss go away. They can even do this and, at the same time, allow you to keep your fuckin' 'greenie credentials'."

"What do they want in return?" asked Houganis.

"All they want is certainty, Tony. Policy certainty. If you can provide that, I can assure you your electoral futures are secure."

"Bull, you're a champion!" said Mendicane, gripping Griffith's hand and pumping it vigorously, Hounganis, more hesitatingly, offering Griffith a wet fish handshake.

"Good. I'll set up a meetin'."

13

A bell was ringing. Incessantly. An alarm bell. Forcing its way into his unconsciousness.

It stopped.

The weight pressing on his body had gone and the hood had gone from his head. Without opening his eyes, he sensed bright lights. Something was over his face. Not the hood. It was hard and smelt rubbery. The thought came into his head to fight it, but his arms were down by his sides and he didn't have the strength to lift them. He felt someone push on his chest; he opened his mouth and, as the pressure lifted, he gratefully sucked in a lung-full of oxygen. More pushing on his chest made him expel it, then he sucked in another lung-full, then another.

He was no longer constrained and realised he could move his arms and legs. Emil blinked his eyes open. He was on a trolley. It was in the back of a vehicle, which must have been an ambulance. There were uniformed Chinese police standing around, outside the open back door. The man who had been pressing on his chest, bent over him and removed the oxygen mask. Immediately, his senses were assailed by the sweet, over-powering smell of putrefying, organic waste. Food waste. He pushed himself up, supporting himself on his elbows, realising as he did, that it was himself, his own clothes, he could smell. They were wet and they stank of it. The waste.

He could see, outside the end of the ambulance, that they were in what looked like a large concrete cave. It could have been the set of a James Bond film. Even down to the operators behind glass panels, in a control room that looked like it was set up in the rock wall. He realised he was still at the Island West Transfer Station.

The man leant over him again, with a stethoscope.

"Please, breathe deeply."

He listened to Emil's chest, then tapped his chest and back in a few spots, while still listening. Emil could read from the man's uniform that he was a paramedic from the Hong Kong St John Ambulance Brigade. The man shone a light in each of Emil's eyes, made some notes on a clipboard at the end of the trolley, then sat down beside it.

Vehicles were approaching from somewhere. Emil couldn't see them from the back of the ambulance. He could hear them, and the blue flashes, on the walls and ceiling of the facility, identified them. They pulled up, out of sight, the uniformed officers coming to attention. Emil felt exhausted and slumped back down, closing his eyes and happy to receive the oxygen mask over his face again. There was a discussion going on outside the vehicle. A number of people speaking Chinese. Someone spoke to him in English, from the open door of the vehicle.

"So, Mr Pfeffer. You have a very interesting way to occupy your evening."

Emil looked up. The expressionless face of Senior Inspector Tang looked back.

"Oh, it's you."

"Perhaps you can tell me how you managed to get into a waste barge, wrapped up like a mummy?"

"How did you find me?"

"I did not find you. I was at the Aberdeen Marina Club. There was a disturbance there, earlier this evening. I was called there when it became apparent that *you* were the cause of that disturbance. You are very fortunate that the master of the barge was watching the containers being filled. He noticed the movement and told them to stop. If they had closed the container, next stop for you was the landfill. You should thank him, for saving your life."

Emil lay back and took another drag on the oxygen before trying to respond. He felt weak, light-headed.

"I was walking on the midlevels. Near the top of the escalator. Conduit Road. That's all. I don't know why this was done to me, why they tried to kill me."

"Who are they?"

Emil didn't answer. He left the oxygen mask over his face.

After a brief conversation with the paramedic, Tang left. It was clear to him this round-eye was up to more than the reason he gave for being in Hong Kong. This incident made it even clearer that he was involved in what happened to the lawyer, Cheng. First Cheng murdered, now an attempt to kill the round-eye. Tang felt sure that solving one matter would get to the bottom of the other. There was no doubt in his mind that they were related. But the last thing he needed was for a foreigner, even worse, a United Nations official with whom he was dealing, to be murdered under his nose.

Emil spent the remaining hours of the night at the hospital, for observation. In the morning, he was escorted back to his hotel to get clean clothes, before being taken to police headquarters in Arsenal Street and the waiting Senior Inspector Tang.

"Why did Cheng visit your hotel several times, Mr Pfeffer?"

If Tang was tired after his late night call-outs, he didn't show it. Emil, on the other hand, felt decidedly worse for wear and disinclined to be helpful.

"How is that related to what happened to me last night?"

"That is what *you* will tell *me*, Mr Pfeffer."

"I don't know, Senior Inspector. When you find out, can you tell me?"

"What is it you are hiding from me? I will find out, in the end."

Emil shrugged his shoulders. "I don't know what you mean."

But as he said it, he was thinking of the DVD, now safely in the pocket of the clean trousers he was wearing. His hand was moving to feel for it, for reassurance, when, realising what he was doing, he stopped himself. All the while Tang, like a predator, was watching him; a big cat stalking prey, a leopard or a jaguar, readying itself to pounce.

"Why did you go to the Marina Club last night?"

"I wanted to speak to someone."

"What happened?"

"He didn't want to speak to me."

"Is that why you were shouting at him, causing a disturbance, so you were expelled from the premises?"

Emil weighed up in his mind, as he had many times already in the past week, whether now was the time to tell Tang about the DVD.

"He was rude and refused to speak to me."

He was still uncertain about where it would get him with Tang, whether it would make Tang more favourably disposed to helping him find the blonde, or just become another wasted opportunity. Better to wait, for the moment.

"So why did you go to Conduit Road?"

"I followed him there. I was trying to speak to him."

"What did you want to speak about to Mr Howard Law, at that time of night?"

So he knows, Emil thought. Of course he would know. He would have had that information from the staff at the Marina Club.

"If you aren't already aware, he was the chairman of the arbitration panel in the legal dispute, the reason that I was called to Hong Kong. I wished to speak to him about matters concerning those proceedings."

"What 'matters', Mr Pfeffer?"

"I'm sorry, Senior Inspector, but that's confidential."

"Previously, Mr Pfeffer, you told me that you were not

directly involved in these proceedings; that you were not even allowed into the room where they were being heard. How can there be confidential matters concerning the proceedings that you now need to discuss with the chairman? In the middle of the night."

"Well, there are, Senior Inspector, you'll just have to take my word for that."

His brain was still too dulled to think of a better response. Tang was sharper than he'd given him credit for being. Tang's face remained impassive, but Emil thought he could sense anger, contempt, even disgust, behind the visage. It's not me you should have contempt and disgust for, Emil thought, returning the stare. You should be focusing a little closer to home.

*****

Emil was the victim of a crime, not the perpetrator. There hadn't been a complaint about the incident at the Marina Club, so there wasn't much else Tang could do, but let him go. Emil returned to the lobby cafe in his hotel and tried to eat something. Not that he felt hungry, after his near death experience, but it was almost midday and he hadn't eaten the previous evening, so he thought he should have something. It would give him time to think.

This was where he had last seen Cheng. It was where Tang had confronted him with news of her disappearance. Maybe sitting here he would be inspired to come up with a plan, concoct a strategy, to salvage something from his time in Hong Kong. His phone rang: from the display he could see it was Betty G. He let it go to voicemail. Then he saw that it was the third time she'd called since the previous evening. Hmm. He didn't want to think about it.

He found himself watching the crowd in the lobby, the sandwich and coffee he'd ordered useful as a cover for him while he looked. Tang would, undoubtedly, have people here watching him. He scanned the lobby, cafe and bar areas. There were probably about twenty people who could have been Tang's officers. But were there others watching him, too, sent by whoever sent the waste collectors for him, last night? Sent to finish the job of getting rid of him. If there were, he would need to find a way to flush them out.

He finished the food and went to his room. Everything seemed as he'd left it. Not that he expected the people who'd ransacked the previous room to return. They would have realised by now that the DVD wasn't there. Returning to the lift, he took it down to the level where the pool was located, several floors above the lobby. He waited there a few minutes, then took another lift to the level where the gym was, on the floor below the lobby. He waited there for five minutes. Didn't seem to be anyone following him, so he took the stairs down the single flight to the hotel exit into the shopping mall.

They'd be onto him soon enough, but at least if he could get a head start, he might have a chance. He raced down the escalator, exiting the mall onto Queensway, hailed a taxi and directed it to the Exchange Centre: scene of the recent infamous arbitration disaster. Premises of the Hong Kong International Arbitration Centre. And location, on level thirty, for the offices of 'Howard Law, International Arbitration and Dispute Resolution'.

His luck was in: at level thirty the lift doors opened just as the chairman himself, walked out of his office heading towards the toilets. He didn't even notice Emil come out of the lift and follow him. It was a small space, with a single cubicle, a single urinal and only just enough space for two people to fit in front of the hand basin. By the time he entered, the chairman was already in the cubicle.

He had him cornered, without needing to lay a hand on him. The only way out would be past, or over, Emil. He waited for the flush. The cubicle door opened.

"We meet again."

For a split second, there was a look of surprise on the

chairman's face. Then rage. He flung the door back and lunged at Emil, fists bunched in front of him. But he wasn't a street fighter and Emil easily parried the feeble assault, forcing the chairman back with his forearm, pinioning him against the wall of the cubicle.

"Wrong move, you filth."

"What do you want?"

"You to be punished for your disgusting crimes. But first, you can tell me about the blonde."

"I don't know what you're talking about."

"Yes, you do. The blonde in the video. The blonde escorting you and that poor child into the apartment block, where you raped him."

"I don't know her, she brought the boy, that's all."

"Not good enough." He pushed harder with his forearm on the chairman's chest. "Hope you haven't been paid for the arbitration yet, because you'll just have to pay it all back. There's a growing list of people who are going to be interested in your starring video performance. Hong Kong police, Australian Government, various professional bodies…"

As he was saying it, Emil was applying more and more weight onto the chairman's chest, making it harder for him to breathe. The jowly face was crimson, watery eyes protruding. Emil eased back.

"Just tell me where I can find her. And her associates."

"Alright," he gasped. "Alright." Emil eased the pressure a little more. "She lives in that block."

"Which apartment?"

"Twelfth floor. 1203. There are some others, associates of hers, also living there. In other apartments, in the tower." As he finished speaking, he jerked forward, vomit projecting over the hand basin and onto the floor, spattering Emil's shoes and trousers. Emil got his arm and face out of the way just in time.

"Oh, you fucking bastard!"

He stood back and spun the chairman over the basin in time for it to receive a second, stinking disgorgement.

"Rotting waste last night, vomit today. Just about sums you up."

He grabbed the back of the chairman's neck, forcing his face down over the basin, close to the acrid puke half filling it.

"You'd better be telling the truth. Don't try to contact them. Don't tell them you've spoken to me. If you do, you won't live out the day."

He released the pressure on the chairman's neck and got out of the little space as quickly as he could, before the smell made him throw up, as well.

*****

It wasn't late, but it was dark by the time Emil resumed his place from the previous evening at the viewing seat, just along Conduit Road from the entrance to the apartment block. He'd been a little more discreet this evening, remaining around the top of the midlevels escalator, rather than hanging around – too obviously – on the roadway in front of the apartment building. There was a bus stop, which he'd used as a reason to loiter for a while and, so long as the shops there stayed open, he'd used them as well. But there hadn't been any sign of the blonde.

With the onset of evening there were fewer people about, but he'd give it another hour or two in the hope of intercepting her, if she arrived or left on foot. Earlier, he'd checked the residents' directory for apartment 1203 but, just like a number of the other apartment buzzers, it was blank. The bench seat was his best option now, as he could see both the entrance to the apartments and a fair stretch of the footpath leading to it from the escalator, without being too obvious. And after the previous evening's episode, he was keeping a cautious eye on his surroundings, so as not to get jumped again.

The night was balmy, cooler than it had been, not at all humid. More like the usual conditions for the time of year. There was a three-quarter moon high in the sky, hidden by buildings from where he sat. He'd been on the seat less than half an hour when he noticed someone approaching from the direction of the escalator. The footsteps sounded like a woman's. He strained to see through the shrubbery, but the person approaching was hidden by shadows. Still, it might be her.

He was concealed by the foliage of the gardens and there was still a distance before the person would come fully into sight. He stood waiting, anticipating. Suddenly, car wheels were squealing around Conduit Road. Two transit vans, only a couple of metres apart, raced past the approaching pedestrian, coming to a screeching halt directly in front of Emil, blocking his view. Before he had time to react, the side doors had been noiselessly slung open, three, four men in black, faces hidden by balaclavas, jumped out, guns pointing at Emil, gesturing for him to get his arms in the air. As his arms went up, they were immediately grabbed, and he was dragged into the first of the vans, a black clad figure jumping in on top of him, then they were moving again, very quickly. It was over in seconds.

Shit! Two nights in a row. How could he have been so stupid?

But he was conscious. He wasn't being restrained. And once they reached Magazine Gap Road, far enough away from the apartment block to be safe, the kidnappers removed their balaclavas. What sort of abduction was this?

"Who are you? Where are you taking me?"

"Just be quiet. You are under arrest."

"For what?"

They ignored him. But pretty quickly it was clear they were heading for Arsenal Street, Wan Chai.

He was escorted into the front reception. The desk sergeant placed a plastic tray on the counter.

"Empty your pockets," he said, indicating the tray.

Emil patted his jacket pockets. He took out his wallet, some small change and his hotel room security pass, placing them in the tray.

"Is that everything?"

Emil looked at the sergeant. Then reaching into his trouser pocket, slowly he drew his hand out, the DVD held between two fingers. He placed it in the tray.

14

There was no processing, no fingerprinting, no mug shots. Just removal of the items he'd had on him, then he was taken straight through police headquarters and out the other side to a small interview room in another building. He managed to extract from the black-clad officer keeping watch over him that they were undercover police, who had the apartment building under surveillance. Emil had been detained for interfering in their surveillance, he was told.

So, no longer arrested, only detained, he puzzled. It didn't make sense – if they were watching the building, where were they the previous evening, they could have prevented him from being grabbed and dumped at the transfer station? But the man didn't stay with him long enough for Emil to ask. He was replaced by a uniformed officer who ignored Emil's questions.

An hour dragged past then a more senior officer came into the room. Immediately, he started questioning Emil, aggressively. Emil remembered Tang's words about Arsenal Street being where the "grilling" took place. A single pip indicated he was a probationary inspector. Probably out to prove himself, thought Emil. They've got the DVD. How much of it have they looked at? They might have viewed all of it, which he hadn't. He didn't know how bad it got.

"What were you doing outside the apartment block?" The interrogator shouted in Emil's face. "What were you up to?"

"Have I broken any laws?"

"You can be charged with a number of offences, so just answer my questions! Who are you working with – give me the names of your accomplices."

"I don't know what you're talking about, officer."

"Don't lie to me. Answer me – what were you doing loitering around that apartment block?"

But in fifteen minutes, he didn't once mention the DVD, or child pornography, or anything related to it. He seemed to be focused only on Emil loitering around the apartment block, demanding Emil confess his 'criminal intent'.

"I don't know what you're talking about. Am I under arrest? If not, can you return my possessions and let me go now?"

"No, you cannot go!' the policeman shouted at him. "What you were you planning to do at that apartment block?"

Emil had had enough. He gathered himself to shout back in the man's face, but before he could the door swung open and Tang strode in. There was a brief, animated discussion between Tang and the probationer. The probationer left and another policeman appeared with the tray of Emil's possessions. Everything except the DVD.

"Mr Pfeffer, come with me," said Tang.

Emil collected his items and followed him. Tang's manner was curt, more abrupt. None of the cordiality of their first meeting remained. The argument with the probationer seemed to have put him in a bad mood, if he wasn't already. Emil said nothing. Now they had the DVD, he was up shit creek without a paddle. He'd have to come clean, since he'd lost the advantage of being able to give the DVD to Tang, rather than have it taken from him.

Leaving Arsenal Street in an unmarked car, they crossed to Kowloon, Tang next to Emil in the back seat. They travelled in silence, Emil's mind buzzing with the possibilities: maybe there was a special facility for people caught with child pornography; or was he being taken to where the really serious 'grilling' took place, off-site, so there could be no political repercussions. No point in asking Tang. It seemed he'd already determined Emil's guilt.

The journey took them far up into the New Territories. It was all new territory for Emil. He'd never been into this part before. If it hadn't been under such circumstances, he would have found it interesting, but he was worried about what awaited him, wherever it was they were going. They passed cluster after cluster of pencil-thin apartment blocks, some of them huge with dozens of buildings, others containing as few as half a dozen; but all of the buildings forty or fifty stories reaching up from the orange mist of the sodium street lighting. He was trying to follow the names on the expressway, but he didn't recognise them, so it was a pointless exercise. It was just a way to take his mind off his predicament.

What he did know was that they'd taken the eastern harbour tunnel crossing, so they'd started somewhere to the east of Kowloon. Just after a sign indicating they were approaching a place called Shek Wu Hui, they turned off the expressway and onto a series of minor roads, surroundings becoming more and more rural, moonlight rather than sodium lights, the road running past spindly thickets of bushes, swampy-looking ground denuded of the mangroves that probably once covered it, the occasional settlements. The buildings they passed now were all only single or double storey. At a roundabout, he saw a sign for Luk Keng Road; a few kilometres further on they pulled into a small fishing village and stopped in front of a ramshackle, once whitewashed building by the edge of a large body of water. He guessed they must be very close to the border with Shenzhen. Across the water in the distance he could see the lights of a port facility, a flock of cranes all brightly lit, tall legs supporting box-shaped bodies from which extended long crane necks.

Tang, still silent, gestured for him to get out. They went up a flight of stairs to a room looking out over the water, towards the cranes. There was a wide balcony the full length of the building, with a columned balustrade. Once it might have been a nice place to sit with a cold beer in summer, he thought. But industrial effluent would have been permeating the sediment below for probably the last sixty years, so he doubted that would still be the case. With the tide low, a pungent sulphurous smell filled the air that hung heavily on the water. The place had a damp, decaying feel to it.

A Formica-topped table stood in the middle of the room, surrounded by four simple aluminium frame chairs. Tang indicated he should sit.

"What are we doing here, Senior Inspector?"

"Just be patient. You will find out."

Before long, a vehicle pulled up outside and they were joined by a softly spoken fellow. Tang introduced the newcomer as Zhong, from Beijing. Tang and Zhong had a long conversation in Chinese. When they finished, Zhong addressed Emil:

"You have been outside the Pearl Gardens Tower apartments two consecutive evenings. Can you tell me why?"

"As I told Senior Inspector Tang, I wanted to speak to a person there."

"But the man you told Senior Inspector Tang you went to see last night, was not there tonight. You should know that because you went to his office today."

"It was a different person I wanted to speak to tonight."

Tang didn't introduce Zhong as a policeman. Being from Beijing, there was a very good chance he was a government official. Perhaps an official who dealt with truculent foreigners. The clandestine, remote nature of the meeting place was making Emil uncomfortable about where the situation was heading.

"But let me ask you: why am I brought to this secret place to be questioned by a government official from Beijing?"

"Alright, Mr Pfeffer. You work for an international agency that is supported by my government, so I will be open with you. In return, I hope you will show the same respect and be open with me."

Emil acknowledged the offer with a nod of his head. He

looked over at Tang, whose impassive eyes were locked onto Emil's face like a weapons guidance system on a target.

"We are concerned about the activities – commodity trading activities – of a certain investment bank in Hong Kong. Sometimes organisations that have foreign staff in Hong Kong find apartments for those staff in the same block. The people in relation to whom our suspicions have been raised reside in the building you were outside for the last two nights. We have it under surveillance. That is why you have been brought here to explain yourself."

"Is Mr Howard Law one of the people you are watching?"

"There are many comings and goings – we cannot be sure, yet, which relate to activities of the people at the bank. He does not live there."

Zhong looked at Tang, but he remained silent, watching Emil.

"He does not work for the bank," Zhong continued. "We are unaware of any connection he has with commodity trading. Are you aware of a connection, Mr Pfeffer?"

"No."

"What about the second person you were looking for – does this person work for a bank? Are they involved in commodity trading?"

"Not so far as I'm aware. I don't know who they work for."

"What we would like to know, Mr Pfeffer, is why you are waiting outside this building, in secret? Your behaviour arouses suspicion. Why do you not call the person you wish to see, or ring the apartment number and go inside? Why did someone take you from there last night and put you in a waste barge bound for the landfill?"

It was cool by the water. The room covered the entire first floor, probably once had been a bar, being open all the way, as it was, along the side facing the water. Emil shivered. He realised the back of his shirt was wet with perspiration, something Tang would have noted already, for sure.

"I'm as mystified as you are."

"I don't think you are, Mr Pfeffer. We are aware of your history. We know what happened in Papua New Guinea. We know that you took matters into your own hands. You are lucky to be alive. And lucky to resolve that situation. Now, why are you carrying out activities unrelated to your work, again, here in Hong Kong?

"Those activities were my work! If you know so much about it, you will know that."

"What about now?"

He shrugged, but didn't answer. What was the point? They'd know he was lying, if he did. Having Tang watching him was like being hooked up to a human polygraph – except that Tang was likely to be more accurate.

Zhong was thoughtful, silently watching Emil for a time, before he spoke again.

"Do you have any connection to Globalreach Americas? That is the name of the bank. Do you know people connected to it?"

"No, I've never heard of it. Who are they?"

"It is a relatively new organisation – a regulated entity in Hong Kong less than ten years. The parent company is registered in the US state of Delaware. They have some large US energy companies on their register of shareholders. We have been watching their trading in energy commodities: coal and oil. There have been instances recently that look like the market is being ramped. Possibly they are engaging in round trip trades and other illegal market practices. You might be interested that there have been irregularities in relation to trading in carbon certificates, as well."

"That is of interest. If you have information, you can share it with my organisation. In fact, as a signatory member, it is incumbent on your government to report suspicious trades to my unit."

"Certainly. However, Mr Pfeffer, we are interested in what information you would like to share with us."

"I don't know what you mean. My organisation provides

information to all member countries through the usual channels."

"Not the organisation you work for!" snapped Zhong, suddenly irritated. "*You*, personally!"

"I think you do," interjected Tang. He stepped up to the table. "Perhaps you could begin by telling us about this," he said, placing the DVD on the table top. "Telling the truth."

Emil sighed. This point in the conversation was always, eventually, going to be reached.

"That is what Ms Cheng delivered to the concierge at my hotel, Senior Inspector." Tang continued staring at him. "Everything else I told you is the truth. I never spoke to her when she was at my hotel. On the earlier occasions, it might have been reconnaissance she was making. I don't know. We'll never know now."

"Why would Cheng have this, this … filthy thing?" Tang sneered.

"I don't know. I think Howard Law is being blackmailed with it. That's why I tried to speak to him. If he was compromised, then the arbitration result is invalid and must be challenged."

"If you are telling the truth, why did Cheng leave this for you, at your hotel?"

"I've been asking myself that question ever since she did, Senior Inspector. I still haven't arrived at an answer. I can't understand why she chose me, not one of the Australian lawyers."

"And I do not believe she would do so, if you were a stranger to her. I cannot believe you did not have some form of relationship with her."

"Well, I can't help you then, Senior Inspector. Maybe she felt safer giving it to someone less involved in the arbitration. I've told you the truth. You can choose not to believe me, if you want to. The only person who could answer that question is Cheng herself, but she's dead."

"How do I know you didn't kill her – to recover the disk?"

I didn't kill her. You know she left the disk at my hotel – the concierge would have told you that."

"Who is the second person you were waiting for outside Pearl Gardens?" asked Zhong.

"The other person who appears on the video."

Zhong shot a glance at Tang. Emil realised they hadn't even noticed her. Damn it! That was the trouble with being too honest. Zhong opened a laptop. He tapped some keys then turned it around towards Emil.

"Go through these photos. Tell me who you were waiting for."

Emil scrolled through the photos of people he'd never seen before, all except one. It wasn't the blonde. But it set his mind racing, the second he saw it.

"She's not there. But who are these people, what do they do in the bank?"

To his surprise, Zhong quickly obliged, running through the faces, putting names and positions to them. He stopped at the photo Emil had recognised.

"This is the person who we think is arranging the corrupt trading practices. He is an Englishman. His position is Executive Director for Commodities. His name is Mr Rodger Beckwith."

Beckwith. An avalanche survivor, evidently. Although he already knew it, the sound of Zhong pronouncing the name made Emil instantly self-conscious. He looked up at Tang, whose stare was more intent than ever.

"Why don't you arrest him?"

"That would not be appropriate. We do not know enough about what they are doing. Beckwith has recently flown to Australia. Apparently, for business meetings."

"Which reminds me – that's where I need to be, too. So, Senior Inspector, when can I leave? Can you please return my passport? I have important meetings with the Australian Government to attend for my work. I have told you what I know, so why detain me further?"

"Two reasons." Tang pointed to the DVD lying on the table next to the laptop. "Cheng's murder and this."

"Look, Senior Inspector, whoever made that video, did it to blackmail Howard Law. Cheng did not like this and tried to expose it. That's why she was killed. It's obvious. Whoever made the video killed her. They must know she gave it to me, so they tried to eliminate me, too." He stared at Tang. "Find who made the video and you have the killer."

Emil continued staring at Tang. Zhong spoke.

"Yes, I think you should go to Australia, as soon as possible, Mr Pfeffer. That is a good idea."

Emil looked at him, surprised, then at Tang, whose expression disclosed no emotion.

"Globalreach Americas has an office in Sydney," Zhong continued, "perhaps that is where Mr Beckwith has gone. For his business meetings. You must go there and find out what you can. Then report back to me."

"I can't do that. I have meetings to organise and attend myself. Besides, I have no reason to go to this company, I have nothing to do with them."

"Go in an official capacity. Say your organisation wants to check something – about their trading in carbon certificates. Make up a story they will believe," Zhong insisted.

"I can't do that! I have no authority. My organisation has no power to do that. We only work with governments, you should know that."

"Then you need to devise a plan how to do it." It was Tang who spoke. Emil expected him to object, but instead he appeared completely in agreement with Zhong's proposition.

"We have suspicions, Mr Pfeffer, well-founded suspicions. But we know too little about this bank and what other companies are associated with it," said Zhong. "We are conducting surveillance, but it is difficult for us to take more direct action. It is difficult for us to gather information outside China, without arousing their suspicions. Someone in your position can help us find out more, without making them wary. For example, we have heard them use an expression – 'cough', or 'café'. They use it frequently. We think this is a code for what they are doing. If you could find out what that is – that would help us."

"Even without asking who 'us' means, which in itself is a concern, I can't. I've told you. I have no reason to visit this company. It's not part of my work. And my work there is important, I must attend to it. I'm not your, your … agent."

It was Zhong's turn to stare intently at Emil.

"If you do not assist me, you will have no work. We will have you brought back to Hong Kong and you will face prison here. Possession of offensive material such as we found on you is a serious matter in Hong Kong, in all of China. It is a serious matter for United Nations organisations such as the one you work for."

"Ms Greenhaugh will be the first to know," said Tang. "She will not help you."

"Either you help me," said Zhong, "or you are finished."

15

The wheel felt light in his hands. He gripped it tightly, trying to maintain concentration.

It was monotonous; there was no escaping that. Long shadows, cast by the roadside gums in the late afternoon, flickered constantly across his face. It was irritating. And dangerous: they were seducing his tired eyes to close and stay closed. Parched, yellow-brown grass along the verge; the long, slow rises and falls of the undulating hills of the southern tablelands seemed to continue interminably, as the Hume Highway carried him back from another fruitless visit to the national capital.

He squeezed his grip again in concentration and checked the speedometer: just over one hundred. That was safe. Even though he hadn't driven this route for many years, he was alert to the ever-present danger posed by the police highway patrol and their radar speed guns. And to the risk of dozing off. It wasn't that warm now, the sun having almost set, but he turned the air-conditioning up full for a blast of cold air to revive himself, then pushed his foot down harder on the accelerator pedal as the highway began ascending another, steeper incline.

A sign flashed past telling him he had just entered the Southern Highlands. When he was young, growing up in a forgettable outer western Sydney suburb, winter trips to the

Southern Highlands brought the promise of log fires, walks in forests of ghost gums, European pines and other exotic tree species, thickly misted nights and clear crisp days. And, at least once a year, snow. From what he could make out now in the fading sunlight, bushfires over the most recent summer had reduced parts of it to a near lunar landscape. He'd read that the fires were coming much more frequently, even the indigenous bush finding it harder to cope. As for the exotics, well they were fast dying out. So much for memories. He checked the speedometer again and focused his mind back on the road.

He'd been back in the country of his birth almost two weeks, setting up and attending meetings, shuttling between government offices in Sydney, Canberra and Melbourne. So far, however, he had been unable to meet with a single minister. They seemed to be permanently tied up in meetings and unable to find time for him. He'd met only senior public servants, or ministerial staffers, all of whom were tight-lipped. They'd told him nothing useful.

The media was full of speculation about the big policy announcement being prepared by the government and Betty G, who seemed to spend her every waking hour trawling the internet for news, was getting more and more agitated, the longer the process was drawn out. The tension was starting to get to her and that meant, by proxy, to Emil.

On arriving in the country, he'd been spurred on by the renewed prospect of cornering Beckwith, assuming he could find him there. Now that his chance of getting Hudson had evaporated, that was what he had to cling to. But that would have to wait. First, he must satisfy Betty G that he was pulling out all stops with the Australian Government.

And then, of course, there were the Chinese. They had a noose around his neck and the end of the rope was held firmly by Zhong.

The next evening Emil called in on Loftus at his Phillip Street chambers. At least he had time for Emil. In fact, as he told him, since the arbitration debacle in Hong Kong, Loftus had a lot of time on his hands. His formerly substantial practice advising the government had evaporated overnight.

"I'm not that fussed, to be perfectly honest with you. I needed a break, anyway, after the intensity of that matter. And it's a good discipline for me to re-hone my skills in some other areas. I do feel sorry for the others who were involved. One thing this current administration is never short on is retribution. They're dishing it out with spades."

"I hope my boss in Frankfurt doesn't take a leaf out of their book. She's not very happy about my failure to meet any ministers since I've been here. I keep getting fobbed off onto their subordinates. She's pretty anxious about the direction this new policy might take."

"Aren't we all, Mr Pfeffer, aren't we all," Loftus mused, his gaze drifting into the middle distance.

"I keep getting told the ministers are in meetings, but they can't be in meetings around the clock, day after day."

"Yes, that's what I've heard, too," said Loftus, snapping back to the present. "And I'll tell you what else I've heard: the place is overrun by Americans. Yanks. They're the ones the ministers are meeting, apparently. Prime Minister and his Cabinet seem to have been with these new US 'advisors' constantly for the last couple of weeks. And if they're not, then it's part of the strategy to say that they are, so that they're simply unavailable to anyone else."

"That's pretty extraordinary, isn't it? Who's running the country? Have these yanks taken over – Washington coup by the back door?"

"Oh, I don't think they're from Washington. At least that's what my sources tell me. I don't have a reason to go down to Canberra anymore, so I can't say I've seen them in person. But from what I've been told, they're more like a bunch of oilmen than Washington insiders. In fact, amongst the chattering classes down there, I'm told, they're referred to as 'the Texans'."

Emil looked around the room where they were sitting, taking in the simple functionality of Loftus's chambers.

During his time in London, he'd occasionally briefed barristers from Middle Temple, Inner Temple or Lincoln's Inn. Loftus's chambers had none of the same trappings of antiquity. The bookshelf lined walls probably the only thing they'd have in common with the English counterparts. His desk looked more like a kitchen table. Simple and practical, a surface on which to place things and work, rather than a statement of authority and importance.

"I have a confession to make," he announced.

"I'm not a priest," said Loftus, looking a little bemused. "St Mary's is just a short walk from here, though."

"It concerns Ms Cheng."

"Don't tell me *you* killed her?" said Loftus, suddenly alarmed. "If you did, I don't want to hear it. In case you want me to defend you."

"No, no, relax. I may need to call on you to defend me at some stage, but I didn't murder Cheng."

Loftus sat back, watching Emil. "In that case, I'm all ears."

"Do you remember when we had a drink at Kerry's Bar, just before you flew out?"

"Yes." An eyebrow raised.

"And I asked about what would happen if you found out the panel chairman was bent – that he'd found against you because, say, he was bribed, or even blackmailed?"

"Yes. I recall giving you a very clear answer."

"You did, you did indeed." Emil paused, considering how best to put what he had to say. "Cheng called in to my hotel the night before she disappeared. I saw her in the lobby. I don't know if you remember. I don't think I told you or the others, but Senior Inspector Tang might have. It was the night before the decision was handed down. She left something with the concierge, for me."

Loftus didn't move. He didn't even seem to be breathing. It was as if he'd been turned into an Easter Island monolith.

"What she left with the concierge was a DVD on which two video files had been recorded. They showed the panel chairman in what could only be described as the proverbial 'compromising situation'."

"Elaborate."

"The film shows him raping a young Chinese boy."

Loftus's pallor became greyer than it already was, the blood draining from his face.

"I didn't know what to do with it at the time. I was trying to work out why Cheng had given it to me. Not you, or Rita or Marianne. I think it's pretty clear that whoever made the film was using it to blackmail the chairman. I think it's also pretty likely that's who killed poor Ms Cheng."

"Do you have this DVD?"

"No."

Loftus sat forward. "Where is it?"

"Tang has it."

Loftus sat back. He lapsed into thought, looking down at his hands resting in his lap.

"Hopefully, that means it's safe. But we need to get a hold of it. We need to get a hold of it and make an application to the Hong Kong High Court to set aside the decision."

"That might be difficult. You see, I didn't give it to Tang. He found it on me. He's holding it as evidence for a potential prosecution – possession of child pornography."

"Hmm. I see now why you might need me to defend you. I need to think about this," said Loftus, thoughtful again. "Rita and Marianne said they will be in Sydney later this week. We should have a drink together. I might have come up with something by then."

"Yes, that would be good." Emil got up to leave. "Oh, one last thing: do you know anything about an investment bank called 'Globalreach Americas'? They're Hong Kong based, but they've got an office here, down near Chinatown, in Goulburn Street."

"No, not my area. You might ask Rita and Marianne when we see them. That's more the sort of thing they'd be in touch with."

16

"That concludes my presentation, gentlemen. Now, I'm sure you'll have some questions?"

Davis Crooter stood at the end of a long, elliptical, teak conference table, looking up and down at the Australian Government ministers and their department heads – all men – sitting either side of it. Halfway up on the left, at the widest part of the table, he could see the taut, white shirt front of Tony Houganis straining to contain his belly, pressing up against the edge of the table. Houganis was leaning back, so his head and shoulders were hidden from Crooter's view by those next to him. Even though it was the worst possible vantage point at the table for seeing the screen at the end of the room, Crooter was thinking, he was sure Houganis had sat there because it gave him easiest access to the plates of biscuits arranged in the centre.

Houganis suddenly swivelled around in his chair and leant forward, exposing his sceptical, frowning face to Crooter. "Yeah, I've got one," he said. "Your forecasting for these global markets is at the pessimistic end of the range, based on the International Energy Agency's modelling and our Treasury's modelling. Your analysis is all very impressive, but I'm not sure I can swallow the assumptions you've based it on."

That's funny, thought Crooter, by the look of it you don't

have too much trouble swallowing most things. "And your question is, Tony?"

The look on the Treasurer's face told Crooter that he was going to make things difficult for them; that he'd already pigeonholed them as competitors, rather than collaborators.

"How do you justify your assumptions?"

"Okay, good question, Tony," Crooter beamed back at him. He'd just spent the last ninety minutes explaining their rationale and why it made sense for the Australian Government to get on board. Now this fat turkey was essentially asking him to repeat it. "Our team will be going through all of this in detail with your Treasury analysts, but just let me give you a quick synopsis."

Crooter looked down at the table in front of him, gathering his thoughts. A frown continued to furrow Houanganis's forehead.

"Certain developing economies' state-owned wealth funds are acting and unless checked, will continue to act, systematically and cohesively to control the remaining global fossil fuel resources that can be economically recovered." He paused to let his words sink in. "This has been a long-term strategy on their part, we suspect they've probably been acting this way – secretly – for the last five to ten years. They are doing this while, at the same time, trying to constrain developed countries, such as your own, and my own, from doing so, by promoting global imposition of this 'two degree warming' limit. And with that limit, a retardation in the development and bringing to the market of new, traditional energy resources – oil, gas and coal. Their campaign to influence and mobilise public opinion in developed countries has been very effective, as you well know, here in Australia."

Crooter looked at the faces around the table, judging each one's reaction to what he was saying. They all seemed to be on board: all, except for Houanganis.

"In the United States, those of us who have our eyes open can see the disturbing parallels between this infiltration of the public consciousness with, for example, the so-called peace movement of the late nineteen sixties. It undermined US government policy so much we lost the Vietnam war. Fifth columnists have been active for years now: the *Guardian* newspaper, the *Washington Post*, organisations in the United Kingdom like Carbon Tracker, and others, in the US and here in Australia, intent on destroying us from within. Our great concern is that, if these developing countries succeed with their strategy, they will control the remaining development and supply. And with it, the global energy agenda into the intermediate future – the next thirty to fifty years, let's say."

"China's just announced that its fourteenth five-year plan will continue the low-carbon economy roadmap they started in the twelfth," blurted Hounganis. "How does that fit in with what you're saying?"

Crooter's eyes returned to Hounganis's face.

"This is an economic war, Tony, that we cannot afford to lose," he said slowly, deliberately. "It's the war to decide who will lead the world into the next phase of global development, for the rest of this century and into the next. Like any other war, there are strategies, tactics, feints, and deceptions. That's why it's critical that your great country should be accelerating, not slowing, the economic recovery of its fossil fuel resources. Right now. We need to wrestle back control of these markets, convince the pundits that there are no long-term structural declines in coal, in oil; continue recovering wealth from them for as long as we can. In that way, *we* can control the evolution of global energy production to new models. Not the Chinese. Not the Indians. Not any of the others."

Crooter kept his focus on Hounganis, who Buddha-like, sat staring back at him.

"Our assumptions are based on in-depth knowledge of what the Chinese, the Indians, Brazilians, the Russians are really up to. Not the propaganda they put about. Our analysts have been carefully following their policies, trading and investment activities of their sovereign wealth funds, for years.

They are the new Seven Sisters. That's how they act – like a cartel, colluding. Secretly. There are clear patterns discernible, which support our conclusions. We have strategic information and insights, provided through excellent links into our own country's security apparatus. This is what our assumptions are based on."

Tony Hounganis shot a quick look at his department head next to him, who without giving any indication that he'd noticed, wrote on the pad in front of him 'NSA' and positioned it so Hounganis could read it.

One of the other department heads asked how the proposal that had just been put to them would affect the government's renewable energy policy. Crooter's colleague, Richard Yorkton, answered.

"At CoFFE, we believe a balance needs to be struck. A sensible, economic policy balance. Our advice has been the same to all the other governments that have joined our program. Investment decisions on energy generation, including choice of technology, are best made by industry, given its insights into market needs. The Australian Government needs to maintain stable and predictable policy settings across the range of areas and that means it shouldn't intervene to promote one technology over others. The market should be left to decide what is most cost competitive.

"Also, in Australia's case, after the arbitration in Hong Kong, we advocate a gradual pull back from carbon trading. Show the public cause and effect. It's a simple message they will understand. Lay the political foundations for a phased ramping up of support for industries such as mining that continue to earn export revenue. Another element is to ratchet down subsidies for solar and wind power: they've had a good run, but like other parts of the economy, need to carry their fair share of the economic belt-tightening. And by not reinstating the funding cuts you've already made to research in these fields, those savings can be redirected back into mining sector research – call it carbon sequestration – something positive for the environment."

More questions followed. They were muted, relating to matters of detail that Crooter left Yorkton to deal with, his team would follow up. Crooter thought he had been subtle, introducing the patriot–traitor theme obliquely, but it had been enough for this lot. It was a political trap for any troublemakers, as the Treasurer seemed to be shaping up to be. Most of them were savvy to it. The others all seemed to be falling into line, but there was always the one recalcitrant who had to be encouraged, manoeuvred or even, sometimes, coerced into position.

The meeting broke up, the CoFFE people departed with a number of department heads in tow, leaving only Hounganis and his colleague the Minister for Mining and Energy, Barry Phelong, in the room.

"Well, Barry, you're responsible for these blokes getting in here, what did you make of that?" said Hounganis, eyeing the selection of sweet biscuits for one he hadn't yet tried.

"I can't take all the credit, it was mostly Bull's doing. He's got business links with them."

"Yeah, but what d'ya think about what they're saying?"

"It's disappointing, I can't deny that."

Hounganis grunted his concurrence.

"But they're good. I think what they're saying makes a lot of sense. They're offering us a positive way forward if we throw our lot in with 'em. They seem to have the Indonesians and South Africans signed up already. That's a fair bit of coal market clout, if we join. Where are you on this, anyway?"

"I don't trust 'em. Crooter especially. And that Yorkton character. He's too smooth by far, for my liking."

Phelong looked Hounganis up and down. "That wouldn't be hard. You jealous?"

"Fuck off, Barry! Just because he wears a smart suit and slicks his hair down doesn't mean he's any good. Just that he's paid too much. I didn't like his ideas on rebalancing our policies. Those fuckwits on the left will see through it in two seconds. We'll get torn to shreds in the media and that'll be the end of the election. We'll be out on our ear."

"You're getting a bit ahead of yourself there, aren't you Tony? What they're talking about to begin with is getting the budget and finances sorted out. That's what we go to the election with. The other policy stuff comes after."

"I'm the fucking Treasurer, Barry. Sorting out government finances is my job, not these yanks you've brought in here!"

"Well, you better bloody-well get moving on it Tony, because the clock's ticking on the election and things don't look too good from where I'm standing. You ought to get over your pride and accept help when it's offered!"

"Just for the record," said Hounganis, "the 'policy stuff', as you call it, can't all just get pushed back until we get re-elected. What are we going to do about the next meeting on the Climate Change Convention, eh? It's shaping up as another vote in support of the two-degree limit. That means caps on emissions, Barry. And it's before the bloody election. How are we gonna deal with that?"

"Calm down, Tony. I'm sure 'Coffee' has factored that into the plans."

"I am calm, Barry. I am *fucking* calm! Just bloody concerned over where this is going. You might recall we've got the small matter of a state visit from the Premier of the People's Republic of China coming up soon. It'll be the biggest trade delegation they've ever brought here. Energy'll be top of their agenda."

"Yeah, but you heard what Crooter said. He reckons their recoverable coal reserves have been grossly overestimated. They'll be coming cap in hand."

"That's a big call, Barry. Sounds to me like it could be just a bit of wishful thinking on Crooter's part. I hope for our sake he's bloody-well right."

"You heard the man, Tony: strategic information. From their security contacts."

*****

In the car taking him and Richard Yorkton to Canberra

airport, Davis Crooter was still chewing over the attitude problems, as he saw them, of the Australian Treasurer.

"We need to very careful with Tony Hounganis. He's well placed in the party and not without his own business connections. Bull was right, if any of them will give us trouble, it'll be him. We need to get him on board, at least until we get through the first phase and the election. After that, we can white-ant him, if necessary."

"He'll be alright. Don't worry. It's healthy to have a sceptic or two about; it will keep us on our toes. Besides, how did Shakespeare put it? 'Give me men around me who are fat, sleek-headed men, such as sleep well o' nights ...'"

"Yeah, that was Caesar, wasn't it? Just before he was stabbed about fifty times. No thanks!"

"I'm more concerned that some of the other lightweights in the Cabinet will run off the rails. If they blow it in the run up to the election and lose, we're finished here. The other side won't want us."

"No, they won't, but that's the risk we run. By the way, Barry Phelong mentioned to me this morning that he's being pestered for a meeting by someone from the GCMO – Emil Pfeffer."

"When was this?"

"Apparently Pfeffer's been hanging around, trying to see him, as well as Mendicane and Hounganis and some of the others, for a couple of weeks."

"We don't need this. If those amateurs in Hong Kong had finished the job they were asked to do, he wouldn't be irritating us now. I certainly don't need it."

"Well, that's your responsibility, so sort it out. It's lucky your paths haven't crossed. You should be careful we don't bump into him when we're here. If he sees you, that'll cause all sorts of problems."

"Don't worry. I'll make sure that doesn't happen. We should have got rid of him when we had him in Zürich, last year, instead of pussyfooting around."

"Let's not get into that – hindsight is twenty–twenty vision. We weren't to know back then he'd become such a goddam nuisance."

"And damn lucky!"

Crooter's mobile rang. He answered it and listened for a minute, then grunted a response before ringing off.

"That was Beckwith. Pfeffer's been into their office, looking for him. Asking questions."

"Pfeffer! Pfeffer! Pfeffer! How in hell did he find out Beckwith's there? What did Beckwith say to him?"

"He didn't see Beckwith. The others said they didn't know who Pfeffer was talking about and got rid of him. Beckwith's not sure he bought it. It's put the wind up him."

"Beckwith's easily spooked. After Frankfurt, I'm not surprised, to tell the truth."

Crooter looked over at his associate. "We need to close off that PNG episode. That means Pfeffer, as well. Once-and-for-all."

17

Emil was sitting in an armchair, looking out the window. The serviced apartment he'd taken was in the Rocks, the old colonial part of Sydney. This was his first visit to the city of his birth for a long time. When he'd been growing up here, never could he have imagined staying in such a location, this close to the harbour. This was a place for rich people, not less well-off 'westies', from the outer fringe suburbs, like him. Sitting here now, he didn't feel like he'd climbed the social ladder, or become anything special. It was funny, but he didn't feel any different now, from how he'd felt then.

The sound of a train crossing the harbour bridge broke into his memories. Back in those days, a trip into the city would have been quite an outing, not least because the trains were so old and unreliable. And if anything, public transport hadn't improved much, given the appalling traffic jams he'd experienced since arriving. In fact, it seemed to have regressed in the intervening period. The city was beholden to the motor vehicle, making the harbour bridge both an asset and a scourge. Every day it carried hundreds of thousands of vehicles, cramming its bitumen to get into or out of the city centre and earlier in the week there'd been a multiple car accident on it. The resulting gridlock across the central business district lasted the entire day.

His negative thoughts, as he sat there, reflected the fact that his visit had become the trip of meetings that hadn't happened. He was yet to get to meet even one of the ministers he'd come to see and about which Betty G was calling him constantly. Like her, he was starting to get irritable, but in his case, out of frustration that the tiny threads of hope of getting a lead on Johanna's whereabouts would appear, then slip through his fingers just as quickly, before he could grab hold of them.

"Betty, if they aren't available, they aren't available," he'd told her, on her latest call. "And there's no policy announcement yet."

"It's gotta be coming soon, Emil, surely. It's been weeks since the Prime Minister flagged it. And from what you're saying, the executive's been locked away, working on it ever since."

He assured her – again – that he'd keep trying.

Nor had he managed to see Rodger Beckwith – the real source of his frustration. The Globalreach offices were in Goulburn Street, near Sydney's Chinatown. He couldn't get over how busy that part of town had become – pavements jammed with pedestrians, Goulburn and lower George streets clogged with buses and cars. The visit had been fruitless, as he had suspected it would be, but that didn't stop him hoping for something positive out of it. He'd arrived there late afternoon, just before close of business, when he thought their guard might be down. He'd asked to see Beckwith, announcing himself as an old acquaintance from Europe. It didn't work.

"Rodger who? Beckwith? Beckwith? There's no one here by that name. Are you sure you have the correct address?"

The woman on the front desk had been briefed in advance. Clearly. The denials came too readily, were too emphatic, he thought, confirming his suspicions that Beckwith was there, somewhere, hiding from him. When Zhong called again, he reported back.

"They denied knowing anyone of that name. The receptionist said there was no one called Beckwith working for Globalreach."

"Rodger Beckwith is registered as an employee of Globalreach Americas in Hong Kong, Mr Pfeffer!" said Zhong.

"Listen, I know that! You don't need to tell me, okay? I'm reporting to you what they said. That's all!" he replied. Then added, less irritably: "They must be hiding something."

What he didn't tell Zhong was that Beckwith would be hiding from him, not from the Chinese. He left Zhong to puzzle over this suspicious behaviour and rang off.

Betty G would not be so easily thrown off the scent, so he headed off to meet Rita and Marianne, to see what he could find out from them about what was going on in Canberra, before his next journey there.

*****

The cork came out with a satisfying pop.

"You'll like this Coonawarra Cab Sav, Emil. Big flavour, good nose, full-body – that's what we like to see!" said Rita, patting her own girth with a grin. "It's a very nice drop and not too hard on the pocket, either," she assured him. She wasn't wrong.

"I still haven't managed to meet even a solitary minister," complained Emil. "They're constantly in meetings with these 'Texans'. Loftus said you might have a better idea what's going on."

"We're all in the same boat, so don't take it personally. Unless you're on the minister's staff or a department head, you won't get to see them," said Marianne. "They still want all the usual briefings, but only in writing. From what we're hearing, it's the same for Treasury, Justice, Mining and Energy, PM and Cabinet. Being on the minister's Christmas card list just isn't good enough anymore, you don't get a look in."

"Ah, and not only do the Texans get in," said Rita, "but they are asking for lots of background policy information, which makes me very suspicious."

"So what's new?" asked Marianne.

Rita frowned at her in mock offence. "Well, in this case, with good cause. I've heard from a contact in the Treasury that – as I suspected," she said, pulling a face at Marianne, "the Texans have taken to advising on economic policy. Our beloved Treasurer is not very happy about it, but he's been overruled".

"By the Prime Minister?"

"That's a very good question. The PM seems to be fully committed, but it would be unusual for him to do something like that. In the past, those two have been joined at the hip on everything. That's why they've worked well as a team."

"Seems to be a bit of a rift opening," added Marianne.

"Does anyone know what organisation these advisors are from, what their agenda is, anything about them?"

"You know Canberra, rumours abound," said Rita. "Some say they're from a highly thought of Washington think-tank, other say not Washington at all. But one thing's for certain, they're from the US, which might give you an idea of the direction the government is going."

"Not from the point of view carbon trading, it doesn't, unfortunately. The US is on board, but there's still a wide gap between the two sides of politics there. So really, it could mean anything. If you can find out more about them, it would be much appreciated."

Rita drained her glass and refilled it from a second bottle that had miraculously appeared without them needing to order it, before topping up the others' glasses.

"Loftus is running a bit late, you'd better save some for him," said Emil.

"He rang. He's caught up on a matter and won't make it. So all the more for us," said Marianne.

"And besides," said Rita, stroking the bottle like it was a cat, "they do have a cellar full of this stuff!"

"You two are getting more and more like an old married couple, the way you bounce off each other."

"Excuse me, not 'old'," said Rita.

"Newly married, if you don't mind!" chipped in Marianne.

"Really? Are you serious?"

Marianne smiled, like she'd just let out a huge secret.

"That's wonderful, congratulations!" said Emil, raising his glass and clinking it with each of theirs. "I never even picked you as a couple – shows how unobservant I am."

"We've been together for a few years actually, but working in the same department, we don't advertise it," said Rita. "There are some real bitches around Canberra. You can never be too sure who might be about to knife you in the back".

"When did you tie the knot?"

"After a year working in Hong Kong together, we decided the time was right, so we had a little ceremony when we got back," said Marianne.

"Speaking of Hong Kong, did Loftus mention to you what I told him?"

"No."

Emil told them about the DVD, playing up his indecision over what it all meant and how he hadn't been able to decide what to do before they left, carefully avoiding any mention of the blonde. They didn't seem put out by it.

"I'm sorry I didn't tell you about it sooner, but I was a little bit thrown by what it all meant. Why did she give it to me, not one of you? Maybe this explains her visits to my hotel. Did I tell you my room was ransacked that night we had a drink together in Wan Chai, the night the police found Cheng's body?"

"No, you didn't. Was anything taken?"

"Nothing, thankfully. They were probably looking for the DVD from Cheng."

"Well, now we can do something about the decision."

"Loftus said he'd contact the Hong Kong police."

"I hope they're willing to play ball."

"I hope so, too," said Emil. But he doubted it. Very much. "Don't suppose Loftus mentioned this investment bank I asked him about? Globalreach Americas? They're Hong Kong based, but have an office here in Sydney. Have they ever come across your radar?"

"Can't say they have," said Rita. "But we can put some feelers out, on the 'sisters network'."

"Very tentative feelers, mind you," said Marianne. "We're *personae non gratae* after Hong Kong. Certain people are looking for opportunities to 'get' us."

"Yes, that's true. Things are a bit tense, especially with these advisors in town. But, we can see what comes up."

"That would be great. Thank you."

So there weren't any hard feelings. He felt the urge to share his suspicions with them, particularly after not having told them sooner about the DVD. But it probably wouldn't have meant much to them, unless he recounted full details of his PNG experiences the previous year. And told them about Johanna – something he really didn't want to go into. Besides, the business of not telling them about the DVD was water under the bridge.

"Let's get another bottle," he suggested. "This is an excellent drop."

He hadn't noticed that there was another, open and waiting, already in Rita's hand.

18

He tightened his grip on the wheel again. It helped his concentration. It was early morning and he had to be careful, the last thing he needed was a speeding ticket and this time of day was exactly when the highway patrol would be out with their radar guns. The sun had only just risen and the dead grass along the verges occasionally glistened at him, as the sun's flat rays caught the frost covering it. He checked his speedometer again. If he kept it around one hundred he'd be there in plenty of time. He was meeting Rita and Marianne in a café near their flat in Kingston, before the meeting at Parliament House. Hopefully they'd have some information for him. Might even get time for some breakfast, if he was lucky.

The previous day he'd woken thick-headed after a night of red wine, too much red wine, with them. Worse still, he'd woken to the sound of Betty G's voice on his mobile. Word had been filtering back to her, through her various sources, that the policy announcement was imminent and the word was that it wasn't looking good for global carbon trading. It was making her *very* anxious.

"Emil, I don't care how many meetings you organised where the ministers didn't show. I only take heed of results and at the moment, you're not getting any!"

"But Betty …"

"Don't *but Betty* me! If you can't manage to meet these

ministers and find out the way things are going, I'll come out there and do it myself. Then we can have a discussion over what your future role is with this organisation, while I'm there!"

"Betty. I've got another meeting lined up with the Treasurer and Minister for Energy and Mining tomorrow. This is the third time it's been arranged. Their offices have promised me this time they'll show. Just leave it with me. I'm doing what I can, but the feedback I'm getting is that members of their own departments haven't been able to see them since these Washington think-tank guys arrived in town."

"And we could do with some background on who these people are."

"I know, I know. I'm working on that too, but it's like classi-fied information in Canberra. There's only so much I can find out – the government's very sensitive about it."

She rang off. If she had such great contacts, why couldn't they find out and tell her? Why did he have to be here? He felt lousy. Rudderless. Then he realised he'd been dreaming about Johanna when he'd been woken by the call – dreaming they were married. His subconscious adapting the Rita and Marianne conversation to his own situation. He wanted to be out searching for Johanna, not wasting time trying to meet politicians who didn't want to meet him. It was one of those mornings, but he didn't have long to dwell on it. His phone rang again almost immediately. This time it was Zhong.

"Are you working in tandem with my boss?"

There was a pause at the other end of the line.

"I don't understand, Mr Pfeffer."

"Don't worry about it. What do you want?"

"Have you found out any more yet? What Globalreach is doing in Australia?"

"Not yet, but I've initiated inquiries through my sources in the government." That might placate Zhong for a while, he thought. There was a longer silence at the other end of the line. "Hello, hello, are you there?"

"Yes, I am here. We need you to do more than that, Mr

Pfeffer. We know that a substantial number of the Hong Kong-based personnel from this company have recently travelled to Australia. Clearly, something is happening there. You need to find out what it is and tell me."

That couldn't have just happened overnight, Emil thought. They're under surveillance, Zhong would have known in advance exactly when they went to the airport and where they were intending to travel. What was he playing at?

"How many? When did they leave Hong Kong? When did they arrive in Australia?"

"You do not need to know that detail. You just need to find out what they are doing. Do you understand?"

"That's what I'm trying to do, if you'd just give me some time to do it!"

"Time is not mine to give you, Mr Pfeffer."

With the pressure being cranked up by Zhong and Betty G, he'd arranged another meeting with Rita and Marianne. They may not have had enough time to find out much, but he had to keep trying. Information was what he needed, but at the moment it was in very short supply.

In the end, sticking to the speed limit meant he hit Canberra's morning rush hour traffic. Consequently, he didn't have as much time as he thought he would have. It wasn't as bad as Sydney or Melbourne, but enough to delay his progress all the same. He had to settle for just a coffee, no breakfast. Good thing he wasn't a breakfast person anyway.

"Don't suppose you can get anything in writing on this?" Emil was scribbling notes as quickly as he could.

"Sorry Emil, not at the moment – just too risky. It's a representative office. Small set up, but they have big plans: there have been discussions with the Securities Commission and the Prudential Authority about setting up a commodities exchange, believe it or not," reported Marianne.

"It helps if you've got the sort of money backing you up that Globalreach seems to have," observed Rita.

"That's very helpful. Thanks," said Emil, thinking: helpful

in getting Zhong off my back; if they knew where it's going, they may not be so forthcoming.

"What about shareholders?" he asked. "I heard they're linked to US energy companies."

"They might be, but the ultimate investors are half a dozen individuals – all of them US billionaires."

"Got any names?"

Marianne showed him her handwritten list, which he quickly copied down. When he'd finished, she tore up her list.

"Can't be too careful."

"That's great, thanks. Any update on the policy announcement?"

"Don't you listen to the news, Emil?" asked Rita. "The PM's doing an early morning media briefing at this very moment."

*****

"Come in, come in Mr Pfeffer," said Tony Hounganis, crossing the floor of his office, hand extended. "Do you know Barry? Barry Phelong, Minister for Mining and Energy."

They sat at a meeting table and coffee was delivered. Emil guessed the office was about ten times bigger than his office in Bad Eschbach. And considerably better furnished.

"Have you seen this yet?" asked Hounganis, holding out a press release for Emil. He took it and scanned the first few lines.

"No, I hadn't. I heard the Prime Minister briefed the press earlier this morning."

"And he'll be making a statement to Parliament later," said Phelong.

"What I'm interested in, gentlemen, is your position on carbon trading. Has it changed?" He held up the press release. "Is it mentioned in here?"

"Well, yes," Phelong sounded uncertain, "but not in detail."

"What is the detail, Minister?"

"We've decided after that Hong Kong mess," Hounganis

cut in, "we need to review our commitment to carbon trading. Holistically, that is, as part of our overall energy and climate change policy package. What that means in the short term, is a phased pull back from our current level of commitment."

"So you're not exiting the market completely?"

"No, no," Barry Phelong spoke up firmly. Then more quietly, "Not for the moment."

Hounganis looked at Phelong as if to say shut up, you idiot.

"A review has been made of all our bilateral trading arrangements," said Hounganis, "and those, where the Attorney-General advises there is further potential exposure, based on the Hong Kong clause, will be terminated at the earliest possible opportunity. We'll then review the situation again, going forward."

"Are you able to give me an idea of how many agreements are affected in this way?"

"It's about half of them," said Phelong. "But don't look so downcast, Mr Pfeffer, it's not the end of the world."

Hounganis shot another filthy look at Phelong, just as there was a knock at the door. A staffer poked his head around it with a questioning look. Phelong nodded to the minion and the door opened wider. In strode Bull Griffith.

"Mr Pfeffer, have you met Barry Griffith? Also known as 'Bull'."

Emil hadn't. He was surprised at the size of the man. He'd only seen photos, or television footage of him. Griffith looked older – and uglier – in the flesh, but moved like a younger, fitter man. The significance of his nickname dawned on Emil – it was like a big, powerful alpha male had strutted into the room.

"We invited Bull to join us because he's affected directly by this business over the coal loader," said Phelong. "The subject of the arbitration. Given your involvement with the team in Hong Kong, we thought it might help for you to get a more personal perspective from him on the situation."

Emil looked at the three of them. Hounganis didn't look

at all like he thought it would help. He looked uncomfortable. Phelong, on the other hand, seemed to have receded into Griffith's shadow. Emil held his hand out and Griffith shook it.

"So Mr Griffith, what is your perspective?"

*****

The answer, Emil was told, he would learn the following day, in a helicopter, looking down on central Queensland from a couple of thousand feet in the air. After the Parliament House meeting, Emil accepted an invitation to fly with Griffith in his personal jet to the port site that afternoon, spend the night there and do a tour of the mine before returning the following day.

During the flight, Griffith regaled Emil with all the facts concerning the number of jobs, the export revenue, the development opportunities that would be lost, on top of the cost of the arbitration loss, if the development didn't proceed. The town itself, Griffith had asserted, would shrivel and die.

"This place might be on the coast, adjacent to the Barrier-bloody-Reef, but let me tell you, Pfeffer, it's a mining town. Always has been a mining town, always will be a mining town."

"But what about the tourism industry? Judging by the number of boats out on the reef, when we flew in, it looks to be flourishing."

"That's nothin'. Compared to the money coming into the local economy from the mines and related development around the town, it's a piss in the ocean. This town would die a lingerin' death if the mining to the west of here stopped and it had to rely on tourists."

"The coal will run out sometime – either that, or it won't be recoverable. With climate change, it may have to stay in the ground."

"That'll be over my dead body!" Griffith's great bulbous

neck seemed to inflate as he said it, like a warning of an imminent attack. But the sudden emotion receded just as quickly as it had come and, with it, his neck. "Listen, Pfeffer, I grew up here, I'm the son of a share farmer turned coal miner and I grew up workin' down the mines from the age of fifteen."

They were in a seafood restaurant. The best in the town, Griffith claimed. Although he would, wouldn't he, since he owned it. And most of the other waterfront properties adjacent to it, he boasted.

"I was the youngest of nine kids. The old man worked and drank himself into an early grave, so we had nothin'. None of us finished school – we had to get out and earn a livin', support our mother. She had a hard life. Didn't live long enough to see how things turned out for me. That's one big regret of mine. I would have liked to make her comfortable, at least for a bit of her life."

"I grew up in the outer western suburbs of Sydney. That was working class, Mr Griffith. And poor. No privileges there, I can assure you."

"I was lucky gettin' into coal mining when I did. It's given me everything. I'll be buggered if I'm just gonna let it all go because the bastards down south are worried about losin' their holidays on the Barrier Reef."

In spite of himself, Emil felt, if not a rapport with Griffith, then at least a grudging respect. Once he'd overcome the initial belligerence – which he suspected was a defence mechanism to cope with social situations where he felt uncomfortable – he found Griffith interesting. He wouldn't go so far as to say good company – the rags-to-riches mantra wore a bit thin after five or six hours. Maybe everyone was like that, once they'd banked their first billion, Emil mused, as he settled into bed that night in the beachside hotel, another part of the Bull Griffith portfolio.

It was an early start in the helicopter, next morning. At the helipad he was advised something had come up, meaning that Griffith had returned to Brisbane so would not be joining

Emil. They took off to the east, below them the azure waters of the reef, before gaining height and swinging back inland, skimming over an olive carpet of bushland.

Below, Emil could make out the railway line from the mines, a steel band that sliced its way through the bush, into the distance. A loaded coal train, probably a couple of kilometres in length, was making its way along the line to the existing port: the one deemed inadequate and a block on the development of the region. The port looked pretty big, from where he sat looking back down at it. Squinting into the reflection off the water, in the distance, lying at anchor – hopefully outside the reef – he could make out a dozen massive vessels. Coal carriers waiting to load up. Bull Griffith had already quoted him chapter and verse on the existing port's inadequacies, as they flew up the previous afternoon, finishing with the advice:

"I'm gonna get that fuckin' port extension, Pfeffer, come hell or high water. Nothin's gonna stop me. Nothin'."

The queue to dock, presumably, bore out Griffith's argument.

Ahead, the olive carpet was patch-worked with great asymmetrical areas of red dirt, some of which had centres of black: the open cut faces of the mine. Others housed long, straight mounds of black – capable of being distinguished as stockpiles waiting for shipping even from the height they were at. Around all the areas of black, haulage trucks and other vehicles, like the ones in toyshops, moved backwards and forwards, a swarm of busy little ants fussing around its booty.

The helicopter was making a circuit of the vast expanse of the entire resource field. "Is all of this owned by Bull Griffith?" he asked the pilot as they flew over more and more areas cleared of vegetation.

"No, only the first couple. He had the rights over all of these areas, but he sold a lot of them off in the last few years. The rest of these are held by some big overseas mining groups. I think they're US or Asian investors. Would be easy enough to check."

After an hour, they returned to one of the first of the cleared areas and descended onto a helipad near some site buildings. The pilot directed Emil to head for the buildings, shouting over the noise of the engine that he would return to collect him when it was time to leave. Emil got out and the helicopter lifted, creating a whirlpool of red dust as he ran towards the building, hands covering his face.

Now that he was back on the ground, the scale of things changed. It was like being Alice in Wonderland; his surroundings changing from tiny to gigantic. The toy trucks he'd seen from the air were enormous, their huge tyres alone four metres in diameter. Through the dust and noise a figure approached him from the buildings. He was presented with a hard hat and safety glasses, then led around the buildings to where a number of normal sized four-wheel drive vehicles were parked. His driver, Terry, one of the site managers, began a circuit of the mine workings.

"Aren't you worried about driving in and out of these monsters?" Emil asked as they waited for several haulage trucks, each loaded with a couple of hundred tonnes of coal, to pass before pulling out onto what seemed to be the main road on site.

"You've just got to keep aware of where they are, as they can't see us. It's not that difficult, since they're pretty hard for us not to see!" Terry shouted back over the roar of the passing giants. "When they're fully loaded it's not too bad, it's when they empty that they're dangerous. Can move pretty quickly."

"I understand your boss owned most of the prospecting and mining rights here at one time."

"Yeah, smart bloke for someone who never finished school."

They tailed some loaded haulage vehicles for a distance before Terry pulled off to the side of the road.

"They're heading for the central coal handling facility. We can't go there in a vehicle this size – too many of those big fellows about. Basically, that's where the coal from this site gets stockpiled for loading onto trains to the port. Any high ash content coal gets washed, then it gets put back in the stockpile. It all stays there until loading."

Terry pointed out the stockpile mound that Emil had picked out earlier from the air. The long black mound stretched for a kilometre and over fifty metres in height.

"That's a huge amount of product, waiting to be sent."

"We're at our peak production rate on this site, it'll be over fifty-five million tonnes this year. That's just this mine. There are another five further west of here, either already in production or coming online in the next year or so."

"Yes, I could see them from the air."

"Well, that gives you an idea of the scale – upgrading the rail line has started – should be finished in the next twelve months, provided this bloody government can sort out what it's policy is. Then there's the port expansion."

They drove to another higher vantage point. Terry pointed into the distance, past the mine workings.

"There's a new village being built over there to accommodate about fifteen hundred workers. It'll have all the services – shops, health, sports and recreational facilities. Work's started on an airport, just past the village, further north."

"That's a lot of infrastructure."

"And it costs megabucks."

Undoubtedly, thought Emil, but whose? Was the Hong Kong money being invested here, as well as at the port facility?

They followed an empty haulage truck back in the direction of the coalface, pulling up by the edge of the access road where they could see the workings in the distance across the pit and below. In front of them, the earth sloped away down to the floor of the pit, over one hundred metres beneath. In the distance, the other sides were tiered, like Japanese hillside rice paddies, but black, showing the huge bands of the coal seam.

"This isn't just one pit, it's actually a series of pits," shouted Terry. "As the mine moves further along the seam, the plan is to gradually rehabilitate behind it, but we haven't started that phase yet. So what we're on here is replaced, compacted overburden." He indicated the direction away from the pit. "Rehabilitation is starting over there and moving this way."

The access road ran around the top for another kilometre or two, before gradually curling its way down each tier to the floor of the pit. It seemed to be the only route for the empty haulage trucks returning from the processing facility. There was a regular stream of them passing.

"I didn't appreciate how enormous these pits are," Emil shouted over the outside noise.

"Yeah, it's about four kilometres long by two and half wide."

Terry's phone rang as he spoke. He looked at the screen, then ignored it. It stopped ringing.

"And about a hundred metres or so deep."

Terry's phone rang again. He looked at it, then got out and walked away from the vehicle to answer it. Emil sat looking out across the cavernous expanse of the pit. At the far end, there was blasting taking place, causing sudden eruptions of dirt and rocks, with clouds of dust whorling hundreds of metres into the air. He was thinking it was too far away to hear, when two loud thuds rattled the vehicle in quick succession. He looked over at Terry who had walked thirty metres away and was standing with his back turned, phone still held to one ear, fingers in the other. He hadn't even noticed the blasts. Must be commonplace for mine workers.

Terry turned, still talking, then looking up, stopped, eyes wide, and started waving his arms. Waving frantically. With a surprise, Emil realised he was waving at him. Sudden panic hit him. Twisting in his seat, he caught sight of the dusty rubber tread of a gigantic wheel as it filled the back window, then blocked the light from it. The vehicle shuddered as it hit, with a jolt shunting forward, tipping up backwards. There was the sound of exploding glass as the back window disintegrated. Metal crushing. Emil fumbled with the seat belt release, the belt recoiling across him. Door. Another fumble, the handle. Shit! Door lock was on. The front of the vehicle suddenly jerked further upwards, violently, outside the windscreen only sky visible. Noise deafening. The huge mechanical beast was almost on top of him. He flicked the door lock off and pulled the handle again, shoving his shoulder into it as he did. The door swung open, Emil squirting out like a pip from a lemon. The front of the vehicle banged back down, the huge wheel rolling over the roof of the cabin, where he'd been a split second before, flattening it completely, behind him, above him, the front and side windows of the cabin exploding as it did. The engine block of the vehicle was being flattened into the ground: there was a wrenching sound as the chassis bent and buckled under the weight of hundreds of tonnes. The vehicle was wrapped around the massive rubber tyre like an aluminium drink can around a foot that had stomped on it.

19

He'd hit the ground with a thump, knocking the air out of his lungs. But he'd hit it rolling, across the dirt, away from the agonised scream of the metal, away from the danger. He'd kept rolling. Then he was sliding, down the side of the pit, loose rocks and stones dislodging on his way through, following him down the slope, banging into his head, his shoulders and arms, then careering on, building his own mini avalanche as he slid. Fifty metres down the slope he came to rest in a cloud of dust, partially buried by his trailing train of dislodged scree.

Late afternoon, four days after his close encounter with the two hundred and forty tonne haulage truck, Emil was sitting in a cafe in Goulburn Street. On the other side of the street, the entrance to the building that housed the Sydney office of Globalreach Americas.

This was his third day staking out the entrance to the building. The first day back, he hadn't been able to leave his apartment – barely been able to get out of bed, he felt so sore. Sitting there now, he still did. His face and hands bore scratches and scabs from his slide down the scree into the pit. Yellowing bruises marbled his thighs and he had an especially painful one of his back, under the shoulder blade. Seemed to be in just the position where the intruder in Stuttgart had hit him, twelve months earlier. Stuttgart. Made him think of Johanna. As if he wasn't already thinking of her. He remembered her rubbing liniment onto his shoulder. He needed her. He had to find her. Sitting there, watching, he had too much time to think. For someone in his frame of mind, having too much time to think was bad news.

The previous day, his patience had been rewarded. Not by Hudson. Not by Beckwith. But by the blonde. Finally. Now he knew for certain, it was her. Another avalanche survivor, obviously. She was just as sexy as she'd been in Zürich, when he and Dominik visited the BKZ offices. She was still turning the heads of every guy she passed in the street. Just like she had at the events she'd attended with Beckwith. Leered at by the salivating Gerry Johnstone. That two-faced bastard. His time would come.

Right now, however, time was something Emil knew he was dangerously short of. Before returning from Queensland, he'd updated Betty G on his Canberra meeting. She was unhappy about the trading pull back, but seemed resigned to it. Then, on his return to Sydney, she'd rung to announce that in light of developments, just as soon as arrangements could be made she would come in person to try to dissuade them from pulling out of the market completely. He didn't have long before she was due to arrive, meaning he had to pull out all stops to find Beckwith and get a lead on Johanna. Betty G's presence would severely curtail any scope to carry out such activities.

Then there was Zhong. He was pestering Emil almost as much as Betty G. He'd called again, straight after Emil had spoken to her. Those two must be the same star sign, or something. They seemed to operate on the same cycles and patterns of behaviour. At least Emil had been able to throw Zhong some crumbs of information, to get him off his back. He'd become very excited when Emil told him about the discussions to set up a commodities exchange. Actually, he was more agitated than excited, Emil reflected on the conversation. It had bought him a little breathing space. Zhong wanted more.

His attention was drawn back to the building across the street. A gaggle of office workers was spilling out the doors and down the steps. The workday was finishing. They looked like they were heading for the Irish-themed pub on the corner with George Street. Another couple of groups followed, going in various directions. Then a single blonde woman came out. Gisela. Seeing her walk out of the building now, left him in no doubt that it was her on the DVD, despite the quality of the recording. Watching her, there was something about the way she moved that made her intensely desirable. And the allure wasn't just for older men. She turned younger men's heads too. The previous day he'd followed her, to find out where they were staying. Darling Harbour. An apartment in the old Goldsborough Mort building – walking distance from the Goulburn Street office. Emil had worked out the best place to make his move. All he could do was hope that she'd repeat the routine. If she did, today was the day to act.

He left money on the table for his coffee, stood stiffly and stepped out onto Goulburn Street. His body ached all over as he hobbled after her. The pavement thronged with people, moving quickly around him, office workers heading for buses, or to the railway for their trains home. He settled into the crowd, not far behind, relieved she was heading in the direction of the apartment. She slowed a couple of times to look in shop windows: he prayed she wouldn't divert in to any. Would just complicate matters. She didn't. But she was taking her time, in no rush to get where she was going, which was good for him. Made it easier to keep up. He managed to keep a discreet distance behind her, without incident, until she was a hundred metres from the apartment building.

It was a straight stretch of Pyrmont Street, leading up to the entrance to the building, tree-lined and with little traffic noise. Now that they were away from Chinatown and the main thoroughfares, there were few other people around. She was wearing high heels, walking at an easy pace. Forcing his unwilling limbs to move faster, he drew level with her.

"*Guten tag, Fräulein.*" He didn't look at her, just keeping pace with her. "You've made Frau Beckwith very angry."

She slowed, turning.

"Who are you?"

"Don't you remember me? I visited your office in Zürich. Remember? The bank was called BKZ, surely you remember that?"

She remained silent, sullen, pace slackening even more, staring at him.

"I found your lover boy in a sack, on the roof, when the PNG ceremony was attacked in Frankfurt, remember that?"

Still no response.

"Your employer has tried to have me killed a couple of times, do you know about that too?"

"I don't know what you're talking about!" she blurted. "You look like you've been fighting with a cat. Go away, or I'll scream."

"It's pretty deserted along here, so that may not do you a lot of good. Besides, I want to help you."

"I don't want your help. Go away."

"OK, but if I go, the Hong Kong police are going to issue an arrest warrant for you. You *must* remember that little boy you took to the apartment in Hong Kong. For Howard Law to abuse. You were very stupid to let yourself be filmed with him. Beckwith will go down with you, too. Was it filmed in the apartment you share with him?"

She'd stopped walking and was looking at him, her face white. Even in the early evening half-light, he could see her tanned skin had lost its lustre.

"I wasn't ... you're ... you're lying!"

She looked like she was about to cry.

"I'm not. I've seen it. It was given to me. Now the Hong Kong police have it."

She started blubbering, tears turning her perfect eye make-up to blotches of black that she smeared, across her cheeks, with the back of her hand.

"Keep walking, we'll see if we can come to an arrangement. Maybe we can help each other. Just listen to me. Where is Johanna Dorn?"

"Who?" The word squeezed out between sobs.

"My girlfriend. Johanna Dorn – Hudson, or Gerry Johnstone, or one of their thugs, grabbed her off a plane in Singapore. They're holding her. Where is she?"

"I don't know. I don't know anything."

But she didn't deny knowing Hudson or Johnstone. They'd almost reached the entrance to the Goldsborough Mort building. He stopped and grabbed her elbow, holding it tightly enough to make her wince.

"Listen, you little ..." he was about to say 'slut', but checked himself, "... marriage wrecker." With sudden self-consciousness, it occurred to him that he probably sounded like Lesley Beckwith. "Listen to me. You and Beckwith are going to tell me where they have taken her – what they've done to Johanna Dorn. If you do, I won't tell the police in Hong Kong who you are. If you don't, then you're finished. You hear me? Completely fucked. Your life will be over. You'll end up in a Chinese gaol!"

As he said it, he thought: that could just as easily apply for me, too, if Tang and Zhong get nasty. He looked into her terrified face, speaking through clenched teeth:

"Don't tell Hudson or any of the others I've contacted you. The Chinese will get you even sooner, if you do!"

He released her arm, then turned and started walking away briskly, leaving her staring at his back, shaking.

"I'll be in touch," he called over his shoulder.

He retraced his steps back along Pyrmont Street, to get clear of the apartment building as quickly as possible. He didn't think Gisela would know what they'd done to Johanna. Beckwith may not know either – he didn't expect that was the sort of information Hudson would share with a weak link like Beckwith. But he'd need to find out.

Threatening people didn't come easily to Emil. It wasn't in his nature. Especially not a woman. But it had to be done. He was getting desperate. The thought of Johanna with Gerry Johnstone – that he had directed her to him – was making him more desperate every time he recalled it. Which was all the time. He had precious few options left; they seemed to be closing off almost as soon as he identified them. If this didn't work, he'd be back to square one, without any leads on where or how to find Johanna. The Singapore police. That would be it. And so far, they'd come up with a big, round zero.

He strode away, not thinking to look around, to check in case he'd been seen by anyone. If he had looked, he might have noticed the person loitering in the shadows of the trees on the other side of Pyrmont Street, thirty metres away, standing behind the vehicles parked there, watching him.

20

The Intercontinental was at the eastern end of Bridge Street, overlooking the Opera House and botanical gardens. Betty G arrived, deposited her bags in her room, then summoned Emil to the cafe in the atrium of the converted nineteenth century building that formed part of the entrance to the hotel.

"Nice place, Sydney. I haven't been here for almost twenty years – since the early two thousands," she said, sipping coffee while feverishly spooling through messages on her mobile phone.

She reminded Emil of a sparrow, or a canary. Relaxing didn't come easily to her. Her natural state seemed be one of high level, nervous energy. She looked up over her half-moon glasses and saw him watching her.

"We need to get down to Canberra, A-S-A-P. Can you make the arrangements?"

"Who do you want to see? It's unlikely we'll get either the Prime Minister or Treasurer, at such short notice."

"I already lined up both of them, before I left Frankfurt."

Emil you idiot, he thought, of course she would have.

"I've got a car. We can go whenever you like." He had to humour her, but it was fast becoming a balancing act between her and Zhong. The Canberra trip was important – not least because it gave him a chance to badger Rita and Marianne for more information. But it would take him away from Globalreach Americas and Beckwith.

Betty G put her phone down and took off her glasses, rubbing her eyes with the backs of her index fingers. She looked as tired as she usually did after her normal fourteen-hour day in the office.

"I haven't found out anything about these advisors," she said. "My contacts have all drawn blanks, which makes me nervous. And just a little bit suspicious."

"I agree. Totally. On the other hand, the fallout from the actual arbitration decision hasn't been as bad as it could have been. Dominik said market impact, so far, seems to have been fairly muted."

"It won't stay that way, Emil. Especially if the Australians pull back, as they propose. I think we should plan for the double whammy: the direct impact of their withdrawal, and then the repercussions as others react to it. We need to persuade them to moderate their response."

"It'll help if I can get some background on who these advisors, these 'Texans', are."

She grimaced. "I hope they aren't real Texans!"

"I'll try to see my contacts while we're down there. See if they've found out anything more."

She nodded. "So tell me about this Bull Griffith character. And your trip to Queensland."

He recounted the meeting with Hounganis and Phelong, where Griffith had been wheeled in.

"It seemed to have been set up by Phelong. Hounganis looked like his nose was put out by it – like he'd been upstaged. It also seemed a bit like it was a set up to get rid of me, out of Canberra, away from the politicians. But it was interesting talking to Griffith, even if he then dumped me onto his underlings for the mine tour."

"So how'd you end up with all the scratches?"

"Our vehicle lost an argument with a mine haulage vehicle – you know, the two hundred and forty tonne sort. I had to take evasive action for self-preservation."

"Without the 'cryptics', please."

He recounted how they'd stopped to view the pit, how Terry had got out of the vehicle and walked away from it to take a call, then had seen the two hundred tonne monster bearing down on the four-by-four in which Emil had been sitting.

"I got out in a real hurry. But then slid halfway down into the pit. It's all loose rocks – some of them are pretty sharp. The jacket and trousers I was wearing were ruined. At least Griffith picked up the bill for their replacement. I had to get them straight away, so I'd have something to wear. He owns the shop they came from."

"How many close shaves have you had now? Better be careful your nine lives don't run out!" she said, smiling.

"Actually, that reminds me. There was something I wanted to mention too you," he said, sitting up. "Griffith seemed to own just about every property worth anything – all the shops, restaurants, cafes, in good locations along the waterfront. I didn't hear one person mention Hong Kong investors the entire time I was there. It was odd, given the arbitration. Apparently he originally held all the prospecting and mining leases, too, although he's sold off a lot of them."

"Hmm. I think the Australian lawyers would have picked up on it, if anything wasn't right, don't you?"

"I guess so." But still, it seemed odd.

The rest of the time was spent discussing how to approach the meetings in Canberra. Emil didn't think they would achieve anything, but he didn't push that opinion too far. It would suggest that Betty G was wasting her time, that her presence wouldn't have the impact she obviously thought it would. His mind wandered, replaying over and over an incident that his recounting the story of the accident had made him remember.

After he was recovered from fifty metres down the scree, Emil and Terry had been taken back to the site building where they'd begun. As he waited for Terry to get keys to another vehicle, he could see back down to where the accident had occurred. The monster haulage vehicle was still there, with their crushed vehicle wrapped around one of its front wheels. The driver was standing in front, looking at the damage.

What Emil was replaying over in his mind was that, sitting in the driver's cab with a leg out the door, had been a powerfully built guy in a white t-shirt, crew cut hair, and sunglasses, talking on a mobile phone. Emil had wondered where he'd come from. He hadn't noticed him at the scene of the accident. Had he shown up to investigate, or was he there when it happened – in the cab, maybe, with the driver? The man had seen Emil watching him and withdrawn into the driver's cab, closing the door behind him. At that point, Terry had shown up with the replacement vehicle.

Initially, he hadn't thought much of it. Now, reflecting on it, even though the fellow had been quite a long way away, he seemed to fit a certain stereotype with whom Emil had crossed paths before. In Luxembourg. In Hyderabad. He certainly looked like he came out of the same mould.

"Have I lost you, Emil?" Betty G snapped him back to the present.

"Sorry, Betty, I was still thinking about Bull Griffith and all his assets," he fibbed.

She would fly off the handle if he started introducing apparitions of Hudson and his thugs. But, now that he recalled the incident, the fellow's appearance did give him cause to ponder.

21

"We've got a name for you," Marianne whispered over the top of the rim of her orange juice.

Having dropped Betty G at the US Embassy, where she was meeting an old friend, Emil headed off for a breakfast meeting of his own. It had taken him a while to find them. Not sitting at the front of the cafe as previously, this time Rita and Marianne were at the very back, in a dark corner. Emil hunched over his scrambled eggs on toast, listening. This was becoming all very conspiratorial.

"At risk of breaching whatever legislation binds you, can you tell me what it is?" he whispered back.

"That's not very funny, Emil," said Marianne, "that's probably exactly what we'll be doing."

Rita lifted her coffee cup. "Coffee."

"I'm right for the moment, thanks."

She had the cup to her mouth. "That's the name, you wally!" she said through the froth.

He looked at her. Her upper lip had a white moustache and she was pointing at a piece of paper she'd slipped onto the table. It looked like the agenda for a meeting. The date showed it had been held a couple of days earlier. Between the senior management team of the Department of Mining and Energy and representatives of the 'Coalition of Future Fuel Enterprises (CoFFE)'.

"Can I take this?"

"Yeah, sure, it's from another department. But if anyone asks, you found it blowing around in the wind."

"And you never met us," added Rita. "Okay?"

Before joining Betty G for their meetings, he did some internet research. It seemed that CoFFE was pretty low-key – 'discreet' might be how it would describe itself. An energy policy think-tank, based in the US state of Virginia. His searching revealed little, so he called Dominik on the prepaid mobile. Apart from quickly bringing him up to date on the lack of developments, he asked him to do some digging, see if he could find out who was behind it.

Already alarm bells were ringing in Emil's head. He remembered what Zhong had said at the meeting in the New Territories: listening into Globalreach in Hong Kong had thrown up frequent mention of a 'code word': something like 'cough', or 'café', he'd said.

Not a code word, Zhong, old boy, an acronym.

After a friendly, almost chummy meeting with the Prime Minister and his chief-of-staff, Emil and Betty G progressed to a more business-like, but equally unsuccessful meeting with the Treasurer. In both meetings, the politicians listened politely to the case Betty G put to them. They indicated they were willing to engage in discussion. But ultimately, it seemed they were not going to budge from their position. There would be a pull back and they would give no guarantee that the country would not withdraw from the market altogether.

"Emil, I admit you were right to have reservations. This situation is disastrous." Betty G looked more worried than he'd ever seen her. "These guys could be starting the final collapse of the carbon market and they don't seem in the least bit concerned about it."

They were on the road, heading out of Canberra back to Sydney. Emil was quiet, concentrating on driving, on not exceeding the speed limit.

"We need to review our strategy. We need to formulate a

GCMO position, to deal with the impact when others appreciate the significance of the Australian position," she was saying.

"From the way Mendicane was talking at the end, we won't have long. Sounds like they're going to pursue this withdrawal pretty aggressively."

Betty G lapsed back into her thoughts, staring out the window at the bushland flitting past.

"I didn't have a chance to tell you earlier, my contacts came good: I got a name for the Texans. The Coalition of Future Fuel Enterprises. C-o-F-F-E. Do you know them?"

"Never heard of them. Zippo."

Before they had set out, after meeting the Treasurer, Emil had managed another brief, clandestine meeting with Marianne. They met near the building where she worked, a rather strange looking, blue glass monstrosity of the sort favoured by business park planners in the 1980s. Its most notable feature was the awning over the front entrance, which looked like an upturned boomerang, above which was what looked like a billboard sporting the nation's coat of arms and proclaiming the name of the government department in residence. All very functional.

"Emil, whatever you do, please be careful with this. Rita thinks she's being watched in her office."

"Do you?"

"No. I might be the pedant, but Rita gets a bit paranoid sometimes. Still we've got – you've got to be really careful. This stuff is sensitive."

She'd slipped him an envelope in which he'd found copies of the resumes of the consultants now advising the government on its policies. The names of the two principals meant nothing to him: Davis Crooter, Richard Yorkton. Impressive academic qualifications, extensive experience, references.

"Look, I really appreciate what you're doing. But can I ask you for one more thing: photos – sorry, two more things: if you can find out what these guys are advising the government, that would really help."

"Jesus, Emil! You're not asking much!"

She was nervous. Rita had been too, at their breakfast meeting. He was asking a lot. Probably for them to break the law.

It would be better if Betty G didn't know about the documents, given the dubious nature of their provenance. If he got hung out to dry for receiving them, that was one thing; but if he implicated her, Betty G would never, ever forgive him. And he didn't want her as an enemy for the rest of his life. As for his suspicions over a connection with Globalreach, that would have to stay his secret, too, for the moment.

"Actually, now that I think about it," Betty was continuing, still looking out at the scenery, "as we have a response from the government, what does it matter who is advising them?"

"I think we should find out more about them, Betty. This organisation has influenced the position that, as you just said yourself, could precipitate a market collapse."

"That may be so, Emil. But the Australian Government can obtain the advice of whomever it sees fit to consult. That's its prerogative. I can't interfere with that. The GCMO can't interfere. This consultancy, think-tank, however you want to call it, they're free to offer their services. That's the market. The electorate will decide whether they like the way the government's going. So what's the problem?"

"Just because these guys have the government's ear, doesn't mean we should back off. If there's no carbon market, if it collapses because the government here follows these guys' advice, then we will have singularly failed fulfilling the charter of our organisation."

"So what are you saying?"

"We need to keep pushing them, Betty. Encouraging, cajoling, supporting. I think you need to meet more of the ministers, emphasise how important it is that the market continues. And get value out of the time you've taken to travel here."

He wanted her around the ministers' offices in Canberra, as much as possible. But he had ulterior reasons. He needed time to get what he could out of Beckwith.

"We also need to know who we're up against. I've asked Dominik to see what he can find out. Let's see what he comes back with."

"I'll see what I can find out, too," she said distractedly, looking out the window.

The discussion petered out after that, Emil assuming that meant he had her tacit concurrence. Then he realised she'd fallen asleep. She stayed that way until he turned into the driveway of the InterContinental. As she got out, he suggested she take the night off, get some rest. She nodded and left.

He parked near his apartment, contemplating an early night for himself. He wasn't used to all the driving and the long hauls between Sydney and Canberra were exhausting. And he was pushing the friendship with Rita and Marianne, too. Maybe he'd gone too far. As he approached the entrance to the apartment building he could see someone was standing there, their back turned so he couldn't see their face. As he got to the entrance, they turned around. Emil almost jumped out of his skin. It was Zhong.

"Jesus, you gave me a fright! What the hell are you doing here?"

"Waiting for you, Mr Pfeffer."

"What? How did you know I was staying here? What are you doing, stalking me?"

"Stalking? No, not stalking. Catching up with my asset, that's all. What information do you have for me?"

"I'm not your *fucking* asset!"

"In that case, I will go to the InterContinental now."

"Why? What for?"

"I am staying there, of course," said Zhong, for a moment the mask of inscrutability slipping and a suggestion of what might have been a grin crossing his face.

"That's bullshit. You'll be staying up town near your Consulate."

Zhong turned to leave.

"Okay, okay. I have something for you. But I need time to get more evidence. To prove that I am correct."

Zhong turned back.

"The government is being advised on its policy review by US consultants."

"A-ha."

"The organisation is called the Coalition of Future Fuel Enterprises. What you thought is a code word, "cough' or 'cafe', when you listened to Globalreach telephone conversations, is probably the acronym of that name: C-o-F-F-E. I don't know yet for sure, but if my suspicions are correct, I think this means there is a link between the advisers and Globalreach."

Zhong looked genuinely surprised.

Emil suddenly wondered whether he'd given too much away. But he had to tell him something. Otherwise he could pull the plug on him.

"That might explain why so many people from Globalreach travelled to Australia recently. When can you get information to prove that you are correct?"

"Look, I found out what the 'code word' means, that's what you said you wanted. That's enough, isn't it?"

"No, you are very good agent, Mr Pfeffer. You must continue, or I go to see your boss now!" said Zhong firmly. "So when will you have proof of the link between Globalreach and these advisors?"

Zhong was a bastard, but he was too tired to argue. "I don't know. I'm trying, but I don't know. I'll let you know. Do not come here again. Understood?"

"You have small time only remaining," said Zhong. Then he turned and walked off into the evening.

In a car parked far enough away to be unnoticed, but from which there was a clear line of sight to the entrance of the building, the person sitting in the front passenger seat stopped filming, lowered the camera and read out the time. His colleague in the driver's seat, handwriting notes of their surveillance on a clipboard resting on his lap, added the time to the notes. He handed the clipboard to the passenger and started the engine. Then the vehicle drove off slowly, in the direction Zhong had taken.

22

There was a queue at the front desk and already the BridgeClimb premises were congested. Busy little business, thought Emil, as he eased his way through the crowd of various nationalities. Asians, Europeans, Americans, tourists from all over.

He discerned a distinct demarcation that split the people milling about into two broad categories: the bigger one, those exhibiting excitement – or was that nervous anticipation – and a smaller one of those exhibiting exhilaration: the first group of the day – the dawn climb – had just returned. The 'befores' and the 'afters'. Seeing them, just the thought of climbing the Sydney harbour bridge, was giving him sweaty palms.

It was early Saturday morning, probably one of the peak periods for the climb, but that wasn't the reason he was there. He certainly wasn't going up the bridge, if he could help it. He'd done it years ago, when he was a student, well before the business started. In those days, it was a popular lark to get up there and climbers were rarely apprehended. These days, given the level of security everywhere, they'd be quickly caught, arrested, prosecuted and fined. Which was certainly good news for this booming little business. Back then, he'd done it to confront his morbid fear of heights. He'd succeeded in getting up and back okay, but it hadn't fixed the phobia. If anything, the condition had become worse with age. No, he was here for an altogether different reason. This was where he'd arranged to meet Rodger Beckwith.

He was early and there was no sign of Beckwith, so he mingled in the crowd, checking out the visitor centre display and souvenirs for sale. As the next group moved off to do the climb, more were arriving, so his failure to join the group heading towards the climb wouldn't be obvious to anyone, unless they were specifically watching him.

After the unexpected appearance of Zhong, he'd become concerned that he was being watched. That bastard Zhong must have been tracking him for a while, to know where he was staying and where Betty G was. Even though his apartment was only a short walk from the BridgeClimb 'base', as they called it, in Cumberland Street, this morning he'd walked a long, circuitous route around the waterfront to Circular Quay and back, frequently doubling back and checking, to see if Zhong was following him.

Beckwith entered the premises. Emil stood at the front window, looking up and down the street for signs that he might have brought back up, or been followed. Satisfied Beckwith was on his own, he moved as far back from the street windows as he could, where Beckwith joined him.

"Where is she?"

"I don't know. I can't just ask them. I don't know how I can find out."

"Do you know where Gerry Johnstone is?"

"No, but that I can probably find out. I think he's still working for us."

"Who's 'us'? Globalreach?"

Beckwith looked at him with a mix of suspicion and caution, gauging whether this was a test or genuine inquiry.

"Well?" Emil drew himself up to his full height, standing over Beckwith to intimidate him, looking down on him threateningly.

"The Coalition."

"CoFFE? You mean you're in with this lot advising the

government?" said Emil, flushed with the satisfaction that his suspicions were accurate. Beckwith gave a barely perceptible nod of acknowledgement. He was frightened, not by Emil's posturing, but by the thought that he may already have said more than he should.

"Where's Hudson? Is he in on this?"

At the mention of Hudson, Beckwith looked even more frightened.

"Look, what's worse, telling me what I want to know, or an extended stay in a Chinese gaol for you and your girlfriend?"

"Hudson will kill me. He'll kill us both!"

"Not if you tell me where I can get him first."

"He's been part of the consulting team. But I haven't seen him for weeks. I don't know where he is now. He might have left, for all I know."

That's funny, Emil thought. Hudson wasn't mentioned in the information Marianne had given him. Either Beckwith was lying, or the information from Marianne was incomplete. He'd check with her.

"I'll give you three days, that's it. Be back here in time for the twilight climb on Tuesday. And if you can't tell me where they're holding Johanna, you better be able to tell me where Johnstone and Hudson are. Otherwise the Chinese get you and your girlfriend!"

Emil made to leave, then turned back. "Wait here a couple of minutes until I get clear, just in case some of your buddies are hanging around outside."

Emil walked out and looked up and down the street, before turning right and heading back towards Circular Quay. He would probably need to check in with Betty at some stage that morning, but – even though he wasn't normally a breakfast person – it was a beautiful morning and breakfast, or at least a couple of coffees, around near the Opera House, seemed like a better option right now. And if Zhong was lurking about somewhere, it would divert him away from Beckwith.

He passed 'The Glenmore' pub, trying to remember the quickest way down to the Quay – Gloucester Street, probably, next on the left – seemed to recall there was a set of steps somewhere there, down to George Street. As he approached the corner, he looked over at 'The Australian' pub on the opposite side. They did breakfast there, too, and there were a few early morning punters hanging around.

Looking at them, suddenly he realised they weren't there for breakfast. Crew cuts, sunglasses, muscles on their muscles. Casually dressed, but they had military, or security forces, written all over them, like full body tattoos without the ink. They certainly weren't looking at menus.

As soon as they saw that he'd seen them, they started for him. But after his experiences with Dominik in India, he'd realised that in such situations one reacted before thinking. He spun around and was running back down Cumberland Street, before they had a chance to manoeuvre themselves around the breakfast tables and street furniture, sprinting across the street, back in the direction he'd come. His first thought, go all the way down to where it passed under the bridge and around into The Rocks.

Suddenly he saw Beckwith, a hundred metres further along, walking towards him. In the same instant, Beckwith saw Emil running towards him, saw the two chasers and froze.

The entrance to the bridge steps was immediately on Emil's left. He darted into it, vaulting up two or three steps at a time, hopefully leading the chasers away from Beckwith. He reached the first landing, instantly realising the mistake he'd made: instead of running up the stairs, he should have gone straight through the passageway under the bridge roadway, to the western side, to Observatory Hill. Plenty of ways to lose them over there.

Now he had only two options. Neither very attractive. Both dead-ends, more or less, where he could be cornered. If he took the exit to his right, he'd be on the bridge footway, the only way off at the Milson's Point end. If he made it that far. These days there were security personnel all over it, who might grab him just for running.

He took the other option, darting up the next flight of steps, to the footway heading away from the bridge along the side of the Cahill expressway, curving around over the top of Circular Quay. Limited exits here, too. He could hear his pursuers, powering up just a flight of steps behind him. His hesitation had let them gain on him. He raced to the top and out onto the walkway, sprinting back towards the city. Unlike the bridge walkway, there was no high wire cage mesh, topped with razor wire, separating pedestrians from the roadway; just the original waist high cement parapet and thick steel rail. He vaulted onto it, eliciting a barrage of horns from the vehicles in the adjacent lanes. Across the other side, he could see the Observatory and the Moreton Bay fig trees in the park surrounding it. But there were eight or ten lanes of traffic between him and it.

A break was coming in the two lanes nearest him. Grunts alerted him to the pursuers emerging from the stairwell – they were almost on him. He had to go. He jumped down onto the roadway, just missing the tail of a passing car, swaying back from the next one. Horns blaring continuously. The smell of burnt rubber from urgent braking. A muscled hand swept over the parapet to grab him. He ducked. It missed. He squatted so the hand couldn't reach him, the gap in the traffic arrived and he shot across the two lanes of the Cahill heading around over Circular Quay.

A wider traffic barrier separated the next lanes, giving him breathing space. A quick look around behind him. The two hulks were clambering over the parapet, holding their hands up like police, trying to avoid being clipped by the cars whizzing past. Horns blasting them. The southbound lanes heading to the western distributor fanned out from two to four, vehicles picking up speed. He darted out across them to a cacophony of horns and screeching brakes, reaching the safety of another lane divider just ahead of an articulated lorry.

Traffic in the northbound lanes was moving more slowly, as multiple lanes converged into two, separated by a barrier from another two. Behind him, the horns and screeches of brakes told him the pursuers were close. He quickly stepped across the first two. A couple of bridge maintenance crewmen, whose truck was in a parking area adjacent to the lanes, were moving to intercept him. Had to go before they got close enough to nab him. A small gap in the traffic opened and he was across it and sprinting towards the park, away from the maintenance men and away from his pursuers.

Hurdling the wooden railing, he ran into the Observatory Hill Park. Behind, it sounded like his pursuers had caused a collision trying to cross the northbound lanes. He didn't look to check, racing through the park to where the Agar Steps led down to Kent Street. The thought ran through his mind that he might be able to flag a taxi there. He wasn't thinking where it would take him. Just away from these thugs chasing him.

Reaching Kent Street, he scanned both directions. No taxis, not even outside the Observatory Hotel. But two white sedans were racing very quickly up from the harbour end towards where he stood. Shit! Must have come around from Cumberland Street. He darted across Kent into High Street, up to where it turned the corner to run back down towards the main harbour. There were steps down to Hickson Road, a long way directly below.

Down the first of the two straight runs he could hear the cars pull up, doors flung open, the clatter of shoes rapidly starting down behind him. He had a good lead on them. Jumping two or three steps at a time down the second long run, he reached Hickson Road. As he came out of the stairway, two more white sedans mounted the footpath, blocking his progress, occupants throwing the doors open and jumping out to grab him.

They weren't Hudson's thugs.

They were Australian Federal Police.

23

Wedged between two burly federal officers in the back of one of the sedans, Emil was driven uptown. The vehicle turned into Goulburn Street, it suddenly occurring to him that he'd been duped, that these were in fact Hudson's men just posing as federal police. But they drove straight past the building housing Globalreach Americas, two blocks further along turning into a side street, then into the underground parking beneath the grey and blue glass box that was the Australian Federal Police building.

Arriving on an upper level, he was shocked to see Betty G sitting in an office. She appeared to be unimpressed. No, that would be a substantial understatement, he thought. She gave him a short, dismissive look, then turned away. He sat down next to her.

"What's going on?"

"That's what you're gonna tell us, Emil. It better be good."

The two 'goons' from outside The Australian pub, that Emil had run from, came in and sat down on the other side of the desk. They produced identification. They were from the Australian Security Intelligence Organisation – ASIO, the domestic security apparatus.

"So Mr Pfeffer, what were you up to this morning?"

"What do you mean? I was out for an early morning walk, when you two chased me."

"You ran that's why we chased you. You've left chaos on the bridge."

"No, I didn't. You two did. I got across without causing an accident. If there's a problem, it was caused by you."

"Emil! For Chrissakes! Just answer their questions," Betty G hissed through gritted teeth, staring at him angrily.

"Betty, you weren't there!" His default response when under attack: attack back. He looked at her. Her face told him the situation was far too serious.

He sighed.

"Alright, alright." He looked at the two ASIO men. "I had a bad experience last year, in my work. There were attempts to kill me. Some guys, who looked pretty much like you two look from a distance, chased me and a colleague. If they'd caught us, they would have killed us. As it was, they killed two other innocent people. That's why I ran."

"You left your apartment very early this morning."

"It's Saturday, I was getting some exercise, I went for a walk – looking for somewhere to have breakfast. That's not a problem, is it?"

One of the men took a portable video camera out of a bag. He turned it on and opened the viewing screen. Shit, they've got me with Beckwith, he thought.

"Can you tell us what you were doing meeting this man?" he said turning the viewing screen so Emil could see it.

Emil moved to his side, so Betty G could see it too.

"I've seen it," she said.

He looked at it. It was him and Zhong, the other night, at the entrance to the apartment building.

"I wasn't meeting him. He was waiting there when I arrived back. He's harassing me."

"We know he was waiting there. We have him under surveillance."

So it was Zhong they were interested in. His best option was the truth. Or at least part of it.

"Why would he be harassing you?" said the second man.

"I was in Hong Kong recently, with the legal team running an arbitration case for the Australian Government. You know, the Prime Minister held a press conference about it, because it's such a big deal. The one they lost, that's prompted the big policy review."

A brief nod from one of the men told him to get on with it.

"A young Chinese lawyer – on the other legal team – disappeared, then was found murdered, just after the decision was handed down. You can verify all this with the Senior Counsel, SJ Loftus, if you want. His chambers are in Phillip Street. He headed the Australian team. The Hong Kong police treated me as a person of interest, because the victim showed up a couple of times on closed circuit television in the lobby of the hotel where I was staying. I hadn't met her, or for that matter, spoken to her. But they kept me in Hong Kong while they investigated – Ms Greenhaugh here can confirm that."

"Well, that was the reason you gave for not leaving," said Betty G.

"Then Hong Kong police introduced this character, Zhong," he said, gesturing at the screen.

"That's what they called him?"

"Yes. I think he's a bureaucrat from Beijing. He's interested in a Hong Kong based bank that has an office here. He convinced the police to let me travel to Australia, on the condition that I find out what I could about the bank for him."

"Cheesus, Emil!" Betty G. hissed.

"Which bank is that?"

"It's an investment bank, called Globalreach Americas." He was getting dangerously close to giving them too much information.

"Why is he interested in it?"

"They have it under investigation."

"Did Zhong say why they have the bank under investigation?" asked the first of the ASIO men.

"He said they were concerned about its commodities trading, including in carbon assets. This would normally be investigated by the domestic authority, before they get us involved."

"What did he want to know? What have you told this Zhong?"

"He wanted to know what they are doing here, but I couldn't find out much. I went into the bank's office and asked some questions on the pretext of investigating their carbon trading operations," he lied. "But it's not our organisation's job to deal with private companies like that, so I couldn't get very far. Zhong is still threatening me, but I don't have anything I can give him."

"How is he threatening you?"

"He says they'll get me back to Hong Kong, on a murder charge, if I don't cooperate."

Betty G drew breath sharply. He gave her a quick look. The ASIO men exchanged a look.

"Why didn't you tell your boss any of this?"

"I didn't want to drag her into it. It's my mess to sort out."

"Too late now," muttered Betty G, under her breath.

"What I can't understand," said the second man, who until then had let his partner do most of the questioning, "is why this Zhong needed you to do this, why couldn't he make the inquiries himself?"

"I don't know. Maybe he doesn't want the bank to know that they're under investigation by the Chinese authorities. I really can't say. Why are you so interested in Zhong?"

"Mr Pfeffer," said the second man, who appeared to be the more senior, "we have very strong reason to believe that the man you know as Zhong is from Chinese state security. We've been watching him since he arrived. If he contacts you again, we'll be watching and listening. We're very concerned because the Chinese Premier is making a State visit here next month. A diplomatic incident, at this time, would be extremely unfortunate. But we can't let Chinese state security operate inside Australia".

They probably do it all the time, without you realising, he thought. But he kept that to himself.

Eventually the questioning reached a natural conclusion. Emil was told he was free to go. The dispute over who was responsible for the chaos on the bridge was unresolved, but Betty G backed him up, insisting that they shouldn't have been so heavy-handed in pursuing him.

The moment they were outside, she let him have it.

"I was going to have this morning off. Instead, I get dragged out of my hotel by Australian security agents at some ungodly hour, so I can sit around waiting until they hunt you down and bring you in," she said. "Emil, I'm the head of an inter-governmental organisation. I should not have to sit in while internal security from a member state interviews one of my management team over espionage concerns. I won't have it!"

"I know, it won't happen again."

"You're *darn tootin'* it won't! How do you get into these pre-dicaments? How could you end up in such a situation with the Chinese?"

"I don't know. It was just bad luck that the woman had been to the hotel where I was staying. It gave them an opportunity – they've taken full advantage of it."

Betty G shook her head. "Cheesus!"

"I'm sorry for ruining your morning, Betty. Let me make it up: let me buy you breakfast," he looked at his watch, "or lunch. I know a good place."

He took her non-response to be agreement. They grabbed a cab back down town and since it was a sunny morning, Emil suggested the rooftop café at the Museum of Contemporary Art, adjacent to the Quay. A table on the outside terrace was found, looking out at the side of an enormous cruise ship, berthed at the passenger terminal. A constant buzz of activity permeated the air, as the vessel readied itself for departure. Thousands of passengers looking down from the multiple decks, waving, throwing streamers, taking photos. Betty G surveyed the scene through her Ray-Ban sunglasses.

"It's glary, isn't it?" said Emil squinting.

"I thought you'd be more accustomed to the light here,"

said Betty G. "But I guess when you were out this morning it wasn't so bright. Exactly what were you up to at that hour, anyway?"

It occurred to him to be honest with her, to tell her everything. But then, in the back of his mind, he could hear Dominik's voice urging caution. He had to confess to himself that, ultimately, he just didn't know where she stood on a lot of things. But one thing he did know, she wouldn't want him chasing after Hudson, to find Johanna. As far as Betty G was concerned, frustrating as it might be, the police in Singapore and other places had to find her. That was their job. And he had to stick to doing his. He decided that, for now, it was better to stay with half-truths.

"I was thinking of doing the BridgeClimb – to confront my fear of heights. But in the end, I chickened out."

She looked around in the direction of the bridge. From where they sat it was just possible to make out ant-like figures, moving in groups, up to the top of the eastern arch and back down on the western side.

"That's not a bad idea. I might even do it before I leave. Then I can go back to the office with something to show for my time here," she said ruefully. Her tone changed. "Look, Emil, let me be frank with you. You may or may not remember that the organisation is being reviewed, in the coming year. That means, in case you hadn't realised, a review of our structure. In particular, a decision needs to be made whether the Market Integrity Unit is retained, or just remembered as an interesting experiment. Incidents like this morning's – they're just not on. It's touch and go as it is for the MIU, and you're not helping the case in favour of keeping it, not one iota."

"I'm just trying to do my job."

"You may not have that job soon. If the market contracts as a result of the position taken by the Australians, then the MIU will go. And the rest of GCMO may follow."

"Then we need to keep at them. Cajole, coerce, influence them into reconsidering their position."

"I've been thinking about it. There's no point us trying again with this government. They seem to have their minds set. We'd do better to get back to Bad Eschbach and get working on our strategy to adapt to the impact this will have on the market overall."

He wondered if he should try to convince her otherwise. It was difficult to read her from behind the Ray-Bans. He really wanted her back in Canberra, in and out of the ministers' offices where there might be a chance of seeing Hudson, if he was there. And he needed more time here, to follow up with Beckwith. But she had to make that decision for them to stay on. If he pushed it, he knew she would dig in. He would have to be subtle – not his strongest talent.

He looked around the terrace and at the surrounding buildings. After their morning with the domestic intelligence service, he wondered how easy it would be for some directional listening device to have been picking up their conversation. Their food arrived. They'd decided it was too late for breakfast and so had opted for the lunch menu. Smoked trout, couscous, tomato and spinach salad for Betty G. Barramundi and chips, with a green leaf salad for him. They both stayed on mineral water.

"Are you on a health kick, Emil?" Betty G asked between mouthfuls, eyeing the mound of thick cut, deep fried potato chips heaped over the large piece of fish on his plate.

"At least I'm not drinking. That Hunter Valley Semillon looked tempting, but I couldn't bring myself to start at eleven o'clock in the morning."

He deposited a portion of his chips on her plate.

"Thanks. You read my mind."

They ate in silence for a while, Emil chewing over how to get her thinking she needed to keep trying with the government. Betty G broke the silence.

"Emil, why do you do this job?"

It surprised him, although maybe it shouldn't have. It was a question he'd been asked before. That time, the circumstances were very different – Dominik had just told him that there were people who would try to kill him, because of what he knew, what he was trying to do. He'd been sceptical, but Dominik had been right.

"I'm surprised you ask, Betty. After all, you were on the panel that interviewed me for it."

"Yeah, but really, after all that's happened, why do you want to do it?"

To catch Hudson and his backers; to stop them and people like them, was what he wanted to say. Above all, to get Johanna back safely. But he couldn't say that to Betty G. That wasn't an answer she would want to hear.

"I'd like to think that I'm making a difference, a small cog in the big wheel implementing international climate policy."

She screwed up her face. "You've been speaking at too many conferences."

She paused for a moment or two, then asked: "You think we're doing more than just chewing up air miles? Meeting with goddamned politicians and other bigwigs, who don't want to hear what we've got to say."

"I hope so."

"Playing at being important. Kidding ourselves that we've got a seat at the big table?"

"I might have been silly enough, once, to think it involved prestige, had some sort of kudos. I was having myself on. It's just about getting our job done."

He looked at her, imagining he could see her eyes behind the sunglasses.

"What about you? Why do you do it, if that's what you think? Why do you drive yourself so hard?"

"I don't know any other way but to go as hard as I can. And I care about the outcome." She looked away, out across the water of Sydney Cove to the Opera House, sails glinting at them in the sunshine, now that the cruise ship had gone. "And it may not always be the obvious one, that's most important. It can be a juggling act. Not just people and positions, but relative values."

"Does that mean you think the end justifies the means?"

She thought for a few moments again, before responding.

"Sometimes, it might. You just have to be able to make that call when you find yourself in such a situation."

"Would you take a stand on principle?"

"If I thought it was warranted. Sure."

As to what the circumstances were, that might justify such decisions, she didn't volunteer and he didn't think to ask. He was too busy considering his own situation. Whether he would find himself in circumstances needing to make such a decision. Whether they would justify some radical course of action he might feel he needed to take.

24

In the end he did have a glass of the Hunter Valley Semillon. Betty G did, too. Having waited until it turned midday, they'd ordered a bottle. It was much more acceptable to have a drink in the afternoon. By the time it was finished, she'd forgiven him for that morning's escapade. Forgiven, but not forgotten. He knew it wouldn't be.

Betty G took herself off for a walk around the art gallery and botanical gardens. Emil returned to his apartment. He needed time to think about the predicament he was in. Despite the soporific effect of a couple of glasses of wine sitting out in the sun, he was too worried to doze off.

When Zhong next showed up, he could blow Emil's story apart as soon as he opened his mouth. If the federal police were to become involved, they might pick up Beckwith, or start some heavy-handed investigation of Globalreach, alerting Hudson. He'd simply go underground again, disappear, leaving Emil with nothing and no closer to finding Johanna. It might even cause them to harm her; they may have already.

No. He stopped himself. He didn't want to go there. Those were thoughts he'd decided long ago, on the day he'd received the call telling him to back off, to put out of his mind. They had to stay out. He would find her. He would find her safe and unharmed.

He still didn't know what CoFFE was advising the

government, but if it continued with the pull back from carbon trading, that was the end of his unit. His job, Dominik's and those of all his team would be gone. He felt responsible for them; he had to make sure that didn't happen. The prospects weren't good. But if Hudson was involved with CoFFE, it was worth investigating.

There were three days until he would meet with Beckwith. He may or may not come through with the information Emil wanted. He knew Rita and Marianne were coming up to Sydney the following day. He'd texted them the previous evening, proposing that they get together for dinner the next evening. They agreed to meet at a pub in Chinatown, early evening, Emil insisting it was his treat, recognition of the unreasonable pressure he'd been putting on them to get him information. Then he'd rung Loftus and invited him to join them.

Sunday evening, Dixon Street, Haymarket. Not the best place in the world to meet, if he was to spot Zhong following him. But, then again, maybe that would count in his favour: maybe the ASIO guys might not be able to pick him out of the crowd either. If Zhong did show up, he'd give him short shrift. He couldn't let Zhong bring ASIO blundering in. Being early, as usual, Emil had made a couple of circuits of the restaurants, looking for a place where they might dine. He hadn't made a booking and didn't know whether the others might have had the forethought to do so; judging from the number of people in Dixon Street, they might have trouble finding somewhere if they hadn't. Even on Sunday evening, the place was heaving and it might be difficult to find a table if they left their move too late.

He finished his second circuit at the Covent Garden pub and went in. There were still thirty minutes before the appointed meeting time; ordering a beer, he found a stool by the window, looking out across Hay Street towards Paddy's Market. It had only been a few days since he last saw Rita and Marianne in Canberra, but still, he was hoping they might have something more for him. Photos of the CoFFE consultants would be a good start. And if, as Beckwith had said, Hudson was part of the team, why hadn't any mention of him shown up? But he didn't want to push it; he knew they were taking a risk. Dominik still hadn't come back with information on CoFFE, either. He needed something more to convince Betty G it was worthwhile to stay longer.

Emil took a sip of his beer and scanned the street outside. There was no sign of Zhong or ASIO-type characters. That didn't mean they weren't there. Not with the numbers of people milling about the pavement outside the pub. His eyes were doing a sweep of the people standing about on the opposite side of Hay Street, when a hand rested on his shoulder.

"I didn't mean to give you a fright," said Loftus.

"No problem. I'm glad you're a fellow early bird. Grab a stool while I get you a drink – beer?"

"I wouldn't say no. I walked in from Glebe, so I'm a little parched."

Emil returned from the bar with a glass of beer. Loftus had not made a dinner booking either, but he assured Emil that wouldn't be a problem, as his 'usual table' would be available at the Marigold, whenever they showed up.

"That's what I like to see, a man with connections," said Emil.

"Not in the Alexander Gelman sense, however, I hasten to add."

"Quite."

"Although I could do with some, when dealing with the Hong Kong police."

"Oh, how did you get on?"

"Most unsuccessfully so far, I'm afraid. But, hope springs eternal, as they say. The wheels and cogs of that bureaucracy will turn, in time."

"With the help of some lubricating oil, perhaps? Government-to-government lubricating oil?"

"I've been hoping that we could avoid needing to do that.

I'd prefer to be able to show that arse, the Attorney-General, a thing or two by getting my hands on it first and initiating the proceedings. But we may need to resort to government leverage, after all."

"So you're familiar with Gelman?"

"Only through being an active subscriber to the Sydney Theatre Company. They had a season of Russians, a couple years ago. For some reason that one stuck in my mind."

The conversation meandered onto other plays Loftus had seen, then Emil got talking about the time he lived in London and how frequently they used to attend the theatre. This, inevitably, led him onto talking about Catherine, his partner, at that time. He seldom spoke of her and when he realised what he was doing, stopped, suddenly self-conscious. He looked at his watch. It was thirty minutes after the appointed meeting time.

"Wonder what's happened to Marianne and Rita?"

Loftus consulted his own watch. "Yes, it's unlike them. They're normally quite fastidious about their punctuality."

"Well, it is Sunday evening, so we can allow them a bit of slack."

Loftus bought another round of drinks and they went back to discussing the Sydney theatre scene, of which Emil had never been aware. Eventually Loftus looked at his watch again.

"Well, we've given them an hour. Maybe we should go and make a start. They can catch up when they arrive. They'll know where to find us."

As he was speaking, something on the bar television screen caught Emil's attention. He moved around to where he could get a better view, Loftus following him. It was a 'breaking news' announcement.

A reporter was standing in front of an office building. An awful blue edifice with what looked like a billboard bearing the national coat of arms above the entrance. It seemed vaguely familiar. Emil wondered whether it was one of the ones he'd been to recently. Over the noise of the bar, it was difficult to make out what the reporter was saying – something to do with early morning raids across the national capital by Australian Federal Police. He looked around at Loftus, who was staring intently at the big screen, trying to make out what was being said. He looked at Emil and shrugged. On the screen, the reporter handed back to the news anchor in the studio.

"So there you have it. Dawn raids across Canberra resulting in more than half a dozen arrests. Australian Federal Police are not saying much but our sources tell us those arrested are all public servants, in several instances, senior public servants. Charges relate, apparently, to breaches of the Official Secrets Act, but at this stage that's all we have to go on, except for what the Prime Minister had to say earlier today."

The news anchor threw back to the reporter outside the building. With a sudden anxiety, Emil realised which building it was: the one where Marianne worked. His attention was immediately drawn to the pods of closed-circuit television cameras spotting the building facade like black moles, that he could see over the reporter's shoulder. Jesus! How many of them were there? Why hadn't he noticed them when he went there to meet her? Desperately, he tried to recall exactly the point where they'd met – how close were they to the building? She must have been aware of them. What was the range of these things?

The footage cut to an outside shot of Michael Mendicane, earlier in the day, walking down a broad set of steps, to confront a pack of reporters. Behind him, the imposing brick frontage of Canberra cathedral.

"No chance that was staged!" said Loftus, smirking.

Mendicane was holding his hands up. It looked to Emil like he was impersonating a priest about to give a blessing to his congregation. Or, in Mendicane's case, more likely a cricket umpire signalling six runs. But at the same time, this story was beginning to make Emil feel extremely uncomfortable. He took a sip of beer. It did little to slake the increasing dryness in his throat.

"This is a sad day for Australia. A sad day for democracy and the trust we place in the public sector. I am shocked. Shocked and disheartened at this breach of trust. Senior people, people who have had the trust of governments and the Australian people for decades, leaking confidential information, government secrets. Whether it's for ideological reasons, or for money, whatever the reason, they have been breaking not only our trust, but also the law. They will be investigated thoroughly and they will be prosecuted with the full force of the law."

"Why worry about the investigation," said Loftus. "Sounds like he's decided they're guilty already." He studied Emil. "Are you alright?"

Emil wasn't. He was feeling decidedly nauseous.

He heard Loftus, but he couldn't respond. In the background, Mendicane was continuing to pontificate, resorting to sporting analogies to get him through the rest of the doorstop interview. Emil was catching snippets of it *"... team tactics sheet to the opposition ..." "... pulling the wool over the umpire's eyes ..."*, then he heard *"... foreign agents involved ... more arrests coming..."*. He looked up at the screen, but they'd cut back to the studio and were going to an advertisement break.

"Shall we head on over to the Marigold?" said Loftus.

"I don't feel very hungry. In fact, I think I'll be sick if I try to eat anything."

"What about Rita and Marianne?"

Emil looked at him closely, trying to judge if he realised, had any inkling what Emil was thinking.

"I don't think they're going to make it tonight."

25

Tuesday. He was still free.

There hadn't been any knock on the door in the middle of the night. No Federal Police officers arriving to arrest him for espionage, to arrest him as being one of Mendicane's alleged '*foreign agents*'. They'd have him under surveillance, of that he was sure. It was probably just a matter of time.

He and Betty G each had meetings that would keep them apart all that day: Emil with private sector organisations involved in the carbon market; Betty G with state government officials. It was an information gathering exercise, to assess the mood of affected stakeholders following the federal government's announcements. Betty G had been for cancelling the meetings, after their visit to Canberra, but he'd convinced her that it was essential for them to go ahead. Even if nothing came of it, they needed to make a proper assessment of the situation before they returned to Frankfurt.

It was a beautiful day, typical of the warm, still, blue days of late autumn – crisp in the morning and chilly in the evening – that presaged the winter. Unseasonably warm – mid-twenties – considering time of year. The cold would come; it just hadn't arrived yet.

In the end he'd gone to the Marigold with Loftus on Sunday evening, but had eaten little. He'd lost his appetite when he saw the news. As anticipated, Marianne and Rita never showed.

"I'm worried that they might have been among the people they were talking about on the news, the ones that were arrested," he explained to Loftus. "I asked them to find out things about that bank I mentioned to you. And about the Texans. Sensitive stuff. I hope I haven't got them into trouble."

"They're big and ugly enough to look after themselves. Don't worry about them."

"I'll tell them you said that, next time I see them, which will probably be when we're all arraigned together in the dock."

"Very melodramatic. Let's not get too carried away. I agree, from what you've just told me, there's a chance they might be involved. But there are probably also a number of other explanations for their non-appearance. Let's wait and see."

He hadn't told Loftus about his own encounter with ASIO the previous morning. But after that episode, they would be watching him, as well as Zhong. Rita and Marianne may have already been dragged into his problems. He wanted to avoid Loftus becoming implicated, if he wasn't already.

Emil's meetings were in offices dotted around Martin Place. As they were all financial institutions that stood to lose from the government's policy changes, he had receptive, attentive audiences. It was clear there was a lot of opposition on the ground to the government's moves. Whether this would translate into action, depended on the policy detail – the sweeteners the government would throw in, to blunt it.

By four in the afternoon, his last meeting was winding up. Leaving the building, which was at the top of Martin Place, he turned down Castlereagh Street, crossed past an upmarket jewellery store, then turned left into Hoskins Place. It was a dead end, but he'd remembered there was pedestrian access from there to Penfold Place, which ran off Pitt Street. So he would be able to get through, but if anyone was tailing him in a car, they would be blocked.

Across Pitt Street, he walked briskly into the Hunter

Connection mall and the series of arcades running under George Street into Wynyard station. It wasn't peak hour yet, but still there was a solid stream of people heading in the direction of the railway. In his student days, he'd worked in the international hotel that sat over the top of Wynyard. Back then it had boasted over twenty bars and bottle shops in the rabbit warren of arcades that led to the station. With changing times, a lot of the bars had gone, becoming other sorts of shops. But the network of passageways and stairwells, through which they'd been serviced, would still be there.

Maintaining his pace, he reached the last section of the arcade before the station, keeping tight to the right hand wall. About one-third of the way along, he slipped into a doorway and along the passageway that led around the back of what had once been the '747 cocktail bar', a dimly lit watering hole decorated like the inside of an aeroplane. He smiled at the memory of the place. He'd been on lots of 747s, but never once been offered a cocktail. Back then in the 747 bar, there'd been lots of cocktails. And plenty of amorous action amongst the office workers drinking them on Thursday and Friday evenings. It was a Malaysian noodle bar now, with much better lighting.

The passageway ran behind the rest of the shops along that side of the arcade to a set of lifts and stairwell at the far end. Down led to the vast storeroom that used to house the hotel's immense wine cellar and alcohol stock, a place he remembered as being patrolled by squadrons of sewer rats as big as small dogs. If you had to go down there to collect supplies, the rule was make sure all the lights were on and make a lot of noise before stepping inside. Up three flights, there was access to the hotel lobby.

He stood at the entrance to the stairwell and listened. From the end of the passageway he could make out the remote sounds of people passing in the arcade. That was all. No footsteps following him. So far, so good.

If he were being tailed, having lost him in the arcade, they'd probably try to cover all the station and hotel exits. There were lots, so that would keep them busy. And there was one he knew they probably wouldn't think of. He raced up the three flights of stairs to the lobby level. Having made a quick check around the doorway to ensure no ASIO-types were loitering there, he crossed quickly out of the service stairs and down to the lower level lobby bar, from which he could access the hotel's car park. He checked again before stepping into the car park, then headed down the ramp, as if he was there to retrieve a vehicle. At the end of the entrance area, the car park turned to the right and disappeared off into the distance. Wynyard railway station had platforms three to six, but no platforms one and two. These were the old tramway station and tunnels that had become the hotel car park.

Emil checked the time: he didn't want to risk Beckwith arriving and, not finding him, leave, thinking he was a no-show. He picked up his walking pace, heading along the old tunnel in the direction of the harbour. The car park was one long straight stretch to the exit, cars parked perpendicularly on either side. It exited into Cumberland Street – perfect – as it provided cover for most of his route to the BridgeClimb premises. But he still had quite a distance to go.

Behind him, there were footsteps. Where'd they come from? He was maintaining his brisk pace, but the footsteps behind seemed to be catching him up all the same. He didn't dare look around. Crossing the passageway to a sedan on his right, he pretended to be opening the door. He looked up casually. The footsteps had stopped. He heard a car door open and close. Then ignition and a grey coloured hatchback, forty metres back, began nosing out of its parking spot. He let it pass, pretending to be making a call on his mobile. Then he realised that there wouldn't be any reception in the tunnel – the driver hadn't looked at him anyway. Once the vehicle had gone, he ran the remaining length of car park and, checking both directions, out onto Cumberland Street.

He would have been preferred to be more cautious along

here, to make sure there was no-one following, but he was out of time. He'd even planned to stop for a few minutes in each of the pubs, the Australian and the Glenmore, to make sure Zhong, or the ASIO guys, weren't lurking inside. But he'd just have to hope they weren't. He stopped just short of the entrance to the BridgeClimb base and took a long look back up Cumberland Street. Satisfied he wasn't being followed, he went in.

There weren't as many people in the area as there had been on Saturday morning. But he immediately recognised two of them. Over by the back wall, where they had spoken on the previous occasion, he noticed Beckwith, half turned away, reading some of the BridgeClimb promotional material. Standing much closer, to his horror, looking straight at him with an expression that almost said she was pleased to see him, was Betty G.

"Don't look so shocked! You gave me the idea."

"Oh, Betty. Er, you're doing the climb?"

"What else do you come here for?" she beamed. "You here to confront your fears again, Emil?"

"Yeah, ah, something like that," he stammered.

Over Betty G's shoulder he could see Beckwith had stopped reading and was watching him. He turned away and steered Betty G towards the ticket counter. Hopefully, Beckwith would understand what was happening and wait for him somewhere, discreetly.

"It's better to do this with someone you know," Betty G was saying as she purchased her ticket.

Emil stalled. The last thing he wanted to do was the BridgeClimb, and especially not now, not with her. He could feel his palms getting clammy, just at the thought of it.

"They can help you confront your demons."

The ticket seller was waiting. "Twilight climb?"

"I can't do it, Betty," he blurted. "You go. I just can't do it."

"Our guides are very helpful in getting you over any apprehension." The ticket seller could see a prospective customer slipping away. Emil was worrying about Beckwith slipping away.

"No, no. You go, Betty. I'll see you back here. I'll go to the museum in the pylon. Or something."

"People are waiting," said the man behind them. They moved away to stop blocking the queue.

"Okay, Emil. But I'm surprised. I never would have picked you for being such a chicken!" she said, moving off to join the group waiting for the safety induction before the climb.

Thanks for the understanding, he thought. Realising how tense he was, he rolled his shoulders, then looked around to see where Beckwith had gone. He was nowhere to be seen. At least he's got the presence of mind to get out of sight, thought Emil.

He stepped outside and looked up Cumberland Street. The afternoon light was fading fast; on the eastern side it was blocked by the bridge approaches, anyway. It would be a while before the street lighting came on, leaving the street shadowy and dull. Emil strained his eyes, but couldn't see any sign of Beckwith.

He looked down towards the harbour. A figure was just passing out of sight around the corner of the bridge substructure. He couldn't see him very well, but it had to be Beckwith.

26

Rodger Beckwith hot-footed it as soon as he was out the door of BridgeClimb. He didn't know what Pfeffer was playing at, but he wasn't going to stand around in the street waiting to find out. He began making his way back up Cumberland Street. If Pfeffer wanted to talk to him, he could either catch up to him or contact him later. He didn't have anything to tell Pfeffer, anyway, so the meeting was all a bit pointless as far as he was concerned.

He knew he'd have to do something to help Pfeffer, to stop him giving their names to the Hong Kong police – whether that meant finding out where Pfeffer's girl was, or something else. If any of this got back to people in the Coalition, he'd be finished with them. Out of a job – assuming, that was, they didn't just straight out kill him. That thought was making him queasy.

As he walked back up Cumberland Street, in the distance he noticed a white sedan pull out of the car park exit up near the end and cruise slowly down towards him. It pulled in to the kerb just before it reached The Australian pub and sat there, with its engine running.

As he passed it, Beckwith stole a quick sideways glance at the two men sitting it. They were both staring intently down the street, the one in the passenger seat with what looked like a small pair of binoculars on his lap. They didn't even seem to notice him as he strolled past. But he wasn't stupid. They were either police or security – looked like the same guys who had run after Pfeffer the last time they'd met here. Once he was past the vehicle, he gradually picked up his pace: best not to hang around for Pfeffer to catch up, after all. Something was going on and he wasn't hanging around to get caught up in it. He was going to get the hell out of there. Once he was far enough past the vehicle to be out of sight of its occupants, he broke into a run.

*****

In the white sedan, the ASIO officers were looking out anxiously for any sign of Emil. They'd been onto him as far as Wynyard, where they'd lost him. It was a disaster. Their colleagues tailing Zhong had just let them know Zhong was waiting down near Pfeffer's apartment in the Rocks. But Pfeffer didn't seem to be heading back there: he was up to something. This was their chance to catch whoever else involved in whatever Zhong and Pfeffer were up to. A chance to wrap up the entire gang.

But then he'd just disappeared. They'd called in federal police back up to make an extensive search through Wynyard, but still failed to find him. It cost valuable time.

Luckily, he'd showed up on the hotel's closed-circuit television. Exiting the car park, still on foot. From the way he was hurrying, they'd deduced he was on his way somewhere to meet someone – maybe not Zhong – he was going a roundabout way, if he was.

He'd got a head start on them, so he could have gone anywhere – he could have been in one of the pubs, or in the sports complex across from them, or he might have been in one of the old tenements, between the pubs. They suspected he was still nearby. They just didn't know where. He might show again here – or he might show up for their colleagues watching Zhong, who was still sitting outside another pub near Pfeffer's apartment. Pfeffer had to be somewhere nearby.

Cumberland Street was completely in shadow from the bridge. Once it got dark, that would help them stay unobserved, but make it harder to spot Pfeffer. And Zhong, if he got on the move. The street lights probably wouldn't come on for another ten minutes. But they didn't have to wait that long.

"There he is!" said the passenger, who'd been scanning up and down the street with binoculars. "Just out of the BridgeClimb premises."

His colleague put the car in gear.

"Not yet. He's looking this way. Wait. Looking around. Okay. Go. Go. He's moving away quickly. Running. Heading under the bridge to the western side."

Through the radio speaker came a voice. "We'll see him when he comes around the Harbour View."

"Okay. We're following." He spoke into a microphone inside his jacket. "Get the AFP guys into BridgeClimb, check everyone in there. He's probably just met someone there, now he's off to see Zhong."

*****

The figure disappeared out of view around the corner under the bridge, just as Emil turned to look down in that direction. Beckwith. Had to be him. There was no one else around. He started running to catch him. He couldn't afford to lose this opportunity – it had taken too long already, just to get this single lead on finding Johanna. He wasn't going to lose it now.

It was brighter around the other side of the bridge, but by the time Emil got to Lower Fort Street, the figure had disappeared again. He ran over to the cement parapet above where the end of George Street joined Lower Fort Street. No sign of him. So he wasn't going back around towards the Quay that way. And there was no sign of anyone further down Lower Fort. No one in the park under the bridge.

Emil ran back up and stopped on the roadway outside the Harbour View pub, scouring the street for any sign of him. In the distance, he could just make out a figure – in the shadows of the buildings in Trinity Street – where it forked left from Lower Fort. He started running again, to catch Beckwith.

*****

Zhong was pleasantly relaxed. He'd found a nice spot to sit and wait for Pfeffer, at a table outside the Hero of Waterloo pub. It was on the corner of Windmill Street and he was sitting with his back against the brick wall of the pub. The sun had been shining on the wall, so the bricks were radiating heat onto his back. It was a very pleasant, relaxing feeling after his ride.

He'd taken to riding a bicycle as he'd found it quicker for getting around Sydney's inner city traffic. He hadn't ridden a bike for years – it wasn't safe anymore in Beijing – and he was starting to notice a little stiffness in his back. The warmth was just what he needed. The bike was leaning against the pub wall next to him. From where he was sitting, he could see the front of the apartment building where Pfeffer was staying. All in all, this was a good place to wait for Pfeffer to show up. It was good, too, to have a few moments to himself. In Beijing, they were nervous about him using Pfeffer; his bosses were sitting on him for results. The information Pfeffer had provided so far was promising, but without any corroborating documents or proof, insufficient. Unless he got more, very soon, he would be recalled; so this would be Pfeffer's last chance too.

To a passer-by, he would have looked like he was dozing. The small glass of beer on the table in front of him hardly touched, a copy of the Australian Chinese Daily newspaper open across his lap. But he was alert and surprised to see Emil running up Lower Fort Street towards him.

Why is he running? Suddenly, Emil diverted into Trinity Street and disappeared from Zhong's view. He's seen me. He's avoiding me!

Zhong jumped onto his bicycle and cycled around into Trinity Street after him.

*****

Further along Windmill Street, a large four-wheel drive vehicle was parked, with its engine running. In it, sat Gregory Hudson and two of his 'associates' – security men – former US special forces. Waiting for Emil to return to his apartment. It had taken them a while to track down exactly where he was staying. But in the end, a couple of phone calls to the right people had pointed them in the direction they needed to look. Being in an apartment, on his own, was perfect. It would be much easier to deal with Pfeffer there, than if he had been staying in a hotel.

This time, Hudson would take care of Pfeffer personally. That way he knew it would be done properly. If you wanted something done properly, you had to do it yourself. How true that was. They'd had the opportunity to get rid of Pfeffer in Zürich, last year. But they hadn't really appreciated, at the time, what a nuisance he could become. And he didn't know what happened to Wiebe, how he'd been killed; but that entire operation had turned into a total fuck up and somehow Pfeffer had managed to escape. He had to be removed from the equation, permanently: not least because of the risk that he could identify him and blow this new project out of the water. The directors wouldn't be happy if two projects were aborted. Hudson reached under the driver's seat and pulled out the pistol hidden there. He reached in again and pulled out a silencer, which he slowly and precisely screwed onto the barrel. He checked the weapon was loaded, with a round in the breech. Pfeffer had been amazingly lucky in Hong Kong. His luck was about to run out.

Another of Hudson's men was waiting at the end of the pathway that ran between the shops in Lower Fort Street down to a small park in Pottinger Street. He was watching both directions, in case Pfeffer approached from either. When he saw Emil running up towards Trinity Street, he sprinted back to the waiting vehicle.

"Pfeffer just ran past. Into Trinity Street," he said, jumping in next to Hudson in the back seat. "Quick. Down here, left into Kent and left into Argyle. We'll cut him off when he gets to Argyle."

Hudson looked quizzically at him.

"Trinity is blocked – just a footpath through to Argyle."

"Okay. Quickly. Faster," Hudson ordered, even though the vehicle was at the end of Windmill Street already, screeching around the corner into Kent.

*****

"Hey! Hey!" Emil had almost caught up to Beckwith.

At the sound, the man turned around. It wasn't Beckwith! Damn. The man turned back and kept walking towards the pathway behind the Holy Trinity church, stopping occasionally to photograph the old building facades and stonework. God! I've just chased a bloody tourist all that way, Emil thought. He slumped over to recover his breath, the butts of his hands resting on his knees. He hadn't run that far, that fast, for a long time. Probably since he'd gone to the squatter settlement with Robert. And that was a long time ago. He was feeling his age. And his lack of conditioning. Have to lay off the booze for a while, get back into the swimming when I get back to Frankfurt, he thought.

He stood up again and turned to head back, to be surprised by the sight of Zhong rounding the corner into Trinity Street on a bicycle, heading straight up at him. Not far behind him, Emil could see a white sedan just nose into the end of Trinity Street. Shit! Can't afford to let Zhong say anything with them listening.

Emil turned and hurried down the pathway towards Argyle Street. He'd head up into Observatory Hill Park and back through the bridge steps across to Cumberland, to see if he could find Beckwith there – once he'd got rid of Zhong and his friends. He'd almost reached the end when a large four-wheel drive vehicle with tinted windows screeched to a halt in Argyle Street, blocking the end of the path. A sense of *déjà vu* hit him – Papua New Guinea – *sangguma* – *kumo* people – Davies' murder.

Two crewcut thugs jumped out, not twenty metres away and they definitely weren't from ASIO this time. There was no room to get past. They started towards him. Behind them, he caught a glimpse of Hudson, in the back seat of the vehicle.

He turned to run, but Zhong had come up the pathway on a bike and was only metres from him. He grabbed Zhong's handlebar to stop him from crashing into him. Behind Zhong, two white sedans had almost reached the end of Trinity Street, blocking the roadway.

"Help! Help!" he shouted, waving his arm. "Hey, ASIO! Police!"

A quick look over his shoulder, the two hulks had stopped.

He kept waving at the white sedans. "Hey, hey, ASIO!"

Zhong snatched a quick look back at the white sedans. Doors opening, occupants getting out. Pushing away from Emil, he peddled quickly past him and the thugs at the end of the pathway and was gone.

Emil started towards the white sedans, waving his arms. Something hit him in the back. A twinge. That bloody shoulder blade, where he was hit in Stuttgart, he thought – must have pinched the damn nerve.

Another quick glance over his shoulder. The two thugs were hurriedly getting back into the vehicle, which then disappeared from the end of the pathway, heading through the Argyle Cut.

Suddenly, he was very aware of his shoulder. It was hurting. A lot. Becoming more painful with each movement. He reached over with his right hand. The back of his jacket was all tacky.

He looked around: people were standing, staring at him.

A woman with her hand up to her mouth. The tourist had stopped taking photos of the Holy Trinity church, his camera now pointing at Emil. Another man, making a call on his mobile phone.

He noticed the front of his shirt felt wet. He looked down: it was red.

He was feeling light-headed. Tried to squat down on his haunches. As he slumped over, the woman screamed.

*****

Betty G felt exhilarated.

The twilight BridgeClimb was one of the best things she'd done in a long time. It was a pity Emil hadn't joined her: the other people were nice, but she would have liked to do it, to have shared the experience, with someone she knew.

Still, she felt great. After the safety induction and the 'suiting up', they'd gone up the eastern arch, where they'd had fantastic views of the inky dusk settling over the Opera House and outer harbour. They'd crossed to the western arch for the spectacular sunset: the mountains in the distance weren't as clear as they could have been – it was the air pollution, their guide said – but it did make for some vibrant oranges and reds as the sun slipped away.

Then, as if to remind them where they were, they descended to the sounds of sirens and the sight of flashing blue and red lights in the twilight darkness beneath them, somewhere just on the western side of the bridge. Well, at least she'd managed to suspend reality for a little while.

Having 'de-suited' she was surprised to find the entrance lobby of the premises brimming with people. As she tried to leave, she was even more surprised to be stopped by an Australian Federal policeman. She realised that all the people were there because they were not being allowed to leave. Police were taking down everyone's details. She recognised one of the policeman from her early Saturday morning visit to Goulburn Street.

"Excuse me, officer, we met on Saturday morning. I'm Betty

Greenhaugh, from the Global Carbon Markets Organisation. Remember me? I was with my colleague, Emil Pfeffer? What's going on?"

He looked at her for a few moments, then the penny dropped and it dawned on him who she was.

"Oh dear. I think we might've caused these people a great deal of inconvenience, for nothing," he said, looking around for his superior officer.

27

"You're making a habit of this, Emil. If you're not getting squashed in a mine vehicle, you're getting shot."

Betty G was standing beside the bed.

Once he'd recovered from momentarily passing out, he'd been conscious throughout what followed, but his recollections were hazy. The ambulance arriving, bleeding being staunched, being sedated, then police all around, the journey to the hospital, examination and the treatment of his wound, the initial police interview. Now hours later in recovery, he was still a little drowsy, the effect of the drugs administered.

"Yes, Betty. We've been here before, haven't we?"

"Well, that was in Frankfurt. Not St Vincent's Hospital in Sydney, we haven't. But whatever you do, you seem to attract these incidents." She shook her head. "You should have come on the BridgeClimb. Lot harder to get shot up there."

"I get my thrills standing on terra firma," he tried to joke.

"How do you feel?"

"Sore. And a bit out of it."

"The surgeon who fixed you up said the bullet went straight through – in one side and out the other. The police found it embedded in a tree trunk. Said it did only minor damage on the way through. The tissue should heal okay, given a bit of rest. You've been incredibly lucky, Emil."

"I should buy a lottery ticket."

The door of the room opened and the two ASIO officers who had been tailing him came in.

"Up to answering a few questions, Mr Pfeffer?"

Emil tried to shrug, but it only caused him to wince in pain.

"Mind if I stay?" Betty G asked.

"No problem at all," said the first man.

His colleague began. "You want to explain what you were up to this afternoon?"

Emil gave him a surprised look, suddenly more alert. "What do you mean 'up to'? That's a bit rude."

"What I mean is," he said tetchily, "why did you give us the slip in Wynyard? Why did you go to the BridgeClimb? Why did you run, when you left there?"

"You're jumping to a lot of conclusions, aren't you?"

They didn't respond. Standing at the end of the bed, arms folded, waiting.

"If you were secretly following me, it's your problem if you can't keep up, not mine. What makes you think I 'gave you the slip', as you put it? That's bloody insulting. I didn't know you were there to be given the slip, in the first place! Besides, if I'm going somewhere, then change my mind, frankly that's none of your business."

"Okay, so you chickened out, as we've heard from Ms Greenhaugh," he said, acknowledging Betty G. "Why did you run, when you left there?"

"I thought I saw someone that I knew. I was trying to catch up to him, but when I did, it turned out I was mistaken."

"Was that who shot you?"

"No. It was a tourist. I was mistaken."

"So why would someone shoot you?"

"Did you catch them?"

"No, not yet."

"In the back of that vehicle was a man called Gregory Hudson ..."

At the name, there was a sharp sucking in of breath by Betty G. Emil looked at her.

"Betty, he was sitting in the back of the car. They must have been waiting for me – near the apartment where I'm staying. Waiting for me to come back." He looked back at the ASIO men. "This man, Hudson, he's on the run from a PNG government arrest warrant. There's an Interpol Red Notice on him. He's the one who tried to have me killed. Last year."

"You must have made him really angry, if he's followed you here."

Emil hesitated. Be careful, he thought, don't want to give too much away. "Maybe he's been hiding out here."

"Or maybe he's tied up with that bank you've been looking into," said Betty G, giving Emil a hard look. "For the Chinese."

Emil picked up her sarcasm. He hoped the ASIO guys hadn't – if they started down that path, things might start getting complicated. More than they were already. He tried to lead them away from the line that Hudson could be connected to Globalreach.

"Actually, when I saw those guys get out of the car, I confronted Zhong because you said you'd be listening," he offered. "In the end, it was lucky he was there. Ironic, isn't it?"

The two ASIO men stood looking at him, as if they weren't sure whether to believe him or not.

"Can you check the Red Notices – that will help you find Hudson."

"You're saying that the first time you saw us, you thought we looked like those guys who got out of that vehicle near the church?" the more senior of the two ASIO men asked, as they were leaving. "Now we're the ones who should feel insulted!"

They went to check the Red Notices with the Federal Police and see what progress had been made in catching Emil's assailants. After they'd gone, Betty G gave him a further going over.

"Okay, Emil. What's the real story? Who were you chasing after? Was it Hudson?"

The truth, or at least a portion of it, was required.

"I thought I saw Beckwith. Out in Cumberland Street,

heading towards the harbour, after I left you at the BridgeClimb. But, as I said, when I caught up to him, it was only a tourist."

"Hmph." She wasn't convinced. "Well, I can't argue with the fact that you've been shot."

"The rest of it is as I told them. God knows why Hudson is here, or how long he's been following me. It's lucky he showed his hand when he did. Otherwise I'd be dead."

"Your nine lives are gonna run out sometime, Emil. Just try to make sure it happens after you retire from GCMO, will you?"

"Does that mean I've got a job until retirement?"

She raised her eyebrows. "We'll see." Then she left.

He was kept in overnight for observation. The wound wasn't serious, so he was discharged the following morning with instructions on how to care for it until he returned for another examination. That afternoon he and Betty G met in the atrium coffee shop at her hotel, where they'd met when she first arrived.

"I had a call from ASIO, this morning," she said, when the waiter had delivered their coffees and moved out of earshot. "They said there's no record of Gregory Hudson having entered Australia. Not any time for the last twelve months."

Damn it! He's got to be using a false name, Emil thought. Just like in Hong Kong. He opened his mouth to speak his thoughts, and then realising what he was doing, closed it again.

"What were you just about to say?" said Betty, eyeing him suspiciously.

"Er, I was, ah, just thinking Hudson must be using a false name." That was a close call, come on, wake up. "It was definitely him in the back of that car."

"These Red Notices have pictures," said Betty, "so they should know what he looks like, if it was him. Just have to hope that they find him and his associates. Then maybe you'll be able to leave it alone and concentrate on your work again."

They left the matter there and switched to discussing the outcomes of their meetings on the previous day. On this subject, they agreed: all of the private sector and state government people with whom they'd met said the same thing: the government's changes would hurt financially.

"I'm surprised at the opposition, at state level," said Betty G. "They're from the same side of the political spectrum, for Pete's sake."

"And the financial people might not openly criticise the government, but privately they're fuming."

"The state government people said we'd find the same response across all administrations. They're fed up with the changes – the flip-flopping, they called it."

"We know they're on our side. Question is, what are we going to do about it?"

Betty G took her time before responding.

"I can't afford to spend any more time here, Emil. I've got a Governing Council meeting coming up in the next fortnight and I must have a strategy to present to them, setting out our response to this situation. I can't get that sorted out from here, so I'm gonna head back to Germany tomorrow. You can stay on – in fact, why don't you take that break we were talking about? Have a week off, then come back recovered and ready for action. It'll give that shoulder some time to heal."

It seemed like she wouldn't need Emil around in Frankfurt to be consulted on this strategy she was developing. At first, the thought that he was being sidelined stuck in his throat. He had the feeling she was dumping him already. But he put that out of his mind. It could be dealt with when he got back to the office. Besides, his unit had probably already done everything they could to contribute to it. So he agreed to her suggestion to have a break. He had to tie off a few loose ends in Sydney and Canberra, he told her, then he'd have a week's break and see her back in the office the following week.

He went back to his apartment, to work out what to do. He didn't expect Zhong or Hudson would show up again, after what had happened. The incident had exposed them more than either would be comfortable with. His immediate concern was how to set up another meeting with Beckwith where ASIO couldn't follow and listen in. He paced up and down the room, considering his options. There weren't many. He could ring Beckwith. Or he could just wait for him outside the Goldsborough Mort building. But if he did that, it would waste a lot of time and prevent him from doing his other work.

Work! Had slipped his mind recently. Suddenly, he had that Monday morning feeling he used to wake up with as a schoolboy. Work. He hadn't looked at his emails for at least three days. Reluctantly, he logged on. A swollen Inbox greeted him, the most recent hundred or so emails relating to the media coverage of his shooting. He hadn't realised. Betty G hadn't said a word about it. It seemed someone had taken a photo of him, lying prone on the pavement, covered in blood. The sort of photo that makes front pages. Worldwide. It dawned on him. No wonder Betty G had been keen to get back to Germany, to prepare for the Governing Council meeting – they were probably going ballistic. And, no doubt, she'd be preparing for the Office for Internal Oversight Services inquiry that would follow. Another hurdle he resigned himself to dealing with when the time came.

The next couple of hours were spent working his way through the Inbox items, dealing with the matters that needed to be dealt with and filing, or deleting, the rest. He rang Dominik to discuss a number of the outstanding items. Neither mentioned the shooting. When they finished, Dominik asked if he was able to discuss 'other' matters. Emil liked that trait in him: he was discreet.

He called Dominik back on the prepaid mobile.

"Emil, what has been going on? Was that really you?"

"Hudson. That's what's been going on. He shot me. I'm lucky it's not worse."

"Did they catch him?"

"No, that's the frustrating thing. He's done his disappearing act again. It's the same as in Hong Kong. There's no record of him entering the country, so how are they going to find him?"

"I hate to say it, but I did warn you. They're trying to get everyone connected to the PNG sham."

"Yes, payback time. A very Papua New Guinean thing to do. But listen, Dom, we've got to keep being careful. Calls on the work phone are definitely being listened to by the domestic security organisation here. It's not the shooting – Zhong is from Chinese state security. They're onto him. When they saw me, I became a target, too. We need to be extra careful."

"Well, this might cheer you up a little. I've found information on the Coalition of Future Fuel Enterprises."

"Finally! What have you got?"

"They've got a lot of links to all the main players in the US coal and oil industries. Seem very well connected there. They also seem to be frequently used for channelling funds to climate sceptic academics and commentators. Lots of familiar names crop up: Green Globe Association, Centre for Greenhouse Analysis, Environment Fact Institute. But you'll love this: the name that crops up more often than all of the others – guess who it is?"

"Who, Dom?"

"Bradlee Nelson."

28

It made sense. The jigsaw pieces fitting together. Nelson, the climate change denying journalist, sponsored by the companies behind these lobbyists. Hudson lurking in the shadows, his hands on the levers of control, dutifully carrying out their bidding. Kidnapping Johanna. They must be the ones who'd bankrolled the former PNG government; there couldn't be any doubt about that. There was just the small matter of evidence. He had none. But he'd get it. Somehow. He asked Dominik to compile the information he had into a report. They'd build on it with whatever else Emil could find out before he returned to Frankfurt.

But he was back to square one. Even worse, his left arm was in a sling. The only real option he had was to go to Beckwith directly. He'd have to chance it. He rang his number. His phone gave a 'No Service' signal. Bloody thing. He turned it off, waited five seconds and turned it back on, then dialled again. No service. Modern technology. It was a shit. These days, with different service providers, how could you tell whether it was your own phone or the other person's phone that wasn't working? He checked online and found the service difficulties number for his own service provider. Eventually he got through to a call centre. The very helpful person there sounded like a young Indian woman: she introduced herself as Madhu.

"Whereabouts in India are you, Madhu?"

"I'm sorry, sir, I am not in India. I am in Melbourne."

That's what you get for making assumptions. He explained that he was trying to reach a number that had worked last week, but now just said 'No service'. She checked.

"That number is not connected, sir. Is there anything else I can help you with today?"

He thanked her and rang off. This didn't look promising. Why did I mention the bloody BridgeClimb to Betty, damn it, he chided himself. If he hadn't, none of this would have happened the way it had, and he would have got the information he wanted from Beckwith.

He took a taxi uptown to the Goldsborough Mort apartments. No point in trying to be subtle now – after what had happened it probably didn't matter if ASIO found out he was contacting Beckwith. And if the police hadn't caught Hudson by now, he would be long gone. So he shouldn't be a problem.

He pressed the buzzer for Beckwith's apartment. There was no response, so he gave it another long buzz. In the lobby, a person came out of a lift and exited. Emil just managed to stop the door closing with his foot. Inside, he took the lift up to the fifth floor and went to the door of Beckwith's apartment. His knock went unanswered. Unlikely Beckwith would still be in the office at this time. And where was Gisela? And why had his phone been disconnected? The lift returned and a middle-aged woman got out. She stopped at the apartment next along the hallway. He was just about to knock again, as she opened her door.

"I think you've missed them," she volunteered.

He stopped and looked at her.

"If it's the couple from Hong Kong, you're after. I saw them heading off with suitcases this morning. It looked like they were moving out."

On his way out of the building, he noticed the managing agent's number on the notice board in the lobby. He rang it. They confirmed the neighbour's assessment was correct.

Globalreach Americas had terminated the lease early. The tenants had already moved out and the apartment would be cleaned and back on the market by the end of the week, if he was interested. He told them he wasn't.

What a disaster. If Globalreach had terminated the lease, then it was a corporate move. It wasn't just a case of Beckwith and Gisela going on the run. He guessed they would've been sent back to Hong Kong. Beckwith must have decided to take the risk that Emil wouldn't put the authorities onto them, or maybe he didn't have a choice. Maybe they'd been moved somewhere else. Whatever the case, they'd gone, leaving Emil without a lead. There wasn't anything more he could do this evening, so he headed back to his apartment to plan his next move.

The following morning he was up early and caught a bus up George Street, towards Broadway and Parramatta Road. He'd tried to reach Zhong's number several times the previous evening, but the phone seemed to be permanently turned off. Maybe Zhong only turned it on to ring and harass his 'assets'. Emil got off at Camperdown and walked up Missenden Road to Dunblane Street, where the head office of the People's Republic of China Consulate-General was located. It was early and they'd only just opened, but already there was quite a crowd of mostly Chinese people in the waiting area. He took a ticket from the machine and waited.

Forty minutes later his number came up and he went to the nominated counter window.

"Hello. I'm trying to get in touch with one of your consular officials. Mr Zhong. He's been here in Sydney and I need to speak to him."

The person behind the counter finally understood what Emil wanted after he explained it for a third time. They went away to get someone who might be able to help. Ten minutes later another consular official, a chubby woman in a plain grey pants suit, came out of a doorway and asked Emil to follow her. They went into a small room, along a corridor away from the noise of the front counter booths.

"I am Miss Ma," she said, presenting him with her business card, in two hands, with a slight bow.

Emil fished around in his wallet until he found a card and reciprocated the gesture. Miss Ma indicated they should sit down.

"How can I help you, Mr Peeper?"

"Pfeffer. Like 'pepper', not peeper."

"Oh, excuse me." She had a little giggle.

"No problem. I wish to speak to Mr Zhong."

"We do not have anybody in the consulate called Zhong."

"He is from Beijing. I understand he works for Chinese internal security. I know he's here, because I met with him on Tuesday. I need to talk to him again."

"Ah." Miss Ma gave a slight smile. "There was a Mr Zhong who visited recently. But I understand he has gone now."

"Can you tell me where? I need to speak to him."

"Back to Beijing."

Emil thanked her and left, growing more despondent by the minute. He walked back down Dunblane Street and into Missenden Road. As he passed the gate into the Sydney University grounds, he thought about going through the campus – it would be a more soothing walk through the playing fields than next to the traffic. But he let that idea drop and kept walking back towards Parramatta Road to get a bus. He hadn't gone far when a white sedan pulled up next to him. He looked at it: the ASIO guys again. The passenger pushed open the rear door.

"Get in, we'll give you a ride."

The day was going from bad to worse already and it wasn't much after ten o'clock. The ride went as far as the Federal Police building in Goulburn Street. Emil found himself back in the office where he'd been sitting with Betty G the previous Saturday morning.

"Just what are you playing at Pfeffer?"

"What do you mean?"

"What are you doing at the Chinese consulate?"

"Is going there an offence?"

"Don't get smart. Someone in your position should learn not to be so cheeky. I'm beginning to understand why this Hudson guy wants to kill you."

"Have you caught him yet?"

"That's a police matter. I'm sure they've got it in hand."

"From that, I conclude the answer is no."

"Just cut being a smartarse," said the more senior of the two, "and tell us what you were doing at the Consulate."

"What do you think? I was looking for Zhong, the great Chinese spy master."

"You might think you're really funny, Pfeffer, but you're in a shitload of trouble here."

"That's crap. You know it's crap. I was looking for Zhong to try to stop him having an arrest warrant issued against me in Hong Kong, for the murder of Cheng. That's where I'm in trouble and, so far, you two have just been making it worse by chasing him away. So what are you going to do to help me?"

"What can we do about that? That's your problem," said the more senior man.

"You're on your own, pal," said his colleague.

"Okay, if that's the way you want to play, I'll be on my way." He got up to leave. "Oh, by the way, Zhong's gone back to China."

"We know. We watched him board the plane."

"You in a hurry, Pfeffer?" said the more senior of the two. "Sit down. We haven't finished with you yet."

Emil flopped back onto the chair. "What?"

"You were in Hong Kong with the government legal team, on the arbitration matter."

"So? You know that."

"How well do you know them?"

It was like being back with Tang. Emil could feel his sweat glands cranking up production.

"I know they lost. That's why I'm here."

"How well do you know Marianne Carrone and Rita McCarty?"

Thank God he'd put a jacket on this morning, he thought. At least the sweaty patches under his arms wouldn't be too obvious to these two.

"They were part of the legal team." He stood up. "Is that it? You finished now?"

The bluff worked. They had nothing. It was a fishing trip.

Heading back down Goulburn Street to get a bus in George Street, he looked over at the entrance to the building that housed Globalreach Americas. There was no sign of Beckwith, or Gisela, or for that matter, Hudson. Not that he expected there would be.

His phone rang. It was Loftus.

"Oh, I'm glad I caught you. I half thought you might have already headed back to Germany."

"No, still here. And I wouldn't go without calling in to say goodbye."

"Good. That's what I was ringing about. Can you call into my chambers sometime before you go? Sooner, rather than later, would be good. I want to discuss with you the approach we can make to the Hong Kong authorities about getting a review of this arbitration started."

"I'm on my way down town at the moment, how about I call in now?"

"Perfect."

29

Loftus greeted Emil in the reception to his chambers. "What on earth have you been doing to yourself?" he said looking at Emil's arm in a sling.

"Someone from my past caught up with me on Tuesday evening and shot me."

"A cuckolded husband?"

"No, that's not quite my form! It's to do with the bank I asked you about, remember?"

"Oh, I see. You can tell me about it once we get some coffee."

"Yes, excellent. I could do with one. It was an early start this morning."

"Is that why you sounded so tired, when I called?"

"Not tired. Fed up. Depressed. I'd just left the AFP offices in Goulburn Street, for the second time in a week." Loftus looked at him, his expression a mixture of surprise and concern. "Don't worry, it was nothing serious. Just ASIO on my case again. Harassing me."

Once they were settled in his chambers, with coffees in hand and the door closed, Emil elaborated.

"I suppose it would help if I started at the beginning."

Loftus adopted his Easter Island statue pose.

"You remember I was late for our first meeting in Hong Kong? Was soaked from being caught in that storm? That was because I'd been following someone. Someone who'd tried to kill me in Papua New Guinea, last year. There's an Interpol Red Notice on him. I saw him, as I was arriving for our meeting, and followed him into Soho. But I lost him, so I reported it to the police. That's how I first met Tang."

"I always wondered how you seemed to know each other already, when he began investigating Cheng's disappearance," said Loftus, rousing himself.

"This person, his name's Hudson. He must have been operating under another identity, because the authorities didn't have any record of him in Hong Kong."

"Doesn't surprise me. Identity theft is rampant these days. I expect it's pretty easy to become someone else, if you're so minded."

"He's been operating here in Australia, also probably under a false identity. He's connected with that bank I asked you about." Emil paused, looking directly at Loftus. "And, I think, with the Texans."

"So that's how you came to be interested in this bank?"

"Not quite. You remember I told you how Tang got hold of the DVD?" Loftus gave a slight nod. "What I didn't tell you, is that the Chinese have been using it to force me to act as their agent."

"Blackmail?"

"If I don't help them find out about this bank, they're going to issue an arrest warrant for me."

"On what grounds?"

"Remember I told you Tang was holding it as evidence for a potential child pornography prosecution. There's that, then there's Cheng's murder. They've got me over a barrel."

"Hmm." Loftus sat back again, fingertips pressed together, thinking. "That makes things a bit tricky."

"How so?"

"I'm flying to Hong Kong at the end of the week. I have an appointment with Senior Inspector Tang. And I've set the wheels in motion to lodge an application to the Hong Kong High Court, to set aside the award on the grounds of there having been a serious irregularity affecting the tribunal. I was hoping – there might be an outside possibility – you would be willing to join me there."

"I don't know. There's a good chance I'll be arrested as soon as I arrive. Let me think about it. I've given them whatever I've found out about Globalreach, but I just don't know whether it's enough. I haven't anything else to give them. It'd be a big risk, I might end up in gaol." He thought for a moment. "Speaking of which, have you any news on Rita and Marianne?"

"Nothing, I'm afraid."

There was a knock at the door and a clerk came in.

"Sorry to disturb you Mr Loftus, this has just arrived. I thought you might want it straight away, as it was sent secure mail and high priority," he said, handing Loftus a large envelope.

Loftus gave the postmark a quick glance, then tore the envelope open. Inside, there was another, which he looked at then passed to Emil. It was addressed to him, care of Loftus. Emil looked at it then examined outer envelope's postmark: Canberra. Rita and Marianne.

"Speak of the devil, as they say. Looks like your up-to-the-minute answer."

Emil was only half listening. "You mean 'devils', don't you?" he said distractedly, carefully prising open the flap of the envelope. Then he emptied the contents onto his lap.

"If we need to stay away from the girls until the smoke clears in Canberra, I thought Hong Kong might be just the place for us to do that," Loftus continued.

Emil pored his way through the pages of solid gold he'd just tipped out across his lap. He stopped at a photo, labelled Richard Yorkton, and held it up for Loftus to see.

"This is the man who shot me."

There were photos of the other CoFFE consultants, as well. He paused over the photo labelled Davis Crooter. The face seemed vaguely familiar, but he couldn't place it. Maybe he'd seen him at a meeting, or at an event, sometime. And at the bottom, there was a thick document, the top of which was headed 'Manifesto' and marked 'Strictly Confidential – CPSC eyes only – do not copy'. Cabinet Policy Steering Committee only. The inner sanctum of the inner sanctum.

They'd done it.

No wonder ASIO was on to them! God knows how they'd managed to lay their hands on it, but this was the jackpot.

Emil thought for a few moments, oblivious to Loftus. He could never take the risk of being caught with this material. This was exactly what ASIO would be looking for and he was sure they wouldn't stop harassing him until he left the country. When he did, he expected they would search him and everything he was carrying. He sure-as-hell wasn't going to try carrying this stuff out through Customs at the airport. That'd be a good way to end up in the cell next to Rita and Marianne. But that was exactly what he needed to do – get it out of the country. Faxing or emailing it would only leave an electronic trail leading back to him, implicating whoever helped him along the way. He looked over at Loftus, who sat impassively, waiting.

"Okay, I'll join you on your trip to Hong Kong."

"Wonderful."

"But first, can you get me a large envelope, large enough to fit this one?"

Loftus summoned his clerk, who obliged.

"Where are you staying in Hong Kong?"

"I believe I'm booked into the same hotel as you were in last time."

Having sealed the envelope inside the other, he addressed it to Dominik Baumann, care of the hotel, then handed it back to Loftus's clerk.

"Can you make sure this goes out, with the chamber's normal outgoing mail, today."

"No problem."

"How long will it take to arrive?"

The man looked at the address. "If we mark it express and put it in the normal post, three days, four at the outside."

"Well, then," said Emil, turning back to Loftus. "Let's start planning this trip."

As he left the chambers an hour later, Emil looked in on the clerks' post room. The envelope wasn't there.

"There were some items to go out this morning, so I took it to the post myself," said the clerk in response to his inquiry.

"Good, I'm glad it's gone."

30

Had he been right to come back, or was he making a huge mistake? Emil turned the question over in his mind for the millionth time.

The immigration official at the airport seemed to linger over his passport much longer than last time. Not a good start. But he was through. Hadn't been led away to somewhere out of sight, to be held until Tang arrived to incarcerate him. But even when he was through customs and immigration, he had the feeling that every uniformed person – and there were lots in the airport – was watching him.

Was he doing the right thing? What had Betty G said to him over their lunch a week earlier? The outcome. She cared about the outcome. Thinking back again over their conversation, he had the feeling now that she'd been talking in riddles. Maybe it was just because he was tired. He hadn't slept at all on the flight from Sydney. Only just managed to get the last seat in economy, at the very back of the aircraft. He'd been dwelling over her words, on and off, for the past nine hours. It mightn't be the obvious one, that's most important. That's what she'd said. Ends justifying the means. Taking a stand on principle. But she hadn't really said those things. She'd given him the politician's answer. It depends. She was a political animal, of that, he was sure.

Emil's arrival in Hong Kong was preceded by another, more

obvious but less welcome one. A thick, claustrophobic pall of smog had slid down into the Pearl River delta a few days ahead of him and was doing its best to smother the life out of the inhabitants. Waiting on the platform for the MTR express to Central, the air stuck to his face like nitrous-smelling cling wrap, stinging his eyes. He wondered whether it was an omen. The authorities in Macau, Shenzhen and Hong Kong had issued warnings for residents to stay indoors, especially the old and the very young. But how realistic was that? It was bloody hot. Typhoons, a thousand kilometres out into the North Pacific, meant warm air was keeping the toxic blanket intact and motionless in the delta. An unwelcome visitor from the mainland, refusing to leave.

On the train into Central, nothing was visible. Just the grey-brown pollution, occasionally infused by the orange of sodium lights, struggling to make their presence felt. It seemed they were being choked as well. He recalled the asphyxiation he'd been planning for the speaker at that conference back in London. Now he found himself wheezing more with each breath he took. London seemed a lifetime ago.

On checking in to the hotel, he collected the envelope that he'd posted from Sydney. He'd taken the precaution of addressing it to Dominik, as the name wouldn't mean any-thing if someone was checking the mail to intercept items addressed to Emil. Dominik had made a booking in his own name, and then cancelled it, requesting that his colleague, Mr Pfeffer collect any items sent to or left at the hotel for him. Without the Australian Government paying top room rates, this time he found himself on one of the lower floors, which he didn't mind, it meant less time in the lifts. And nothing was visible out the window anyway. Loftus, on the other hand, was up on the executive levels.

Having settled into his room, Emil went to work reviewing the material. He had to devise a plan: how to use it. The more he read, the more he realised how judicious he would need to be. He certainly couldn't just hand the 'Manifesto' over to Zhong. That would be espionage. The other option was to release it publicly – give it to a whistleblowing website, or the media. However, that would spell the end of his career. And Rita and Marianne would be eternally damned, and damn him as well. No, he had to come up with a better idea.

Eventually he ran out of time. He'd been at it a couple of hours when Loftus realised he'd arrived and rang his room. Senior Inspector Tang awaited them at Arsenal Street. There was no time to delay.

At police headquarters, the meeting was short and to the point.

"I am surprised you have returned of your own free will, Mr Pfeffer," Tang greeted Emil. "I anticipated the need to extradite you from Australia or another country."

"I don't know why that would have been, Senior Inspector. As far as I'm aware, I haven't been charged with anything."

"Now, now. Gentlemen." Loftus intervened. This wasn't getting off to the start he'd been hoping for. "We're here to see how we can help each other. Let's not begin by adopting adversarial positions."

"How are you going to help me, Mr Loftus?"

"In whatever way we can, Senior Inspector. All you need to do is ask, just as we are now asking to be able to access the DVD you took from Mr Pfeffer, as evidence in support of our application to the High Court. We need it so we can get the arbitration award set aside. It's evidence of a serious irregularity that affected the tribunal."

Tang took his time responding. "Let me think about how you can be of assistance."

"So you will give us access to the DVD?"

"I did not say that. As evidence in a criminal prosecution, I cannot release it to you. I would be breaking the law if I were to do that."

"Senior Inspector. We both know that there are ways – within the law and within police procedures – whereby you could."

Tang didn't respond. Eventually, he said: "What I can do for you, Mr Loftus, is to provide evidence of the action we are taking against Howard Law. I am willing to do this by affidavit, or to appear before the court in person, to give the evidence you require."

"That's very generous, Senior Inspector. I'm just not sure that will be sufficient for the court."

"Well, I suggest we wait and see whether that is the case."

Tang was immovable and the discussion didn't progress further. Emil and Loftus left and returned to the hotel. They found a quiet corner in the bar and settled over a couple of beers. Emil was wheezing more noticeably.

"We shouldn't have walked back," said Loftus. "If your breathing doesn't improve this evening, you should find a doctor."

"I've got some asthma stuff in my bag. I'll be okay. But you're right, we should've taken a cab."

They'd been there barely ten minutes, when Tang appeared, flanked by three uniformed police officers.

"Did you change your mind about the DVD, Senior Inspector?" ventured Loftus.

"I'm afraid not. Mr Pfeffer, please come with me."

Emil exchanged a glance with Loftus. "Mr Loftus has agreed to act as my lawyer. He should come too."

"That won't be necessary, at this stage. We will call Mr Loftus, when we charge you."

"Can I go to my room first, Senior Inspector? I need to get something for my asthma."

But instead of heading up to his room, Emil went to the hotel's gym, where he collected the papers he'd left in a locker. The convoy of police cars drew away from the hotel entrance where they'd been causing a stir amongst the hotel's guests and consternation for the concierge. It was barely a two-minute journey to Arsenal Street. Tang quickly briefed Emil:

"Howard Law had been in custody since not long after you

went to Australia. His trial will be soon. Beckwith's girlfriend was arrested at the airport on arrival."

"What about Beckwith?"

"No. Zhong said it was better to leave him active."

At Police HQ, Tang showed Emil into an interview room. Waiting inside was Zhong, who greeted Emil like a long lost friend. "Mr Pfeffer, I must thank you. You saved me from a very difficult situation by warning me about the Australian security police." He gestured to Emil's left arm, still in its sling. "But what happened to you?"

"After you rode away on your bicycle, Hudson shot me."

He emptied the contents of the envelope he'd brought with him onto the table and selected the photo labelled Richard Yorkton.

"This is Hudson, he has been operating in Australia as Richard Yorkton. He may have used the same name here. These others are the people on the team advising the Australian Government. I think you will find some of them are also Globalreach employees from Hong Kong." He looked at Zhong. "So, do we have a deal?"

Later that evening, Emil and Zhong made their way up the midlevels escalator to Staunton Street. The Yorkshire Pudding pub was as good a place as any to meet Beckwith. After eleven there were very few people around and the pub had its windows closed, which kept out the foul air and made it less likely that they could be observed by passers-by.

Beckwith looked tired, like he hadn't slept for days. Emil introduced Zhong as a colleague of Senior Inspector Tang. He'd brought him along to see if they could work out a deal to help Gisela. The real deal had already been done.

"I didn't give Gisela's name to the police. They worked it out for themselves."

Zhong nodded his agreement. "I can confirm this is correct, Mr Beckwith."

It didn't take much to get Beckwith talking. The first video file showing Gisela had only been a test, he said, to make sure the recording equipment was working. It was supposed to be deleted.

"Somehow, Cheng must have stumbled across everything before that file could be deleted, then copied both files onto the disk she gave to you."

"She just left it with the concierge at my hotel."

"Gisela was not involved in this business in any way. Nor was I. You must believe me, officer," he said to Zhong. "She was asked simply to walk up with the boy. That was all. The people who organised it were specialists, they work for someone in CoFFE, maybe Hudson. He seemed to be organising everything."

Zhong was quick to see his opening. "Who is CoFFE, Mr Beckwith? Who is this Hudson person? If you want us to help Miss Gisela, you must give us all the information we need to do so."

"But first, our arrangement still stands," Emil cut in. "If you want to help Gisela, I want to know what they've done with Johanna Dorn."

"They'll kill me if they find out I've talked to you."

"They won't. Where is she? What have they done?"

"She's alive. I know that much, from talk I've overheard. I don't know where she is, but I think she's on an island. She was taken out of Singapore by sea, on board a freighter. That's all I know."

Emil felt a huge sense of relief, just to know she was alive. The fear that she wasn't had been buried deep in the back of his mind, waiting there like an undiagnosed tumour. Just to hear Beckwith say the words was enough to shrink it.

"How do I find her? What about Johnstone? Hudson?"

"Hudson's very secretive. No one knows where he is or where he might show up. Johnstone is living in the United Kingdom. They lined up a position as an academic at some university." Beckwith handed Emil a slip of paper. "That's where you can find him."

"If you can convince Gisela to give evidence against Howard

Law and tell the police about the others, they may go easy on her," said Emil. He turned to Zhong, "That's correct, isn't it, officer?"

"Provided you tell us everything you can about this CoFFE organisation and the person called Hudson, that you mentioned."

With Gisela still being held at the police lock up in Arsenal Street until a bail hearing, they agreed that after Beckwith's daily visit, he and Zhong would meet. Beckwith's visits to the police headquarters would be completely understandable and Zhong would have as much time as he needed to pump Beckwith for information, without risk of being seen.

"So now that you have your new asset, you no longer need me, right?" said Emil, getting out of the taxi in Arsenal Street, just after the corner with Queensway.

"Yes. I like this deal very much, Mr Pfeffer!" said Zhong.

He walked the short distance back to the shopping mall entrance below the hotel. On the escalator he checked his phone. There were a number of voicemails from Loftus. They would have to wait until the morning. It was late and he was tired. He was looking forward to his bed. As his head hit the pillow, the room phone on the bedside table rang. He thought about ignoring it, then picked it up.

"Oh, you're back. Finally." It was Loftus. "What happened? They obviously didn't charge you, because you're back here."

"No, no. It was okay. Just a long time. I need some sleep, I haven't slept since before I left Sydney."

Loftus sounded agitated. "We have to meet."

"Can't it wait until breakfast?"

"No, we really need to have our plan sorted out by then. We need to do it now."

He couldn't understand the urgency, but he was tired and couldn't be bothered to argue. "Alright, alright. Give me thirty minutes. I'll see you in the lobby."

Emil showered to wake himself up and got into clean clothes. Loftus was waiting for him in the lift lobby.

"We can go to the office I've rented."

"At one in the morning? You're not serious are you?"

"It's very important," Loftus insisted.

They took a cab, which headed over to Kowloon.

"Where are these offices?"

"Nathan Road. Best I could do at short notice." Emil looked at Loftus. He seemed a little dishevelled and grey around the eyes. "We've got to get that DVD back. It's just not good enough for Tang to give evidence."

The cab stopped outside the locked and shuttered entrance to the Burlington Arcade. It seemed a very strange place to take office space. Loftus produced a key and unlocked a steel door next to the arcade shutter. It led up a steep set of stairs. At the top was a corridor, lit only by the fire exit signs at each end. On either side of the corridor were doors, evidently to offices, broken wooden stud walls and never-cleaned windows. There were chunks missing from the linoleum flooring. Loftus led him to a door at the very end, the back of the building.

"Well, this is a far cry from the Exchange Centre," said Emil looking around the space in the half-light filtering in from outside. "The government certainly isn't wasting tax-payer money here."

"The government's not paying for it."

There was a change in Loftus's voice. The self-confident assurance seemed to be gone.

"Any lights in this place?"

Loftus didn't respond.

Emil's eyes began adjusting to the dimness. He noticed that there were no desks waiting for folders, legal tomes and papers to cover them, as before. There were a couple of overturned tables and a chair or two. Papers and refuse were strewn about the floor. The warning bells started ringing in his head, but all too late.

"Doesn't look like much work'll be done here." He could see Loftus's profile, silhouetted by the neon glow from outside, head down, as if he were looking at the floor. "What's going on, Loftus?"

"I'm sorry," said Loftus weakly, without looking at him.

A voice came from an inner room, which Emil hadn't noticed in the dark. "Howard Law isn't the only one with dirty little secrets to hide, Pfeffer."

31

Not even the vast sodium lighting array of the Kwai Chung-Tsing Yi container terminal was making an impression on the heavy blanket of smog. If anything, along the shoreline around this part of the delta it was sitting more thickly, more hideously impenetrable than ever. The diffuse, dull, orange aura made the place seem sinister, dangerous. Containers were being loaded and unloaded, despite the hour, but the activity seemed remote, only a background noise, muffled by the dense, suffocating air.

Emil wished he'd taken something for his asthma. Walking any distance in this soup was making him wheeze. Fortunately he wasn't the only one having trouble, so the physical exertion was being kept to a minimum. They'd left Loftus in Nathan Road, presumably to return to the hotel. It was better, he thought. Shame could be a harsh taskmaster. Loftus hadn't been able to look at Emil after Bull Griffith had revealed himself.

"He's right," he said, as Griffith emerged from the inner room. "I'm sorry, I didn't really have a choice."

"Everybody has a choice, it's just the one *you* made," said Griffith.

"Easy for you to say, if you're the one pulling the strings," said Emil.

"I really didn't have a choice, if I wanted to keep my career and stay out of gaol," Loftus continued. "You see, I was once very foolish. A young, naïve lawyer working for a very greedy, dangerous man," he gestured towards Griffith. "I did something that was illegal and wrong, thinking it would help my employer. It helped him all right, but there was a price. A loser … two losers, really. The victim and me."

"You were well rewarded," sniffed Griffith. "Financed you becomin' a barrister, didn't it?"

"Yes. And you've been wielding it over me ever since."

"So are you in on Griffith's little – or should I say, big scam with the Australian Government?"

"What do you mean?" Loftus turned to Griffith, but still wouldn't look at Emil.

"Oh, sorry, of course you would have had to be. How else could Griffith have got away with using the Hong Kong investors as a front, without someone on the Australian legal team making sure it wasn't exposed."

Loftus stared at Griffith. "Is that true?"

"What's it matter if it is? I didn't interfere in runnin' the case. At the end of the day, we could rely on Law."

"You're a mongrel!"

"Nothin' to get excited over, Loftus. The arbitration served its purpose. You can get it overturned, doesn't worry me now. I don't need the government's money anyway. They're gonna reverse their policy. Again!" Griffith gave a short laugh. "You can piss off now."

But he wasn't finished with Emil. He had another part of his empire to show him. In Nathan Road a car was waiting to take them to the container terminal. They were now sitting in the captain's stateroom in the Panamanian-flagged *Global Bulk I*. The vessel was empty, having unloaded its cargo, and riding high in the water. Not that it made any difference to what they could see outside. Still, it didn't stop Griffith from trying to point out the extent of his local holdings until the fetid air got the better of him and he, too, started to wheeze. Now that they were inside and he'd recovered his breath, it was time to get down to business.

"You think you're pretty smart, don't you, Pfeffer. Workin' out it was me behind the arbitration."

"If Loftus had done his job properly, he would have been able to find that out easily enough."

"That's where you're wrong, smartarse. No matter how much searchin' he did, he wouldn't have been able to discover my ultimate holdings in Taipan Investments. He would've had to search through a huge number of companies. This vessel's a good example. There's a dozen shipping operations around the world under Taipan Lines alone. But even if he'd sifted through all of 'em, ultimately he would've run up against blind trusts and dead ends. So you shouldn't jump to conclusions."

"OK, so he wasn't in on it. Why'd you get him to drag me out in the middle of the night? Just so you could show off your fleet?"

"You've got a nasty little habit of receivin' stolen goods, Pfeffer. That's what we're here to sort out. Where's the information that was stolen from the government?"

"Don't know what you're talking about."

"There was a Cabinet document, and other papers, removed illegally."

"You act for the government now?"

"I know you've got it. Those two dykes from Canberra sent it to you. Loftus told me."

"That's why he couldn't look me in the eye."

"Where are the documents?"

"They were useless. I dumped them."

"Bullshit."

"Why are you so concerned about them anyway? Are you hooked in with the Texans? The Coalition of whatever-it-is? CoFFE."

"Listen, Pfeffer. You can either give the documents back to me, or they'll come after you to recover their property. And I don't mean the government. This time, if they do, you won't get away. I'm givin' you a chance that, quite frankly, you don't deserve."

"Why are you then?"

"Your little girlie asked me to."

The statement took him completely off guard. Suddenly, he felt like he was reeling backwards.

"What, what're ..."

"Don't think that information will help you get her back."

"What the *fuck* are you talking about?" he said, recovering some composure. "What do you know about Johanna?"

"I know she's not interested in you anymore."

"How the *fuck* would you know?"

"Because she works for me now. Best worker I have, matter of fact. Intelligent. Hard-workin'. Easy on the eye. Your old mate Gerry Johnstone must've been at his persuasive best – convinced her she'd be better off with me than waitin' 'round for a loser like you."

Emil felt like the top of his head had blown off. He started towards Griffith.

"If you want to get out of this fucking room alive, you better tell me where she is," he snarled at Griffith, just barely controlling his rage.

"Ha! I can do better than that," said Griffith, completely unfazed. "She can tell you herself!"

There was a passage to the side of the stateroom, through which the vessel's radio room could be accessed. Griffith led the way through into the radio room. Emil followed, confused, trancelike, his mind swimming. How did Griffith know Johnstone? His mind raced back to the conversation with Lesley Beckwith. It wasn't possible. It couldn't be possible. Again, he raked over the coals of the countless times he'd been through it in his mind already. No. He refused to believe it.

Suddenly he realised Griffith was holding out the microphone of the ship's radio to him. He looked at it, puzzled.

Griffith took it back and spoke into it again. "He's lost for words, so you better say somethin'."

"Hallo." The disembodied voice came from a speaker on the wall above the radio table.

It was her.

"Johanna?" he said into the microphone.

"Hallo Emil."

"Are you alright?"

"Yes, I'm doing fine."

"Where are you?"

There was a crackling on the line, a break in transmission. Then it returned.

"I can't say. Emil, don't worry about me anymore. Just get on with your life. I'm fine, really. Just forget about me. Give Bull whatever it is you have of his, and forget about me."

"Johanna! What are you saying? Why? I can't forget about you! I love you!"

The line cut out. Emil turned to Griffith. "Call her again! How do you get a line? Get her back!"

Griffith didn't move, his face creased by a huge grin.

"Guess that old song was spot on. Words of love won't win a girl's heart anymore. Ha ha ha."

His expression suddenly changed.

"Now stop fuckin' me about. You heard her. I want that information in the envelope you got through Loftus. We know it's not in your room, so where is it?"

Emil stood silently, looking at the floor. Stunned. Confused. Exhausted. Completely exhausted. After a few moments, he looked up at Griffith.

"It's too late. It's gone."

32

'Words of love, soft and tender, won't win a girl's heart anymore.'

He couldn't get the line out of his head. That bastard Griffith. Loftus was right, he was a mongrel. They were going around in his head like an endless loop and, worst of all, each time he realised they weren't, they'd start again.

'If you love her then you must send her somewhere that she's never been before ...'

It didn't help that he remembered the song and knew all the words.

'... worn out phrases and longing gazes won't get you where you want to go ...'

Which was more than could be said for Griffith. He obviously only had a vague idea of the lyrics. Just enough to wind Emil up. The sound of massive trucks and coal digging equipment would be the only 'music' that bastard would've ever listened to.

Returning to the grind of the daily office routine at Bad Eschbach hadn't helped. It was a relief, but also a nightmare. A welcome distraction; but stifling at the same time. He'd left Hong Kong the day after the late night meeting with Griffith. No point in staying. Hadn't seen Loftus again. Loftus wouldn't be able to face him anyway. He didn't care what happened about the arbitration. But he just couldn't believe, couldn't bring himself to accept, that Johanna didn't want to see him again.

Stepping out of the S-Bahn at Zoologischer Garten, he started walking down Kufürstendamm. Checking the numbers, he realised he'd have to walk most of its length. He knew the address was past Nestorstraβe and that the apartment block was above an Oxfam shop. It was colder than Frankfurt, the pale grey sky ambiguous as to its intentions. He didn't mind the cold; it helped him clear his head. The walk would be good too. He needed to stretch his legs after the hours on Deutsche Bahn getting here. Just so long as it didn't start raining – he didn't want to arrive looking like a drowned rat.

Being back in the office had tested his mental resilience. He was doing his best not to be a zombie and get Betty G offside again, especially since he hadn't taken the week's vacation he'd agreed with her he would. She didn't ask why and he wasn't about to volunteer a reason. He was concentrating on work; on motivating the team; on getting his unit's work in order. But to those who knew him better, it was clear that there was more wrong than just the arm in a sling. Betty G might be too preoccupied to say anything, but Dominik wasn't.

"What happened in Hong Kong?" he asked, typically direct. He'd dragged Emil out for a drink. They were in the same Frankfurt wine bar to which they'd gone after the wake for Gordon Davies. Dominik's choice.

Emil shrugged. "No reason to stay any longer."

Dominik was not going to be put off that easily.

"But something happened, didn't it?"

Emil was torn between opening up and telling the entire story, or telling Dominik to mind his own business. He's only trying to help, Emil reminded himself.

"It's okay Dom, I'd really prefer not to talk about Hong Kong just at the moment."

"Do you remember the last time we were here? You mostly wanted to talk about this girl you'd met, and how you could get in touch with her again, don't you remember?"

"Is that why you brought me here?"

"From the way you're acting in the office, whatever happened is clearly something to do with Johanna. It might be better to talk about it. If you bottle it up, it will be worse, don't you think?"

"You're a nosey bugger, Dom, but you're right," he relented, telling him about the meeting with Bull Griffith. And the brief conversation with Johanna.

"But how did she sound, when she said it?"

"Normal, relaxed. Herself. Griffith didn't prompt her. It sounded like she was happy to tell me to get lost."

Dominik thought for a while. "Did she say what work she does for him? Did he say?"

"I told you Dom, it was a very brief conversation. To the point. The message delivered was clear. Then that was it. There was no small talk. No clue as to where she was – she said she couldn't say."

"Hmm." Dominik mulled the next question in his inquisition.

"Dom stop it. Don't ask. Whatever angles you think of, I really don't want to dwell on it any more than I already am." Dominik looked hurt. "I appreciate your concern, but I need some space."

"What about Johanna's family – have you spoken to them?" he asked, not to be put off. "Have they heard anything from her? Maybe you should go and speak with them, in person."

Emil had to admit, he had a point.

So now he found himself in Berlin, about to cross Nestorstraße. He could see the Oxfam shop and next to it the entrance to the apartment building above. The other side of the entrance there was a *Schoko Laden*, so he detoured and bought a box of pralines, before ringing the buzzer of the flat.

"*Ja*, hallo." The voice sounded uncannily like Johanna.

"Hallo, Frau Dorn. Emil Pfeffer."

They'd never met, but she greeted him like a member of the family. He found it disconcerting, but she quickly charmed him. Again, just as when he'd spoken to her boss, Mathias, he had a strange feeling that he didn't really know Johanna as well as he thought he did. Or maybe, it was that he only knew her in one-dimensionally.

"Johanna has told me so much about you, I feel like I have known you for a long time, Herr Pfeffer."

"Please, call me Emil."

"And you must call me Gitta."

"Thanks for making time to meet, I don't mean to impose."

"What do you mean? I am delighted you have travelled to Berlin, to see me. Have you news of Johanna?"

"Yes, I spoke to her a little while ago. She said everything was fine. Have you heard anything more from her?"

"No, just the note I told you about, telling me she would be unable to be contacted for some time. But I suppose I have to put up with that. She's a very naughty girl sometimes. She gets wrapped up in her work – just like her father used to – everything else, including her poor old mother, is forgotten. But you have spoken to her. And she is not in any trouble, as you were concerned when you first rang?"

"No, she said everything was fine."

"And did she explain her disappearance from the flight? Is her boss going to make her reimburse the cost?"

"No, they won't do that. It's all sorted out."

What he didn't tell her was that Mathias' internal investigation had discovered that her ticket hadn't been bought by them in the first place. Emil wondered how much Gitta knew, and how much he should tell her.

"Did she say why she got off the flight? Her poor colleague in Brussels, Mathias, has been very concerned."

Obviously, Mathias hadn't mentioned anything about the ticket.

"No, we spoke only very briefly. Just enough for her to tell me she was okay."

"Did she say when is she coming home?"

"It was only short, we didn't have time for that."

Gitta considered his response, then sitting up straight said: "I am a very poor hostess! Here you bring me some lovely pralines and I haven't even offered you a coffee. After your journey, you must be ready for one."

While she was in the kitchen preparing the coffee, he browsed the photos on the mantelpiece. She came back in and, seeing him there, introduced him to the rest of the family – at least their photos – Johanna's siblings and their families.

"And this is me with Wernher, but as you can see, it was taken a long time ago. Unfortunately he died when Johanna was very young. She has little memory of him."

Gitta produced a bottle of schnapps. "It's almost dinner time, let's have a drink with our coffee."

Shortly after the schnapps appeared, out came the family photo albums. Johanna as a child, as a teenager, as a schoolgirl, school athlete, family holidays at the beach, hiking in the mountains, skiing. After the second schnapps, the stories of Johanna growing up began.

"She was so naughty as a child – and – what's the word I'm looking for? *Frühreif*?"

"Precocious."

"Yes; and very strong-minded. *Willensstark*. And a strong sense of justice. I always thought she would become a lawyer, like her father was. *Rechtsanwältin*."

"I'm sure she would have been a good one."

"Yes, her brothers and sister are very accomplished, but she was always the smartest."

It was just as Johanna had said, they were scientists and academics. But the longer he stayed, the more uncomfortable he was feeling with himself. More of an imposter. Gitta seemed to be treating him like a future son-in-law. In other circumstances, he would have been pleased. He wondered how he could broach with her the subject he'd really come to discuss.

"Gitta, you said Johanna hasn't contacted you since she went missing?"

"No, she hasn't."

"And did she say anything to you about, ah – before then," he hesitated, not sure whether he could bring himself to ask her mother the question, before asking it. "How she feels about me?"

Gitta looked at him, puzzled.

"Emil, that's a very strange question to ask." She thought for a moment. "She likes you *very* much. *More* than very much! But you should know that better than me. Or are you two worse at communicating to each other than I ever imagined?"

That's exactly the problem, he thought. Most recently, Johanna had been crystal clear in her communication. It was just that he didn't believe her. Didn't want to. Couldn't. Being here, finding out all the things about her formative years he didn't know because she hadn't told him, hadn't had the time, the opportunity, made him feel like a sneak thief, stealing his way into her family more deeply than she'd been able – or prepared – to let him do. And, what was worse, doing it after she'd closed the door on him. But he couldn't help himself.

"Yes, perhaps we are," he lied, smiling, then diverting the conversation. A couple of hours later he felt like he knew the family inside out. As for Johanna, the more he learnt about her, the more he wanted to know. He wished she could've been there with them, so he could see her reaction to some of the stories her mother was telling. But he wished, more than anything, she could be there to tell him she didn't mean what she'd said.

The clock on the sitting room wall showed it was after six.

"I'm afraid I must be going, Gitta. I need to check into my hotel. Thank you for a very interesting afternoon."

"You must come again, Emil. Thank you, too. It was wonderful to meet you after all Johanna has told me." She planted a kiss on each cheek.

As they reached the door of the apartment, he noticed a cluster of photos on the wall he hadn't seen on his way in. Johanna as a teenager, with her father. Then he realised it couldn't be her father, he would have been long dead by then.

There was something disconcertingly familiar about the man with her. There was another in which he looked younger – with a young Gitta and Wernher.

Gitta saw him looking at the photos.

"You didn't see these before? That's Johanna and her godfather. After Wernher's death, he was like a second father to her."

"He looks vaguely familiar."

"Yes, Johanna told me. He should be familiar to you. Gordie. Poor Gordie."

Emil couldn't believe his ears, or his eyes. Couldn't believe the photos of the young man he was staring at.

"Gordon Davies?"

"Yes, poor Gordie. He and Wernher were great friends in their student days. They were activists together in the seventies and eighties. We had such wonderful times together."

"Johanna didn't tell me."

"No, she doesn't like to talk about it. Not since Gordie's accident."

"Gitta, you probably wouldn't have heard. There's been a second inquest. It wasn't an accident."

She gave a little gasp. "*Nein.*"

"Gordon's vehicle was run off the road by another vehicle. We don't know who was driving it, but we know who told them to do it." He took her hand. "I'm sorry, I don't mean to upset you. Don't worry, I'm going to find them."

Walking back along Kufürstendamm, the temperature had dropped and snowflakes were swirling lightly in the air. Again, Emil was lost in his thoughts.

They were in the little restaurant, upstairs in the Markthalle in Stuttgart. A waiter had just delivered their food and she'd moved the parsley garnishing to the side of her plate. "For Gordon," she'd said, as she did it. In memory of Davies – his habit. He scanned his memory for other conversations. He couldn't think of any clues she'd given about her relationship to Davies. No wonder she'd been so interested in the inquests. No wonder she'd studied tropical birds, and travelled to Papua

New Guinea. She'd been so familiar with Davies' little idio-syncrasies – he should have realised.

"… poor Gordon," she'd said. "He was such a nice man. He was always joking and happy."

Emil, you unobservant idiot, he reproached himself. He should have realised a long time ago there was something. Maybe she'd been dropping hints, waiting for him to ask, but he simply hadn't picked up on them. Too preoccupied with other – now less important – things.

"He always called in to see us, when he was in Port Moresby," she'd told him. Well, of course he would have, if he was like a second father to her. "He was interested in our work." Without doubt, since he'd set her on that career path in the first place – she'd followed him, not the father she'd never really known.

But why would she do what she'd done? Why now hook up with a bastard like Griffith? The antithesis of Gordon Davies. Why would she do it, especially if he was connected to the likes of Hudson and his associates?

Hudson.

And his associates.

Suddenly, he realised. He stopped in his tracks, halfway along Kufürstendamm heading back towards the Zoologischer Garten. Maybe she was exactly where she wanted to be. Maybe they had unwittingly provided her with an opportunity, which she'd immediately understood and grabbed with both hands. And they had no idea what they'd done. Because they didn't know.

Justice. He remembered a conversation they'd had, one weekend, walking through a village in the Rheingau. Dominik had taken leave and he'd been struggling to stay on top of things – the internal mole investigation, cyberattacks on the GCMO, all his other work. His report on Davies' death and related matters in PNG had been swallowed by the New York bureaucracy and he'd lost focus on it.

"Have you heard any more about poor Gordie?" she'd asked.

"My report has gone off to New York, but so far there hasn't been a peep in response."

"Will there be one, or will all this just be forgotten?"

"It won't be by me," he'd promised.

"Good." She'd kissed him. "Nor me. Somebody needs to get justice for them, however long it takes."

He might not have forgotten, but he hadn't done anything about it. Now she had been presented with the opportunity and he was certain she wouldn't waste it. If he was right, it explained everything. But did she realise what a risk she was taking? How dangerous these people were? He had to find her. He had to help her.

All of a sudden he was aware of the snow falling about him. He shivered at the cold and started walking briskly. There was much to do.

33

A large marquee had been erected in the garden outside the Prime Minister's office and banks of portable air-conditioners were blowing cool air into it. How long it stayed cool was a point of conjecture and already some of the assembled hacks were sketching out opening paragraphs to stories of government waste. The fact that the expenditure was being incurred principally for their comfort would, of course, be lost somewhere in the telling. But why miss an opportunity to put another nail in the coffin of the latest manifestation of the 'flip-flop' government?

The press conference could have been held inside, but then the venue would have needed to move from Parliament House to one big enough to accommodate the small army of journalists and officials travelling with the Chinese Premier. So, in the end, it had been decided to do it in the garden at sunset and hope that the place wasn't completely swarmed out by the moths, mosquitoes, bugs and insects that usually appeared about that time of day.

As it turned out, when the newly installed Australian Prime Minister, The Right Honourable Anthony Hounganis, strode out of his office alongside the Chinese Premier, it was still over forty degrees and way too hot for the flying pests. But the short walk between air-conditioned office and air-conditioned podium was still enough to knock the stuffing out of

Hounganis, and his welcoming address to the Premier was liberally sprinkled with gasps and wheezes. The tension and anxiety of mounting a party room coup to depose a sitting Prime Minister would, for most people, be more likely to cause weight loss but, in Hounganis's case, the result had been the opposite. He'd needed to get a larger suit made in time for the swearing in ceremony. Now, in the extraordinary early summer heat, he looked like he was paying for his sins. He might even be sweating some of them off.

Hounganis paused after his opening words of welcome, to mop his brow and face with a handkerchief, before continuing.

"So, Mr Premier, just let me say again what a great pleasure it is for me to extend to you warmest of Australian welcomes. In fact, the warmest November welcome on record."

Hounganis looked at the crowd of journalists to see if anyone picked up on his attempt at humour, but if they did, they were too hot to acknowledge it. The translator must have, as the Premier nodded and smiled.

Then the new Prime Minister launched into a long – overly long, given the conditions – discourse on the great history of trading relations between the two countries and how the latest bundle of agreements would further cement the strong ties between them.

"So it is today," Hounganis continued, "together with the Premier, I can announce a range of collaborative energy programmes between Australia and the People's Republic of China, including both supply of traditional resources such as coal, liquefied natural gas and iron ore, but also joint development of exciting new research projects in traditional and renewable energy technologies."

He paused, panting slightly and took a sip from a glass of water. Then picked it up again and drained it. An attendant moved in and refilled it and he drank half of that glass as well.

"Got to keep your fluids up in this weather. I hope you've all got some water – there are bottles being distributed."

There was a murmuring amongst the journalists. The Premier took a sip from his glass. Hounganis continued.

"Finally, ladies and gentlemen, I am proud to make two further announcements. Today Australia renews its commitment to limit its greenhouse gas emissions in keeping with its budget under the two-degree cap. I have already commissioned a full review of the national emissions inventory to evaluate the national position, to assess where we stand. Suitable policy measures will be put in place in accordance with the findings of that review. I will announce these in time for the upcoming climate change conference."

He took another sip from his glass.

"Secondly, I want to convey to you my immense satisfaction at the concluding of a new and expanded bilateral carbon trading agreement between Australia and the People's Republic of China, as part of Australia's enhanced commitment to carbon trading." He turned to the Chinese Premier, extending his hand. "And, Mr Premier, I want to thank you for your cooperation and friendship in reaching these agreements."

The Premier received Hounganis's wet fish handshake with good grace, then launched into his response to the welcome, which was brief and business-like. In his small backbencher's office, Michael Mendicane sat alone watching proceedings on the closed circuit television screen. He dialled Bull Griffith's mobile number for the tenth time that day. Again, without success. Returning his attention to the television screen, he stared at Tony Hounganis's glistening, sweat-beaded face. Hounganis stood impassively, listening to the translation of the Premier's response to his welcome. That should be me standing there, thought Mendicane. He fingered the keypad of his mobile phone again, contemplating one last attempt to reach Griffith, then decided against it.

In the sweating, uncomfortably crowded rows of journalists lined up in the marquee, sat one who didn't seem to be taking many notes. He had a pad open on his lap, and a pen in his hand, but the page was blank. There was no need for him to write anything. After all, it was his script both leaders were reading from. And they were reading it out perfectly. Zhong leaned back and crossed his legs, then took a swig from his bottle of water. He was satisfied. Yes, he was very satisfied.

34

Emil sat at a table around the corner of the bar, near the front window, nursing a pint of stout. A couple asked if they could share his table, which was fine with him. Made him all the more inconspicuous, part of the furniture. The pub was filling up and the traditional folk band would start playing down the back soon. They were good and he enjoyed the music they played. Didn't have a clue what the songs were, but he liked what he heard. Pity was it became so difficult to hear the music once the place filled up, unless you moved down the back. But he wasn't doing that, not yet, maybe even not tonight. He wanted to observe Gerry Johnstone's modus operandi a bit longer, before he moved in on him.

He'd been there a couple of days, finally having taken the leave he'd been talking about taking for a long time. Betty G was relieved. In fact, she was more than relieved, she was positively beaming. When news of developments in Australia filtered through to her, she gone straight around to Emil's office.

"How'd you do it, Emil? How'd you get them to change their position? I thought it was a dead duck. We were a dead duck!"

"Well, Betty, I'd like to take the credit, but I can't. When they stopped and thought about what you'd been saying to them, I think it must have sunk in. They realised the error of their ways."

"That's a load of baloney, Emil! You know it is. You did something, I know. I can tell."

But she was smiling. Emil remembered again what Johanna had said about him being transparent. Maybe he was, after all. No wonder Tang and Zhong had stitched him up so easily.

"Remember our lunch in Sydney? Maybe I just put into practice what you said that day."

Betty G stopped, trying to remember what she'd said. That's stuffed her, he thought.

"It was obviously good advice, whatever it was," she said, then headed back to her office, her brow creased in thought.

"Yes, obviously," he called after her.

He'd gone via London, breaking his journey to visit Lesley Beckwith at her firm's offices in Canary Wharf. They had a coffee in the mall below the building. She looked as beautiful as when they first met. He arranged the meeting with the specific purpose of telling her that Beckwith was alive, thinking that at least she'd be able to pursue him for child maintenance. But when she announced that she had left the flat on the river and was now living with the firm's senior partner, somehow it didn't seem that important anymore. Maybe that explained why she looked so good. Besides, if she needed to find out, she could. It wasn't as if Beckwith was using a false identity to avoid detection. Funny, he thought, both times they'd met he'd had the intention of talking about Beckwith, and in the end both times he'd decided not to.

At London City airport the departure lounge had been about as full as it could get. Every available square foot of floor space was covered, but fortunately it wasn't long until the flight was called and the passengers began shuffling across to the stairs to board. It was only a short flight and he'd no sooner dozed off as they taxied for take-off than he was being woken by the announcement that they'd started their descent into Edinburgh. It had been an early start from Frankfurt that morning and he was tired. Travelling was always tiring, but it seemed to wear him out more these days: or maybe he was just doing too much. In the week since his trip to Berlin, he'd been to Geneva, Brussels, Luxembourg and Warsaw. Nor was the workload at Bad Eschbach getting any lighter. But the Berlin trip preoccupied his thoughts and he'd got away as soon as he had been able to do so.

At least Betty G was off his case.

"It's good to have the old Emil back!" she'd told him that morning, before he left.

He'd gone to the office to do some final tasks before handing over to Dominik and, predictably, she'd been there. They'd even had time for a coffee together, before he had to go. Just like old times. But it wasn't. If anything, he mused as the aircraft wobbled its way down into a strong westerly headwind, it was more different now than ever. But maybe it was just his attitude, or frame of mind, she'd been referring to. Then he'd left the office, in his pocket the slip of paper Beckwith had given him in Hong Kong, with the address of his destination: *Sandy Bell's Bar, Edinburgh.*

There were a few details yet to be filled in. Like how they had got Johanna off the flight in Singapore. And what she was doing for Bull Griffith. He had a rough idea now of where she might be, but Gerry would confirm that for him. It might take a lot of drinks to loosen Gerry's tongue enough to get him blabbing, but that wouldn't be a problem. Emil had the time and plenty of experience dealing with Gerry when he was drunk. From the very first days of their friendship. And in spite of Gerry's treachery, he still thought of him a friend. He blamed himself for not remembering what Gerry could be like. So he would give Gerry a chance to redeem himself. Gerry was going to help him, whether he realised it or not.

The music had finished and the crowd in the bar was starting to thin out. Beyond the fogged window, sleet slanted in on the wind, making the cobblestones more treacherous than they would be already after a few pints. Around the end of the bar, he could see that the last of Gerry's harem of student devotees was saying her goodnights. He might be getting on in years, but he hadn't lost his touch yet. Passionate goodnights they were, but it was clear Gerry wasn't getting her into his bed, not tonight at least. Maybe he had slipped a bit, after all.

Emil waited patiently. The bar wasn't closing yet and he knew from the previous nights he'd been there that Gerry wouldn't leave until it did. After a final cuddle, the pretty young law student left and Gerry settled back into his seat with the remainder of his pint and a whisky chaser, staring thoughtfully into the middle distance. Considering, perhaps, the strategy he'd use on her next time. Emil walked around and stood in front of him.

"Hello Gerry."

He looked up, not showing any surprise. He's probably too pissed to be surprised, Emil thought, or even to remember what he did to me.

"Hello Emil. Fancy seeing you here."

"Yes, Gerry, fancy that. Well, let's have a drink – what can I get you? Same again?"

"Why the hell not? The night's but a pup!" His eyes lighting up ominously as he said it.

"That's right. And we've got quite a bit of catching up to do, haven't we?"

For all the information he was going to extract from Gerry, there was one subject he wouldn't broach, one question he wouldn't be asking – no matter how drunk he got. The question that had been niggling his psyche since his drunken encounter with Lesley Beckwith, the one – if he was honest with himself – he most wanted answered. He wouldn't ask Gerry; he wouldn't even ask Johanna, when he finally found her. If she told him, that would be her choice. But first, he was going to help her get justice for Davies.

Appendix

The United Nations Global Carbon Market Organisation

The GCMO is the product of a United Nations sponsored treaty between the participating countries under which the Constitution and the funding arrangements for the organisation have been agreed.

The governance structure of the organisation consists of the Governing Council and an Executive Board, which is headed by the Director-General.

The Governing Council itself consists of the Director-General plus nine Ministers from participating members states, who themselves are appointed on a rotating basis from the General Council, in which the Ministers of all participating member states sit.

The Executive Board is made up of the unit directors and their deputies headed by the Director-General. The Director-General answers to the Governing Council, which represents the General Council of all Treaty signatory members.

Mission/charter:

The GCMO charter is to:

- Improve the functioning of the carbon market by ensuring sound, effective and consistent level of regulation and supervision on a global basis;
- Ensure the integrity, transparency, efficiency and orderly functioning of the carbon market globally;
- Strengthen international supervisory coordination across the carbon market;
- Prevent regulatory arbitrage and promote equal conditions of competition;
- Ensure that the taking of carbon investment and other risks is appropriately regulated and supervised across and between member states.

Roles and functions:

The role and functions of the GCMO are to:

1. Set market policy across carbon markets for the primary objective of maintaining stable carbon prices in furtherance of the environmental policy objective (of limiting the risk of dangerous anthropogenic climate change) (Policy Unit)
2. Gather and publish data across all markets and undertake carbon market analysis (Economic Analysis Unit)
3. Evaluate new proposed market arrangements (MIU) and monitor on-going market operations (MIU) with a view to limiting attacks on market integrity (in conjunction with national regulatory bodies through Liaison Unit)
4. Liaise with national regulators (Liaison Unit)

Glossary of Selected Terms

ADC – Assistant Deputy Commissioner (of Hong Kong Police)

AFP – Australian Federal Police

A-G – Attorney-General

ASIO – Australian Security Intelligence Organisation

BKZ – Bankgesellschaft Kohlenstoffermäßigungen Zürich

BMU – German Federal Ministry for the Environment, Nature Conservation and Nuclear Safety

CoFFE – Coalition of Future Fuel Enterprises

GC – Governing Council (of the GCMO)

GCMO – Global Carbon Markets Organisation

IGO – Inter-governmental organisation

IOS – UN Office for Internal Oversight Services

After the Texans...

MIU – Market Integrity Unit (of the GCMO)

MP – Member of Parliament (Australian Federal Parliament)

MTR – Mass Transit Railway (Hong Kong subway)

NSA – National Security Agency (US)

NGO – Non-governmental organisation

PNG – Papua New Guinea (aka Papua Niugini)

Author's Note

This is a work of fiction. All the characters are fictional and any resemblance to any person, living or dead, is unintended and purely coincidental. The GCMO does not exist, nor does, and never did, the BKZ, Green Globe Association, Centre for Greenhouse Analysis, Environment Fact Institute or CoFFE: they are purely creations of the author. Similarly, places such as Bad Eschbach and the Debepare conservation projects exist only in the pages of these novels. The lines of the song quoted in Chapter 32 are from 'Words of Love' by the Mamas and the Papas.